GAME. SET. MATCH.

a novel by
JENNIFER IACOPELLI

OUTER BANKS TENNIS ACADEMY, BOOK 1

To Mom, Dad and Annie

PROLOGUE

May 11th

St. Catherine's Preparatory School for Girls
Los Angeles, California

The classroom desks were the old-fashioned kind with a small compartment beneath the writing surface. There was just enough room to fit a book or two plus an extra pen or pencil. It was also the perfect height and width to prop up a cell phone on its side, completely out of sight.

Indiana Gaffney glanced up at her physics teacher, Mrs. Lopez, standing just a few feet away, oblivious to the rebellion going on just inches below the scraped and scarred wood of Indy's desk.

"The first part of Newton's first law," Mrs. Lopez said to the class, letting her voice trail off, allowing silence to hang in the air, a cue for one of her students to fill it with the answer.

Indy slouched in her seat, her blue eyes darting to the phone balanced between the lip of the pencil holder and the calculus textbook she'd need for next period. A young female tennis player with a long, brown braid walked across the screen, bouncing a ball against her racket face into the red clay surface of a court in Madrid.

"An object at rest stays at rest," Indy said, glancing back to her teacher, hoping her contribution would be enough to keep Mrs. Lopez's focus on the rest of the class while she watched this final game.

Rolling her neck, Indy flipped her long hair over her shoulder. She leaned her hand against her cheek then slid it beneath the blonde curtain and plugged the small white bud into her ear. Mrs. Lopez was a hard ass and she'd probably get a week's worth of detention for watching a tennis match in the middle of physics, but if Penny Harrison was going to beat Zina Lutrova, Indy wasn't going to miss it.

The commentator was shouting over the raucous crowd. "Penelope Harrison, just eighteen years old, is up a set, a break and 15-Love. Two more serves like that and she'll have three match points."

"It's amazing," the other announcer chimed in. "If you didn't know who Penny Harrison was before today, you sure do now. She's going to take down the number one player in the world and defending champion in the final of the Madrid Open—a huge win in her young career."

Indy felt a small pang inside her chest. Last year she and her mom had watched this tournament on TV together. Her mom had been sure Indy would be playing there one day on that court in Madrid or one in Paris or New York, winning a major tournament. After her mom died, winning tennis matches really didn't seem to matter much anymore. Nothing mattered except she was gone and wasn't coming back. Though she'd probably be pissed as hell at Indy for giving up.

The thought came unbidden from a place in her mind she'd locked away for way too long. Was it time to start again? It was what her mom would have wanted, wasn't it?

The camera zoomed in on the stands where Dom Kingston, Penny's coach, sat, his hands clasped together like he was praying. He was one of the best coaches in the world and he'd wanted Indy to come train at his facility in North Carolina. If she had, that could've been her standing across from the number one player in the world right now. Or maybe she would've been number one already. Indy bit her lip, wondering if Coach

Kingston's offer would stand more than a year later.

"Does anyone know the rest of Newton's law?" Mrs. Lopez asked.

The camera focused on the court again and Indy slipped farther into her seat just as Penny tossed the ball into the air. Her serve was up into Lutrova's body, an attempt to handcuff the Russian, who managed a sharp return, grunting with the effort, sending Penny scrambling.

It was a furious battle, a blistering exchange from the baseline, each girl pounding away like a heavyweight boxer, neither giving an inch. Then Penny seized upon a short backhand and sent a rocket into the corner, perfectly placed. All Lutrova could do was watch the ball cut through the air as it passed her by.

"Yes," Indy said under her breath. If she wanted it, if she wanted to be on that court in Madrid, then AP Physics wasn't going to help her. Neither was playing tennis at St. Catherine's. Maybe she'd put in a call to Dom. After all, what did she have to lose?

"Indiana?" Mrs. Lopez asked, cutting into her thoughts.

Indy glanced at up at her teacher and grinned sheepishly as she provided the answer. "A body at rest stays at rest and a body in motion tends to stay in motion with the same speed and in the same direction unless acted upon by an unbalanced force."

"And an example?" Mrs. Lopez asked, her eyes twinkling knowingly, darting down to the desk and then back up to meet Indy's gaze.

"A tennis ball during a match."

"Excellent," Mrs. Lopez said, holding out her hand. Indy grinned and shrugged, handing over the phone. "Detention this afternoon."

30-Love.

~

Estadio de Tenis
Madrid, Spain

Blinking down at the red clay and the white tips of her sneakers, Penny Harrison swiped her wrist across her forehead and brushed away rivulets of sweat. She tucked the wayward strands of dark brown hair escaping her braid behind her ears. The pleasant breeze swirling through the stadium was overpowered by the tons of hot air expelled from the stands as the crowd squawked their approval. Steadiness was difficult with everyone still roaring. One deep breath and then another, she filled her lungs and exhaled, slowing her heart rate, bringing herself back under control or at least trying to—it was a lot harder than in the past. Then again, she'd never been in a situation this big before, so that made sense, but she couldn't think about that now. Penny reeled herself in, focusing on her next serve, just her racket and the ball, no crowd, no opponent, no TV cameras. Nothing else.

Shuffling footsteps brought a shadow toward her, smaller than her own. The ball girl, expectant, but patient and not much younger than herself, held out her towel and two tennis balls. Penny took the towel first and wiped at her palms and wrists. The last thing she needed was for her racket to slip out of her hands. Now that would be embarrassing, especially since she was so close, just two points from a win against Zina Lutrova, the best tennis player in the world, ranked number one for most of the last two years. This would easily be the biggest win of Penny's career and she would prove all the naysayers wrong. All the so-called experts had blasted her after her loss in Australia. They said she wasn't ready for the big time. Just two more points and they would be eating their words.

The crowd was still buzzing after her last point and she could feel the rush of excitement flowing through her body. A shiver followed, goose bumps rising across her skin. She'd been working for this moment her entire life, and now she was here, on the precipice of something great. Penny took another deep breath, doing her best to quell the adrenaline-fueled instinct to speed up and just be done with it. Rushing led to mistakes and a match could turn on the smallest hiccup, especially a match against the number one player in the world. Her coach was sitting in a box just behind her. She could practically hear his words burning into her from the stands, his voice echoing in her head with the words he'd say if the rules allowed him to shout down to the court. *Once you have her down, you can't let her up again. Never give an opponent hope. Finish her, Penny. Finish her now.*

The first ball was pretty beat up, bits of fluff sticking out of it like a neon green cowlick, red clay wedged into every crevice available. The second was almost new, ready to do whatever she commanded. She tucked the first into the hidden pocket under her traditional white tennis skirt.

Across the net, Lutrova waited, bent at the waist and crouched low like a cobra ready to strike. Facing Zina would cripple most people. Their game would go to hell the second they caught the icy-blue gaze of the Russian superstar, but Penny wasn't scared, at least not anymore. She was about to prove she was as good as the world's number one.

The crowd murmured, an anxious wave of sound, equal parts hope and dread.

The umpire, high atop his chair, said, "*Silencio, por favor.*"

Penny approached the baseline; the crowd's collective voice faded to a distant hum, but they were behind her, pulling for her, willing her to win. Everyone loved an underdog. Her entire body felt loose, almost relaxed and the world slowed down around her, nice and easy, just the way she'd been taught.

One bounce, then two, three and four in perfect rhythm. Her body weight shifted forward and then back, arms up, racket ready, the ball suspended above her head. She pushed into the ground then sprung up and out, racket face hammering a clean stroke, skimming it off the white chalk T in the center of the court.

Penny's feet hit the ground together, balanced and ready for a return that never came. The ball whistled by Lutrova's desperate lunge and pounded into the wall behind her, missing the line judge's ear by inches. An ace.

40-Love.

~

Harrison Residence
Ocean Hill, North Carolina

"And Penny Harrison has three championship points!" The announcer's voice roared through the television set.

Jasmine Randazzo grabbed the bottle of Jack Daniels by its neck and tried to yank off the cap. As much as she was rooting for Penny to win, it still stung a little that the other girl was off winning a huge pro tournament and she was sitting at home after losing in the first round. A warm hand surrounded hers and pulled the bottle away from her.

"Easy there, Jas," Teddy Harrison said, twisting the cap off and handing it back.

"How are you not drunk?" she asked, narrowing her eyes at him. "I'm drunk."

Teddy snorted softly. "I'm not drunk because I do this more than you. Some of us have actual lives off the court, you know."

"I have a life, sort of," she muttered, pouring herself another shot. The whiskey missed the glass, spreading out over the table and Teddy took the bottle away again. He poured out two glasses and handed one to her.

"Yep, sort of."

"To Penny." Jasmine saluted the TV set, then sent the burning liquid down the back of her throat.

"You gotta stop worrying about my sister," Teddy said, settling back on the couch beside her, his arm coming around her shoulders, squeezing tightly.

"I'm not worrying about her," Jasmine argued. "I'm happy for her and she better watch her back once I get on tour."

"How many shots have you had?" Teddy asked, snickering through another shot.

The television camera zoomed in on the player's box. Their coach, Dom Kingston, was there, applauding with the rest of the crowd, and one row behind him were Jasmine's parents sitting beside the Harrisons, cheering on Penny.

"Heaven forbid we make it through a match without my parents being on camera," Jasmine grumbled, leaning her forehead against Teddy's shoulder. He was so solid and warm. She snuggled closer.

"It's good for publicity," Teddy said, probably for the hundredth time that week. "When people see Mr. and Mrs. Tennis out there, they want to come here and train at OBX."

"They aren't nearly as cool as everyone thinks. They're my parents. Totally dorky like everyone else's."

"They're pretty damn cool, Jas."

"Whatever."

"Not whatever," Teddy said, taking another shot. Jasmine frowned. When had he poured another shot? "Your Grand Slam winning, Olympic gold medalist parents are awesome and so are you."

"Damn right I am."

"You want another shot?"

She shook her head and the world spun a little more than it should have. "No, I think I've had enough."

Teddy smiled widely, a dimple appearing in the corner of his right cheek. "No such thing."

Jasmine leaned forward, wrapping her arms around his shoulders. Her nose trailed over his neck, inhaling deeply. He smelled good, really good, like spices and ocean water and soap and Teddy, her best friend. It was nice to be that close to him. She decided that she should do it more often.

There was a buzzing from across the room from the television, a crowd moving from silence to a raucous cheer, as the announcer shouted over them, "Game. Set. Match. Harrison."

"Teddy," she whispered against his skin.

A grunt rumbled through Teddy's throat. "Yeah, Jas?" he asked, his mouth suddenly really close to hers, close enough to feel his breath against her lips. She answered by leaning forward ever so slightly until there was no space between them at all. The kiss was heavy and deep. She hadn't done a lot of kissing, but this was definitely the best one ever. She could feel it in her fingertips, in her toes, and in a lot of other less innocent places, and then he was gone, flinging himself to the opposite end of the couch, staring at her, mouth agape.

For a moment the only sound in the room was their breathing, and the announcer screaming over the crowd. "Penny Harrison has won the Madrid Open and the United States has found its newest star!"

"Jas," Teddy started, but she shook her head. "Shit, Jas, I'm…"

"Forget it," she mumbled, leaping to her feet, her shin brushing against the table, sending the now-empty bottle of Jack over on its side. She stumbled to the doorway and broke into a run. She heard Teddy call her back over the buzzing in her ears, but she didn't turn around. She just kept going.

Game. Set. Match.

CHAPTER 1

MAY 14th

"Crap. Crap. Crap," Indy muttered to herself. She pulled her long, blonde hair into a ponytail, not even sparing a glance for her reflection as she raced past the mirror hanging inside the closet door.

The closet was still empty; its future contents still packed inside suitcases and boxes lining the floor of her dorm room. The walls were bare, no posters or pictures to brighten up the sterile, white sheetrock. The dorms at the Outer Banks Tennis Academy were functional, used as a place to sleep and that was about it.

Besides, she didn't have time to worry about decorating. After arriving the night before and unloading the back of her yellow Jeep Wrangler, Indy'd collapsed into bed, feeling like she could sleep for a week. Unfortunately, her travel-slogged mind hadn't remembered to set her alarm and her body was still operating on California time.

She was supposed to meet her new coach, Dom Kingston at eight, which meant she had five minutes. Indy grabbed her tennis bag, shoving her room key into a small pocket and slammed the door behind her. Then the real panic set in. Looking left and then right, she realized she had no idea how to find Dom's office. Her brain had barely registered her room number the night before when the security guard had shown her the way, let alone memorized the zigzag pathway they took to get here. Then miracle of miracles, the door across the hall cracked open.

"Thank God," she said as a tall boy with a dark tan and even darker hair slipped from the room.

He whipped around to face her, his eyes wide in obvious panic. Lifting a finger to his lips, he eased the door closed behind him. A bright pink, paper daisy was pasted in the middle of the solid wood with the name Katie written across it in glitter. Indy smirked. Apparently Katie, whoever she was, had company over last night. The guy standing across from her smirked back, a dimple appearing in his cheek.

"Morning," he said and then turned, starting down the hallway.

Indy sniffed out a short laugh and then followed. "Wait," she called out, catching up quickly. "I'm late."

"That's nice," he said, but didn't break stride.

She rolled her eyes to the ceiling. "I'm late for a meeting with Dom and I have no idea how to get to his office. Please, it's my first day."

That made him stop, the smile creeping back onto his face. He stepped up to her. "A deal then. I take you to Dom's office so you're not late on your first day and you never saw me here."

Indy grinned. "Saw who where?"

"Atta girl," he said, his green eyes sparkling with mischief. He tossed his head in the opposite direction. "This way. It's faster."

He led her out of the dorms and through a maze of practice courts. OBX had courts in all surfaces, though the blue hard court was the most common, many of which were already in use.

"This is as far as I go," he said, drawing to a halt just outside the main building. "Good luck, New Girl." Then he was gone, jogging through the parking lot and down the street into the neighborhood that sat just next to the OBX property.

Indy glanced up at the main entrance. OBX was written in huge block letters painted navy blue, darkly contrasting the light sand-colored stucco exterior of the building. It stood for Outer Banks Tennis Academy, the best training facility in the world. It looked exactly as it did the last time she'd been there, a year ago with her mom, and starting today, she would be a part of it. It was perfect timing. The junior tennis season was just starting to heat up, and if she could make a splash in OBX's invitational in a couple of weeks, she'd be well on her way to the pro career she and her mother always dreamed of. That is if she qualified.

It had been a long time since she'd played at an elite level. High school tennis definitely didn't count. The last major championship she won was over a year ago. She was crowned the West Coast Regional 16 & Under Champion just a few weeks before her mom got really sick, too sick to even fight her on pulling out of Nationals.

Indy was back now and really, she'd put this off for too long. Watching Penny Harrison kick ass in Madrid was the tipping point. Indy knew her mom wouldn't have wanted her dreams to be put on hold forever. She wouldn't have wanted them to be put on hold at all.

Swallowing back the lump in her throat— one that just wouldn't go away no matter how much time passed since her mom died—she reached for the door handle and stepped into her new life.

"Welcome to OBX," said an older African American man dressed in a dark suit as she stepped through the main entrance. He put down his newspaper and stood from behind a reception desk at the center of the large atrium. Shining, grey speckled tile lined the floor and there was a large wall of windows up on the second level. "I'm Roy Whitfield, head of security. You must be Indiana Gaffney. The night security guard told me to expect you this mornin'." His accent was a little jarring to her ears. Despite the beaches and warm sun, the distinctive twang in his voice was a stark reminder of just how far away she was from home.

"Indy," she said, "just Indy."

"Well then, nice to meet you, Indy. Running a little late this morning, darlin'? Was that Teddy Harrison I saw you walking with?"

"I, um, I guess so. I don't know. I was lost," she stuttered. Was that who he was? Teddy Harrison, twin brother of Penny Harrison, the one the tennis world called, "the normal Harrison" because he was only headed to a full athletic scholarship at Duke and not racing up the rankings of the pro tour?

Roy nodded. "Hmm, alright then."

"I'm supposed to meet Coach Kingston…" She trailed off as Roy's attention was drawn behind her.

"Ah, speak of the devil."

Indy couldn't help but smile when she turned and saw her new coach striding toward them from the other end of the atrium. Dom Kingston was tall and tan, his dark hair a little too long and graying at the temples. As a player he had won both the US Open and the Australian Open, twice.

"Indiana, happy to have you here, finally," Coach Kingston said, shaking her hand firmly. His dark brown eyes met her blue ones, letting her know without a doubt that he meant it.

"Thanks." It meant a lot that he hadn't given up on her and had enough faith in her abilities to bring her on. She'd basically called him up out of the blue, hoping the old cell phone number she had for him was still good. It was and it turned out he was thrilled to hear from her, even after so much time had passed.

"Have a little trouble with the clock this morning?" Dom asked, raising his eyebrows.

Indy laughed nervously and shrugged. "Yeah, the Eastern Time Zone and I aren't friends yet, and then I got lost."

"Teddy Harrison was nice enough to show her the way," Roy cut in, his mouth turning down unhappily. "Funny, him being on campus so early."

Dom pressed his lips into a thin line and hummed. "Indeed." Then he shook his head and focused back on Indy. "You should start getting used to time changes. Success on tour is half talent, half being able to adjust to new time zones, and here at OBX we have a policy: on time is fifteen minutes early."

"It won't happen again," she promised, a twinge of excitement shooting through her at the thought of being on the pro tennis tour and that Dom saw her living that life one day.

"See that it doesn't. Now, Roy, would you be kind enough to show Indiana to the locker room and then drop her off at the training courts?" Roy nodded and Indy quashed down the stab of disappointment that Dom wouldn't be taking her around himself. He must have read it on her face. "I've got a lot of paperwork to catch up on this morning. It all piled up while I was in Spain. You're in good hands with Roy." He strode to a side staircase near Roy's security desk, then turned back. "Welcome to OBX, Indiana. I'll see you out there in a little while. Roy, when Penny gets in, tell her I'd like to speak with her."

"Will do," Roy said as Coach Kingston climbed the stairs and let himself into his second-floor office. "Now, Indy, come on, girl. We'll get you set up with a locker and then off to practice. I've been here since the day OBX opened its doors. You have any questions or need anything at all, you can come to me."

He led her down a hallway off the atrium. OBX had state-of-the-art indoor facilities, both for training and recovery, a full spa, video analysis rooms, and indoor courts. She'd seen it all before, but that didn't make it any less impressive. Then, at the end of the hallway, a large mahogany wall littered with small brass plaques caught her eye. It stretched from the edge of the locker room door all the way to the exit that led to dozens of practice courts.

"The Title Wall," Roy said when he saw the direction of her stare. "Walk past this every day, Indy, and it's easy to stay motivated."

Indy squinted at the plaques, catching names and dates any tennis fan would be familiar with, incredible athletes who came through the doors of this training facility just as she had with the same dreams and aspirations.

The newest plaques were still shiny and bright, not faded like some of the others. They were all less than a year old.

Penelope Harrison – Australian Open Junior Girls
Penelope Harrison – OBX Classic Invitational
Penelope Harrison – French Open Junior Girls
Penelope Harrison – Wimbledon Junior Girls
Penelope Harrison – US Open Junior Girls
Penelope Harrison – Madrid Open

"It's been a good year at OBX." Mostly for Penny Harrison, she added in her head.

"A very good year."

"I'll be up there soon." She was already picturing her name on a brass plate with a huge tournament name next to it.

Roy's eyes twinkled at her. "You win a tournament, Indy, and that's where it goes, up on the Title Wall. Come on now. Let's get you out to the training courts. Workout's started and Coach D'Amato hates tardiness."

"Lead the way," she said, giddy at the thought of her standing in the center of OBX's main court, holding a trophy aloft as the crowd cheered her victory.

~

Indiana's breath came heavy and hard. A knot crept up her throat, choking her as she scrambled to keep up with the dozen or so other athletes racing back and forth, sideline to service line, sideline to alley line and then finally sideline to sideline. Assistant Coach Giulia D'Amato watched them like a hawk as their sneakers pounded from ad court to deuce court and back again.

"All the way through." The smooth Italian accent echoed off the hard court. "Do not stop, run through the line. *Andiamo!*" The tiny woman barked orders like a drill sergeant.

Their feet skidded to a halt near the fence that surrounded Courts 11-15. According to Roy, these were the training courts for all non-ranked players. Right now, however, they were being used for torture.

"This is insane," she mumbled under her breath. As soon as she stepped onto the court, fifteen minutes later than Coach D'Amato had expected her, the entire group, the Junior Elite Girls as Roy called them when he dropped her off, was instructed to complete fifteen "Einsteins." Nothing had ever winded Indy so fast, not the drills her former coaches made her do, not even the matches she'd played as a junior. She thought she'd kept herself in decent shape, running, lifting weights, swimming, along with the fitness program her high school tennis coach put together, but apparently it wasn't enough.

"*Eccellente*," D'Amato called. "Take some *aqua* and then rackets for serving drills."

They jogged to the fence behind the far baseline to grab some water. It seemed no one walked anywhere at OBX. Everything was done at a run. Indy's one consolation was that most of the girls looked as out of breath as she felt. That was her first goal then, step up her conditioning so she could surpass these girls purely on an endurance level.

They drank greedily from their water bottles and stood in a cluster, waiting for Coach D'Amato to call them back to practice.

"Why does she call them Einsteins?" Indiana asked the girl next to her. Shorter than Indy, the girl had a natural tan to her skin and her long dark hair was pulled back in sleek ponytail. She was one of the few not panting and strikingly pretty in an exotic sort of way, the exact opposite to Indy's blonde hair and fair skin.

The girl rolled her almond shaped brown eyes. "Einstein's definition of insanity, doing the same thing over and over again expecting a different result. She makes us do one for every minute anyone is late."

"Sorry," Indy muttered and the other girl's cool façade wavered a little.

"It happens. Just don't let it happen again."

"I'm Indiana Gaffney, by the way, but everyone calls me Indy."

"Jasmine Randazzo. Welcome to OBX."

It took Indy a moment to realize why she recognized that name, but then it clicked. Jasmine Randazzo was the daughter of John Randazzo and Lisa Vega, serious tennis royalty, and founders of this school. Jasmine wasn't quite as tall as she looked on TV and her frame was a lot slighter.

"Oh you're... That's so cool."

"What?" Jasmine frowned.

"That you're..." Indy began, but then realized her mistake. "I'm sorry. You probably get that all the time, your parents being who they are."

"Whatever, they're my parents." The girls standing near them buzzed. Clearly Indy'd said the wrong thing.

"Right and you're totally following in their footsteps. You played in Madrid last week."

Jasmine shrugged. "The Spanish Federation asked me to play."

"Wow." Indy smiled. "That's such an honor."

"Whatever, it's not that big a deal. Besides, the competition wasn't all that great."

"But didn't you lose in the first round?" The words slipped out before Indy even fully thought them. The girls around them gasped. "Shit, I'm sorry. I didn't mean—"

"Whatever," Jasmine said and stalked away, racket in hand. Silently, the others followed her, like little drones trailing their queen bee, most of them without enough guts to meet Indy's eye, except the last two, a short blonde and a tall redhead, who stared at her hard, then tossed their heads and giggled together as they walked away.

Indy pursed her lips. Her stupid mouth, it always got her in trouble, but it wasn't like she was wrong. Jasmine had lost in the first round.

"*Andiamo ragazze!*" Coach D'Amato called. "Girls, line up for serves. Indiana, you first."

Indy caught the ball the coach threw in her direction before moving off to the side to observe.

"Power it up the T," Coach D'Amato said.

She bounced the ball a few times until she felt comfortable, tossed it in the air and put everything she had into firing the ball up the middle of the court. Her serve wasn't quite at the level it had been a year ago, but it felt really good to just let it fly.

Indy stood tall as someone let out a whistle and another added a "Whoa." She turned, let her eyes linger on the line of girls behind her and smirked.

Coach D'Amato cleared her throat, drawing Indy's attention back around. "Again."

She obliged, grunting with the effort of her serve. It had been clocked at speeds averaging between 100 and 115 miles-per-hour, sometimes more. It was the most dominant part of her game and what convinced her mother she could become a professional tennis player. When she started playing big junior tournaments a few years ago she'd never been broken on serve. It's what caught Dom Kingston's eye at a regional championship and the reason he'd invited her to train at OBX.

Five more serves and the line behind her buzzed, the worker bees getting agitated.

"*Grazie,* Indiana. Jasmine, next."

Jasmine just rolled her eyes. Indy ignored her and moved to the back of the line. She watched as Jasmine hit solid, steady serves. Indy recognized the technique from Jasmine's mom, Lisa Vega, two-time French Open Champion. Her serve was good, really good, and suddenly Indy couldn't wait until she and Jasmine went head-to-head. Tennis royalty or not, to prove to everyone she was the best, Jasmine Randazzo was who she had to beat.

CHAPTER 2

May 14ᵗʰ

A beam of sunlight shining through her window warmed her cheek. Penny Harrison pressed her nose into the sheets and inhaled. The fresh scent of the laundry detergent her mother used was a reminder that, for the first time in four months, she was home for more than a couple of days.

"Penny." Her brother Jack's voice carried up the stairs and into her bedroom. "Delivery for you."

She rolled out of bed, feet landing on the plush carpet, a welcome change from the tightly woven, thin carpeting found in most hotel rooms.

She curled her toes into it, relishing the comfort before standing.

When she got downstairs, both her brothers were in the kitchen. Jack, her older brother and more recently, her agent, was digging through the fridge. Her twin, Teddy, was sitting atop the central island, shoveling a spoonful of cereal into his mouth. Beside him was a long, white box wrapped with a bright blue ribbon.

"You want some?" Teddy asked, his mouth full of the sugary crap he called breakfast.

"No thanks."

Penny pulled the ribbon free of its bow and folded it up neatly. She lifted the lid of the box to reveal a dozen long stem roses. There was a note tucked inside the sea of petals.

To many more victories.

Your friends at Nike

She breathed in the aroma of the fresh-cut flowers. Nike was upping their game. They'd been dangling a sponsorship deal since the end of last season when she swept the junior Grand Slams, but they'd backed off earlier this year after she'd lost in the quarterfinals of the Australian Open. Penny wrinkled her nose. Lost was a bit of an understatement. She'd been pounded, losing in a double bagel. A total embarrassment and something she swore she'd never let happen again.

"The flowers are a nice touch," Jack said, pouring himself a glass of orange juice.

"A car would've been a nicer one," Teddy quipped.

"I already have a car," Penny said, tucking the note back inside the box and then pushing his legs out of the way to find a vase under the island.

Teddy smiled, his dimples appearing, making him seem far more innocent than he'd ever been. "Yeah, this new one could be for me."

"Dream on, little bro," Jack said.

"Whatever. Speaking of cars though, can I borrow yours today?" he asked, turning to Penny.

"Nope. I'm going to OBX," she said.

"What? Why?"

"I have to train. The French Open is in less than a month."

"Yeah and you just won Madrid and almost a million dollars. You're not going to take a day to enjoy that?"

"I did," Penny said. "When Jack and I stopped over in New York to talk to potential sponsors I took the whole afternoon off and went shopping."

"Whoa, jump back. You're a real wild woman, Pen."

"I try. Why can't Mom or Dad drive you?"

"Mom's doing some tutoring thing and Dad's working. Please? I've already walked it once today."

"What do you mean?" Jack asked, narrowing his eyes.

Teddy smirked. "I stayed over at OBX last night."

"Did you? Who was it this time?"

"Katie Nelson."

"Ugh, you're disgusting, Ted," Penny said, looking up from arranging her flowers.

"Katie didn't think so. In fact…"

"Don't finish that sentence," she said, reaching for the bowl of car keys on the counter. "Take my car."

"You're the best, Pen." Teddy jumped down from the counter and took the keys from her, then strode out the room and probably back to bed. His training session wasn't until the early afternoon.

"So Nike," Jack said, taking the card from the box. "Looks like your win in Madrid made them rethink their pullback after Australia."

Penny wiped some of the last sleep from her eyes. "Looks like it."

"You know this isn't just an outfitting deal, Penny. They want you to be the new face of their brand. You can't go into a major tournament and bomb out again. Things have to be different at the French Open."

"I know that," she said, crossing her arms over her chest. They'd had this conversation a million times since January. "I'm not playing in Rome or Brussels to focus on the French. I'll be ready."

Jack slung an arm over her shoulder and squeezed. "I know, but I wouldn't be doing my job if I didn't remind you."

Rolling her eyes, Penny shook her head. "What was I thinking hiring my brother as my agent?"

"You were thinking that your big brother is brilliant and that he'd always do what's best for you, even when that means kicking you in the ass. Now go get dressed."

Penny stood tall and saluted him. "Sir, yes, sir."

"Brat."

Twenty minutes later, she climbed into Jack's car and they sped down Ocean Trail toward OBX. Pulling into the parking lot, Jack navigated into her designated spot.

Reserved for Penelope Harrison
World #33

The sign was updated after her run to the quarterfinals at the Australian Open as well as some decent finishes in a few other tournaments. Now, after her win in Madrid, she'd popped into the top twenty for the first time in her career. Rankings were the result of complicated math. They were determined by a points system that reflected the results, good and bad, of each player at every tournament. Some tournaments were worth more than others and Grand Slams were worth the most. When Dom recruited her, convincing her parents to move their family from

Chicago to this tiny town on the North Carolina coast, he promised she would someday be a top twenty player. Now, here they were, just a few weeks away from the French Open where she could hopefully push into the top ten.

Penny grinned, thinking about that last match in Madrid. She'd worked for that win for a very long time. A breakthrough. A crucial step that brought her closer to winning her first Grand Slam.

Stepping out of the car, the sounds of the game she loved filled her ears from over the high fences surrounding the forty-five court complex, the solid thwack of balls hitting racket strings, sharp instruction from coaches, the pounding of feet on the hard courts. Jack went to the trunk to grab his bag, but Penny headed straight in.

She managed only a few steps into the main building, which housed the offices, a few indoor courts and the training rooms when Roy Whitfield caught sight of her.

"Penny Harrison!"

"Hey, Roy."

He was one of the first people she'd met at OBX four years ago and was a kind face during those intimidating days. None of her grandparents were still alive, but Roy was a pretty decent substitute and he did actually resemble her Gramps, her dad's dad. With a quarter of African-American blood in their veins, Penny and her brothers had a creamy, tan-colored skin and dark hair, but all three shared their green eyes with their mom.

"C'mere and give an old man a hug. Welcome home, girl." He kissed the top of her head and gave her a final squeeze. "Jack," he said, nodding at her brother, who had arrived inside.

"I'm glad to be back."

The air smelled the same, rubber from the soles of all the sneakers and the distinct aroma that popped out of every newly opened can of tennis balls and the sharp scent of the floor cleaner. This was home too. OBX was the place that made her dreams a reality.

"Coach asked to see you as soon as you got in," Roy said, tugging on her dark brown braid and nodding up at her coach's office.

"I'm not in trouble, am I?" she asked, as she walked to the stairs.

"I wouldn't call it *trouble*." Roy's eyes twinkled at her, his cheeks wrinkling as he smiled.

"I'm gonna head out, Pen. I'll see you later. Roy," Jack said, walking off toward the back exit. After playing tennis at Harvard, Jack helped out with the coaching whenever they were back at OBX. He said he did it to keep himself in shape, but Penny figured he just missed playing—she couldn't imagine giving tennis up cold turkey. This, plus he could check out the young talent coming up.

Penny took the stairs two at a time up to Dom's office and saw him standing at his window, which overlooked the rest of the facility, and in the distance, the coast with tiny umbrellas dotting the shoreline in various shades of the rainbow.

"Hey, Dom," she said, drawing him from his reverie and tossing herself into the seat across from his desk.

Dom turned and moved around his desk. "P, welcome back. You ready to go?"

"Yep. Roy said you wanted to see me. What's up?"

"Just wanted to talk through the training plan leading up to Paris."

Penny pursed her lips and waited for him to continue. As nice as it was to be home, there were two tournaments between now and the French Open she could be playing in, both of which Zina Lutrova was headlining. It had been Dom's idea to skip those tournaments in favor of coming back to train.

"I've brought in an old friend of mine to be your hitting partner. He's just getting back into full-time training himself, so it'll be the perfect fit for the next few weeks."

Penny raised an eyebrow, but knew better than to question him outright. "Yeah?" she asked simply.

Dom nodded. "Yeah. I want you to focus on your defensive game and building up your endurance. You saw what it was like in Australia this year. Two weeks of tennis is no joke. You can't fade at the beginning of the second week. You need to be peaking for the semis and finals, not for the round of sixteen."

"Right," Penny said, clenching her teeth. She wanted to tell him that endurance or lack thereof had nothing to do with the end of her run at the Australian Open. It was the only time her mental focus had slipped. At the highest levels, the mental game was even more important than physical.

"I am still the world's number one." Zina's Russian accent reverberated through Dom's office. Penny's head snapped to the video screen in the corner and everything else flew straight out of her head. It was an interview from the tournament in Rome where Zina was playing this week. "Harrison played a good match, but I did not play my best. It was a fluke," the young Russian superstar said from the press conference desk.

Dom paused the video as the interview ended. Penny focused on the arrogant smirk Lutrova managed to wear even while discussing a decisive loss at the hands of a player she was supposed to be better than. That expression alone was enough to make her want to grab a racket, fly to Rome, and take Lutrova's ego down a notch or fifty.

"These next few weeks are critical, P. Zina will be gunning for you in Paris. You're going to face her down and you're going to win," Dom said.

"I'll be ready."

"Good. Now go. I'll be out in a few. I've got to pull together the Classic rankings by this afternoon."

"Ranking day. It's that time of year again, huh? Feels like yesterday I won my first one."

"Yeah, well, three years was a good run, P, but looks like we'll have a new champ this year."

~

Penny was halfway to her practice court, one of the very few clay courts on campus, before she realized she hadn't asked Dom who her new hitting partner was. He'd said it was an old friend, but Dom had been in the tennis world for more than twenty years. That didn't exactly narrow down the field. Whoever it was, they were sure to be pretty damn good. Dom would only let her train with the best.

She opened the gate and dropped her bag against the fence before tilting her head in confusion. There was a man sprawled across the court, eyes closed, face to the sun, completely relaxed, except for his hands, which were firing through the air, drumming along with the music she could hear buzzing through his headphones even from the other side of the court.

"Excuse me," Penny said sharply. "This court is reserved." The man didn't move. He was tall and broad, making the large playing surface seem so much smaller than it actually was.

"Excuse me," she repeated when he didn't so much as twitch in response, "this court is..."

She trailed off as she approached. Frowning down at the court squatter, she immediately recognized him, especially since the last time she'd seen him he'd been in a similar state, totally relaxed, eyes closed—though he'd been wearing much less clothing.

Alex Russell, the best player in the world—or at least he used to be. Three years before, at the age of seventeen, Alex Russell was the first British man to win Wimbledon since 1936 and the youngest man to do it, ever—besting a record set by Boris Becker in 1985 by 211 days. He'd won the career Grand Slam at twenty, and since then, his game had gone to hell. Too much partying and not nearly enough training sent his ranking freefalling from number one in the world down into the mid-twenties, and only that high because of his insane natural talent.

He also held the distinction of being the only thing *ever* to distract Penny Harrison from tennis.

Penny kicked at the soul of Alex's sneaker and his eyes flew open. "What are you doing here?"

He pulled the plugs from his ears, the notes even clearer now as a heavy metal song echoed against the court.

"Sorry, what was that, love?" he asked with a wink, his eyes lighting up in recognition and then slipping over her form quickly, his tongue darting out to lick his bottom lip.

The low timbre of his voice sent shivers down her spine and her mind reeling back nearly four months, to the Nike event at the Australian Open she hadn't wanted to attend in the first place. She was midway through the most important tournament of her life and not in the mood for a party, but Jack insisted it was a chance to mingle with her potential sponsors and get her face out there. Plus, it was all for a good cause as proceeds were going to the fight against pediatric cancer. Jack had pulled that last part out of his hat after she flat out refused to go.

Twenty minutes in she'd been ready to go back to the hotel. She'd lost Jack in the crowd and was steadily making her way to the exit when she ran headlong into a chest and narrowly avoided the drink that sloshed out of its accompanying hand.

Penny blinked herself back to the present and looked at the same chest now as Alex stood, running a hand through his sandy hair, his jaw line covered with stubble, just enough to give him an edge. His blue eyes shined down at her.

"What are you doing here?" she repeated, crossing her arms over her chest. Her throat started to close because she suspected she knew the answer already. He was wearing a white T-shirt, streaked with red clay stains, and dark blue basketball shorts.

"Dom didn't tell you?"

Penny's stomach sank. Alex Russell was *technically* an old friend of Dom's. When Alex started on tour Dom was finishing up his long career. They'd met up on the court more than once and Dom's final match—in the second round at the US Open—was against the younger man, who was on his way to his very first championship.

"I'm your new hitting partner or you're *my* new hitting partner, whichever you prefer, love." An easy smile spread across his face.

Penny's eyes narrowed. That was the same smile he'd bestowed upon her that night in Australia. He'd smiled and asked her to dance.

"You're training again?" she asked, raising an eyebrow. She shook her head. "No, forget it. I don't care. This is not happening."

"And why's that?" His eyes sparkled. Actually sparkled, like he was some damned cartoon prince in a Disney movie. "I don't play against has-beens."

The smile wavered and then disappeared completely. "A has-been?"

"Everyone knows the LTA dropped your sponsorship and your agent left you, but besides that…" She trailed off, her eyes lingering on his knee, an angry-looking scar surrounding the top of the joint. He was recovering from knee surgery and hadn't played in a tournament since Australia, but she couldn't bring herself to use that against him. It was every player's worst fear, an injury that pulled him out of competition, maybe forever. He'd supposedly been laying low in London, rehabbing his knee and what was left of his reputation.

"Besides what?" he asked, forcing the issue. His expression darkened as he stepped closer, his chest nearly brushing against hers.

"Your knee…they said…everyone said that your knee was…"

"You should know better than to listen to *everyone*."

Penny swallowed. The implication was obvious. The tour had buzzed incessantly about how they'd left the Nike party together in Australia, but no one knew the truth. The stories ranged from outrageous to obscene, but the reality was even more embarrassing for Penny.

He'd asked her to dance, and staring into those blue eyes and that grin, it had been easy to say yes. They'd danced; their bodies pressed together, the bass of the music pounding through them, his hands trailing paths of fire over her skin and she knew he was feeling what she was, an intense physical connection, burning hot on the dance floor that would become an all-encompassing inferno somewhere more private. His mouth had pressed against her ear, pleading with her to leave with him. Taking a risk for the first time in her life off the tennis court, she agreed and it had been one of the most incredible nights of her life. She'd snuck out the next morning, half out of embarrassment—she wasn't the kind of the girl who did one-night stands—and half because she had a training session. The next night on the news came reports of a motorcycle accident. An

Australian supermodel with an insanely high blood alcohol level had been treated for minor injuries and the man people once thought could become the greatest tennis player of all time had his knee torn to shreds.

Penny didn't care that people saw them leave the party together or that they whispered about it for weeks. She'd brushed off everyone's questions, even Jack's. Alex had just given her a ride back to the hotel, she'd said and she was pretty sure Jack had believed her. Rumors and gossip didn't matter. It stung a little that Alex was with someone else the next night, but what really struck her to the core was that he could've just as easily crashed his bike one night earlier with her on the back. She could've lost everything, and at the time, the risk hadn't even crossed her mind. That was the thought she'd taken with her onto the court for her quarterfinal match and that was what distracted her enough to go out in straight sets against a player not fit to carry her racket bag. Then Nike had pulled back their interest, and her reputation on the court—the only reputation that really mattered—was tarnished. She'd been working her way back ever since.

"Grab your racket." Alex's voice broke through her thoughts.

"What?" she asked, blinking up at him.

He walked to the bench just off the court and tossed his headphones and iPod into the racket bag sitting atop the bench before pulling out a brand new racket, still covered in the clear protective plastic. The distinctive red W was easily visible against the tightly wound white strings. A Wilson racket, what he'd been playing with since he was a junior, not that Penny would ever admit she knew that.

"Grab. Your. Racket," he said again.

"Why?" But she knew why and the thought of facing off against him was both exhilarating and terrifying.

"Love, I'll show you exactly how much of a has-been I'm not. Let's go. You and me, right now."

"No."

"Scared?"

Penny glared at him. He was pushing her buttons, yet her pride won out over the logical part of her mind that told her this was a bad idea.

"Warm up and you serve first."

The confrontation had her blood pumping. Alex ran in place, swinging his arms around, stretching them over his head and behind his back before going through his serving motion, whipping it through the air. Penny slowly went through her measured stretches starting with her ankles and wrists, then working her way inward. She kept her eyes focused on the clay, allowing each muscle to loosen up before moving on. Finally, she looked up at him. He was waiting at the opposite end of the court, racket in hand, bouncing a ball.

Penny pushed up onto the balls of her feet as she waited for what had once been the world's best serve to catapult at her, but then fell onto her toes as a looping volley traveled over the net.

She straightened and caught the ball on her racket. "Has your game really regressed to this level? If it has I'm not going to waste my time," she called out, offended he was going easy on her.

"Alright then. 15-Love."

Shaking her head over the fact he counted that ridiculous serve as a point, she again bounced on the balls of her feet, preparing to receive a real serve.

He stood up straight and ran a hand over the back of his neck. "You sure about this? I figured we'd save it until you improved defensively, like Dom wants."

Penny's eyes narrowed. "Just hit the damn ball."

"Your funeral, love," he muttered before his body coiled and exploded through the ball.

She got her racket on it, but the combined speed of the ball and the tight strings of her racket sent it sailing long.

"30-Love."

That was the best serve she'd ever seen. She'd played against men who could hit as hard, but his serve was in another category all together. A wicked spin combined with the velocity, even with the clay slowing it down a little, made it sheer luck she got her racket on it. Apparently, reports of his knee injury were grossly exaggerated. No one could blast a serve like that on a blown-out knee. Crossing to the other side of her court, she prepared again, taking a step back this time to compensate for the velocity. His face was stone, no emotion—all business.

Alex fired another serve out wide, sending her lunging. This time her return landed in play. Her feet caught up underneath her and changed direction, knowing he would counter cross-court.

She hit the ball in stride, launching it back across the court. For a split second, she watched the gorgeous backhand fly to the opposite corner for a winner. Then her momentum sent her sprawling into the clay. She rolled over, tucking her shoulder and landing on her back, knocking the breath from her lungs. Penny lay there a moment, gasping at first and then breathing slowly in through her nose and out through her mouth. Everything felt okay, so she rolled onto her side and stood up, brushing the clay from her hands.

Alex was on her side of the net by the time she regained her footing. "Are you all right?" he asked, one hand cupping the back of her head, the other sliding down her side to check for injuries.

A tremor slid through her as his calloused fingertips traced her jawline, tilting her chin upward, forcing her to look at him. She shouldn't be feeling like this. Her body ignored her mental reprimand and she ever so briefly leaned into the touch. It was just like that night, magnetism unlike anything she'd ever felt before. His eyes left hers and drifted down to her lips. She wet them unconsciously and he sucked in a harsh breath. It was enough to break the spell.

"Don't touch me." She pulled away, her skin immediately mourning the warmth of his hand. "I'm fine."

"Are you sure? Dom will kill me if you get hurt."

"Thirty-Fifteen." She ignored the pain in her hip—it was just a bruise—hoping to both reassure him and reignite the competition. She wanted to play, even more now than before.

Alex studied her and Penny kept all emotion off her face, not giving away even a hint of discomfort. "Thirty-Fifteen," he agreed, before retreating to his side of the court.

A half hour later, they were thrashing each other, holding their serves, and despite the bruise blooming on her hipbone, she was pleased with her effort. The respect she saw in his expression after she returned one of his serves for a clean winner wasn't a figment of her imagination. She would never admit it out loud, but playing against him every day *would* help her prep for the French.

Drenched in sweat and adrenaline thrumming through her veins, the sound of the gate opening didn't register. She was too caught up in the thrill of the match, of having a fierce opponent, and she relished every point she won, a small revenge for the little part of her that still resented him hooking up with an Australian supermodel the night after Penny was in his bed.

"Got started without me, huh?" Dom's voice rang out, startling Alex as he tossed the ball up into the air. It fell to the ground, bouncing away.

Penny cringed. Dom instructed her to start on her conditioning, not get roped into a full-on grudge match. Her coach stood at the edge of the court, the breeze ruffling his dark hair, looking every inch the elite athlete, still in great shape, even in retirement.

"Couldn't help ourselves," Alex quipped, retrieving the ball.

"Well, next time, wait for me. I'm your coach. Can't analyze anything if I'm not here to watch," Dom said.

"Right," Alex said, laughing. "Haven't had a coach in a while. Might take some getting used to."

Shaking his head, Dom turned his attention to her. His eyes caught the red clay staining her white tennis shorts and blue T-shirt. His thick, black eyebrows lifted up into his hairline, asking the question "What happened?"

"Can I talk to you for a second?" Penny asked, inhaling deeply through her nose, trying to keep from exploding at her coach. He didn't know about her and Alex. This situation wasn't his fault. It was hers. "Privately."

"Say what you like, love. I'm a big boy."

Her back teeth grinded together and she turned to her coach. "We only have five weeks until Paris and I don't have time to waste helping him get back into match shape or whatever. I'm not training with him."

"I don't know. It looks like you two got in a pretty good workout. Any other reason?" Dom asked, narrowing his eyes and crossing his arms over his chest. It was his battle stance. She hadn't seen it in a while.

"She thinks I'm a has-been," Alex said as he started kicking around one of the stray tennis balls, picking it up with his foot and bouncing it off his knee, showing Dom exactly how seriously he took her opinion.

Penny pressed her fingertips against the side of her head, trying her best to ignore him as she led Dom a few feet away, giving her a little more privacy. "I can't train with him, Dom," she said, her voice quieter this time. "He's too... I just...can't." Her words failed her. She couldn't tell her coach she couldn't train with Alex because he was a smug prick who already managed to seduce her once. That no matter how much playing with him could help her game, he would be nothing but a distraction at a time when she could least afford it.

Dom folded his arms over his chest and lowered his head, keeping his voice low. "Listen to me, P. He's the perfect training partner for you." She opened her mouth to interrupt him, but he cut her off. "This is the best thing for you going into Paris, a training partner who can keep up with you, challenge you on a daily basis. Even not having played in months, he's better than everyone here."

"He seems fine," Penny groused, looking up at the sky and sighing in defeat as his words echoed her own thoughts.

"Good then, so there's no problem?" Dom asked, but it wasn't a question and he was already walking away from her, gathering up the stray balls from their impromptu match.

"So, love, what's the verdict?" Alex asked, suddenly right beside her, and despite everything, as his body hovered just inches from hers, her skin started to hum at the proximity. She spun on her toe, their chests nearly colliding. Alex's hands came up to steady her, but she slipped away from his grasp.

"I told you not to touch me." She moved back out onto the court and he matched her stride, his arm brushing against hers as they walked. She pulled away immediately and stepped in front of him. Looking up, she squinted into the sunlight shining behind his head, reflecting off the golden streaks in his hair. "Outside of this court, you stay the hell away from me, understand?" she whispered so Dom wouldn't hear.

Alex grunted, a sound deep from within his chest, a sound she recognized. He'd made it once with his lips buried between her shoulder and her neck, his weight pressing her down into the bed, skin again skin. "Understood," he said, but Penny knew the real test wasn't if he could stay away from her, but if she could keep herself away from him.

CHAPTER 3

May 14th

"Easy, *agevole, ragazze,* easy," Coach D'Amato called as the Junior Elite Girls jogged around the practice court, cooling down from their practice session. "*Va bene, va bene.* That is all, *eccellente.*"

Jasmine, leading the line, slowed to a walk and then made a beeline for her racket bag resting against the fence that surrounded the court. She'd had a good practice and her muscles were tingling, a good hurt. It was the perfect way to start off Classic Rankings day.

"Good practice *ragazze,*" Coach D'Amato said as the girls began to leave the court. "Indiana, *uno momento, per favore.*"

D'Amato pulled the new girl aside and seemed to be explaining something about her footwork, demonstrating a simple crossover step.

Jasmine smirked. Indiana had an insane serve to go along with her ridiculous name, but not much else. Her footwork was a mess. Her forehand was okay, but her backhand was so weak decent players would never give her the courtesy of ever hitting to that side. And of course she started at OBX just before the Classic. She wasn't the first player to try that strategy. They would show up thinking Dom would be so floored by the talent oozing out of their pores he'd just hand over the Classic trophy and all prestige that went along with it, though Indiana was the first to actually show up on ranking day. It didn't make her any less delusional, but still, it was a gutsy move.

No, Indiana Gaffney wouldn't be giving her any trouble during the OBX Classic. Jasmine let her eyes wander over the other girls gathering up their things, almost all of whom looked ready to drop. In truth, none of these girls would give her a problem. Since Penny started full time on tour, Jasmine was easily the best player at OBX. Years of hard work had brought her to this point and now it was her time to shine. Time to live up to her parents' legacy.

"Lookin' good out there, Randazzo." A voice carried from the other side of the fence, breaking into her thoughts. She would know that voice anywhere. Teddy Harrison. Her eyes flew open wide, looking around for an escape route, but the fence surrounding the junior courts only had one other exit and it was four courts away. She briefly considered sprinting in that direction, but it was too late.

"What's up?" she asked, forcing a smile onto her face before turning to look at him. He was standing just behind her, outside the court, both hands up against the top rail of the three-foot fence.

"You ready?"

"For what?" she asked, stalling, looking around for someone, anyone to latch herself onto and give her a plausible excuse to leave, but most of the girls were already off the court, headed for the locker rooms. The only one left was Indiana and hell would freeze over before she asked that girl for anything.

"It's Monday, Jas," he said, "We have a hitting session."

"Oh right, I uh, I forgot." It was only half a lie. She hadn't thought about him at all during practice, but when she woke up this morning, she'd hoped he'd forget about their weekly session. They'd had one stilted and altogether awful conversation after their kiss last week. It was all about how much better they were as friends and how they shouldn't let one stupid kiss change all that. Or at least that's what Teddy said and she'd gone along with it like an idiot because the truth was she'd rather have him in her life—even just as a friend—than not at all. She loved him. It wasn't just a stupid kiss for her. It was everything she'd ever wanted for the last four years, even though she knew Teddy didn't do relationships—ever.

"Right. So, are we going to train?" he asked, bouncing on the balls of his feet, expelling some of the excess energy he always carried around. It seemed like he was willing to just move on and ignore the tension that still lingered, if he even felt it at all. Jasmine felt like her body was encased in quicksand, being crushed under the pressure of loving someone who wouldn't love her back.

Keeping her expression schooled into indifference, Jasmine nodded and moved off the court.

"Hi, Teddy," Indy said as she followed just behind Jasmine.

"Hey, new girl," he said, flashing her a brilliant grin, one that made Jasmine's stomach flip, even if it wasn't for her. "How'd you find out my name? You asked around, huh?"

Indy laughed, yanking her long blond hair out of its ponytail and shaking it out. "More like Roy recognized you through the window."

Teddy laughed and winked. "Sure he did."

Jasmine cleared her throat, forcing down the lump that was practically choking her. How the hell did Indy know Teddy? She'd been at OBX for like three seconds.

"You two know each other?"

"Yeah, *someone* was lost and late this morning, so I showed her the way to Dom's office."

"Right, only after I swore—"

"Sorry, Indiana, Teddy and I have a training session. See you later."

Jasmine pushed past the other girl and started down the path to the practice court she and Teddy always used. She heard him mumble a quick good-bye to Indiana and then the sound of his footsteps as he jogged to catch up.

"That was rude."

She stopped short and turned to him. He nearly crashed right into her, but caught himself just in time, taking a quick step back. "Do you always have to do that?"

"Do what?"

"Flirt with every single girl who smiles at you?"

"I was being polite," he shot back.

"You were flirting."

"Jas," he said, his bright green eyes looking into hers. Jasmine pursed her lips, not impressed that he thought her name and an apologetic expression would be enough.

Running a frustrated hand through his short hair and huffing a breath, he began again. "I'm sorry. I just thought we said we were better off as friends." She could practically hear the panic in his voice, like he was being backed into a corner.

"We did." She tried to pretend she didn't hear his sigh of relief.

"Then why are you freaking out?" He took another step back.

"I'm not freaking out. I just—wait, what were you doing here this morning?"

"I uh…" His eyes grew wide and she knew he was fumbling around in his head for an excuse.

"Who?"

"Who what?"

"Who did you screw last night, Ted? Don't play dumb."

"Shit," Teddy muttered, his eyes locking onto something over her shoulder. She could hear the chatter of girls walking down the path behind her. "Teddy?"

"Walk with me this way." He grabbed her arm and led her down a smaller path, away from the practice courts, near the edge of OBX property that ran along the beach.

"Teddy, what the hell? Why can't you just answer the question?" Jasmine yanked her arm free and turned just in time to see a girl with long, blond hair, a lot like Indiana's, stride past on the main walkway where they'd just been standing. Katie Nelson, another junior player, probably on her way to the late-morning session with Coach D'Amato. She'd be going to UCLA in the fall.

"Sorry, I just—"

"Didn't want Katie to see you," she finished for him.

"Yeah, I didn't want a scene," he said, looking away from her, keeping his eyes trained above her head.

"Why would there be a—oh, it was her?"

He shrugged carelessly. "It didn't mean anything."

"It never does," she muttered.

"What?"

She felt herself deflate, the anger seeping away. They were just friends, nothing more. That's what they'd agreed to, and if she kept pushing this, she'd lose him.

"Nothing, let's just go hit, okay? I need to get another good workout in before Dom posts the rankings. I know my mom and dad will want to go celebrate afterward so I probably won't be around for afternoon session." She was at her wits end, and if she didn't have a tennis ball to hit soon, she was going to use his head for one.

~

"Jasmine, come on!" Lara Cronin, one of the other juniors, yelled from the locker room door. "It's going to be posted in five minutes!"

It was the rankings sheet for the OBX Classic Invitational. Every year Dom invited some of the best young female players in the world to play at the Classic, people likely to make a splash on tour in the next year or two. There were major bragging rights involved, and as they lived in the age of information, the results were almost always big news in the tennis world. When Penny swept through last year's tournament, the media labeled her a player to watch going into the new season. Tournament directors all over the world took notice. Of course Penny was the first Classic winner to ever have so much success in her first year on tour, which just added a whole new level of expectations for this year's winner.

Jasmine gathered her racket bag and met the gaggle of girls waiting for her at the locker room door. They were twittering with anticipation as they all followed her down the hallway, past the Title Wall and out into the main atrium.

"What's all this?" Roy asked from his desk, looking up over the edge of his newspaper. "You girls all here for me?"

A ripple of laughter echoed up into the atrium's high ceiling.

"We're here for the Classic rankings," one of the stupider girls said and Jasmine rolled her eyes.

"Ah, it all makes sense now. Dom's still up in his office. Should be comin' down the pipe any minute though." Roy chuckled, going back to his paper.

They all looked up and saw Dom through his office windows. He was standing in the corner of his office, where his printer sat on a table. He reached for a piece of paper and studied it for a moment, before nodding and disappearing from view.

It was like all the air was sucked out the room. Everyone pulled in a breath and held it, waiting for their coach to appear on the stairwell, rankings in hand.

"I think I'm gonna be sick," one girl muttered.

"Gross, then get away from me," another chimed in.

"Are they out yet?" a voice asked. Jasmine turned and saw Indiana Gaffney standing at the edge of the crowd, long blond hair still wet from her shower and hanging halfway down her back.

"Not yet, Dom just—"

Jasmine cleared her throat, a firm *ahem-hum*, cutting off whoever was responding. She squinted in that direction, but it was impossible to pick the voice out of the group of girls.

"There he is," Lara said from beside her, gripping her wrist. Dom stepped off the last stair and turned to the wall next to the stairwell.

Jasmine pulled away and took a step forward, feeling the girls behind her hesitate and then move with her.

Dom pinned the single sheet of white printer paper to the corkboard and then turned to them. "Ladies, behind me is a draw ranking for the OBX Classic. Remember, not everyone will make the tournament. Some of the best junior players in the world will be attending as well. If you have any questions, I expect you to come see me in person. I will not be taking any calls or meeting with your parents on this subject. Is that understood?"

The girls nodded.

"Good, now one more thing. Some of you might've heard that Penny's back on campus and that Alex Russell is here as well, getting himself back into match shape. He and Penny will be training together leading up to the French Open."

Jasmine's focus shifted from the white sheet of paper behind her coach's head to Dom's face as a few gasps and nervous giggles came out of the crowd around her. Most of the girls were used to Penny being around, although some of them liked to suck up to her once in a while, like her talent might rub off on them if they got close enough, but Alex Russell? That was just insane. Her own parents were a big deal, but more for their relationship off the court than anything else. Alex was only twenty-one and already had the same amount of Grand Slams as her parents did combined.

"I expect you all to behave professionally. No hovering around their practice court and making nuisances of yourselves. Do I make myself clear?"

Everyone nodded again.

Dom eyed the crowd like he didn't quite believe them, but he continued anyway, "Excellent. I'll see you all tomorrow."

He turned around, escaping up to his office, and the crowd pressed forward immediately.

For a moment, Jasmine's vision blurred as she took in the names. She took a deep breath, blinked then looked again.

OBX Classic Rankings

1. Jasmine Randazzo (USA/OBX)
2. Cara Pagnini (ITA)
3. Tatiana Belova (RUS)
4. Indiana Gaffney (USA/OBX)
5. Stella Almanzar (ESP)
6. Jessica McCormack (NZL)
7. Aliya Polina (RUS)
8. Ellie Forester (AUS)
9. Jelena Petrović (SRB)
10. Yulia Markelova (RUS)
11. Laura Wiltvank (NED)
12. Sydney Whitcomb (USA/OBX)
13. Lara Cronin (USA/OBX)
14. Saskia Johnstone (GRB)
15. Daciana Raducan (ROU)
16. Keisha Bernard (USA/OBX)

Behind her Lara squeaked in delight at making the cut, and Addison Quinn, who'd missed the tournament, started sobbing, but none of it really registered for Jasmine. Her eyes were glued to the top of the list.

How was it possible that after one day of training at OBX Indiana Gaffney was fourth? Dom even put her above Stella Almanzar, the Junior Australian Open runner-up, and a player Jasmine lost to on more than one occasion.

Jasmine pushed through the crowd and saw Indiana hovering at the back, her weight shifting back and forth, eyes focused on the board, but not moving any closer to it. It almost seemed like she was scared to look. Their eyes met, but Jasmine just strode past her, across the atrium straight for the door. As she was about to open it, someone pulled it away from the outside.

A tiny woman with caramel skin just like Jasmine's, dressed in a flowing white dress down to her ankles, secured at the waist by a large brown leather belt, and a tall man in jeans and a collared shirt were standing just outside the door.

"Mom, Dad, what are you guys doing here? I thought we were going to meet up later?" she whispered, glancing back over her shoulder to see if the other girls noticed the appearance of the stylish couple.

"We came for you." Her mom, Lisa, practically skipped the last few steps between them, bracelets jangling at her wrists, before pulling her into a hug. "Number one ranked in the tournament. *Mija*, I am so proud of you."

Jasmine lifted her head from her mom's shoulder and saw her dad, John, standing behind them. Her parents were her biggest fans. Tennis was never something she was expected to do. They never even brought up the subject of playing until she begged for lessons when she was seven. Yet, despite all the success they enjoyed in their own careers, the smallest things, like a number one ranking in a junior tournament, had them beaming like she won a Grand Slam. The problem was it was still a number one ranking in a junior tournament and *not* a Grand Slam victory. But she was going to eventually get one—that was the plan—and the OBX Classic was a necessary stop on the path she'd wanted to travel since she was old enough to understand exactly who her parents were.

A lock of salt and pepper hair fell onto her father's forehead. "Dom called me when he put the rankings together. I wanted to be here when you found out."

"Oh my God," a breathy voice said from behind her. "Mr. and Mrs. Randazzo are here."

The crowd behind Jasmine converged around them. Though her parents had founded OBX, they pretty much gave Dom free reign to run the academy as he saw fit and stayed out of his way. So whenever they showed up on the grounds, it was a pretty big deal for the other students.

"Can I have a picture?" Lara asked, holding her phone out and sidling right up to Jasmine's dad, snapping a picture before he could answer one way or the other.

"I watch the video of your French Open win all the time," Katie said to her mom, leaning around Jasmine's shoulder. Jasmine fought down the urge to snap her elbow into Katie's stomach.

"Wait, will you sign my racket bag?" Keisha asked, digging through the bag for a pen.

Her mom shot Jasmine an apologetic grin, but then turned to the group of girls and patiently responded to them one by one.

A small shriek from over by the rankings list echoed over the din of autograph and picture requests and Jasmine's eyes flew to where Indiana Gaffney stood, hand over her mouth, staring at the board. The blond girl turned around, her hand falling away, a huge smile on her face. Apparently, she'd worked up the courage to look at the list. Jasmine averted her eyes. She was ready to live up to her parents' legacy, and if she beat Indiana Gaffney along the way, so much the better.

CHAPTER 4

MAY 14th

Fourth. Dom ranked her fourth in the Classic. Sure, after coming to OBX, Indy had every intention of taking everyone by surprise in the tournament, battling her way into the final and winning the whole damn thing. She just hadn't expected Dom to rate her so highly. He hadn't even watched her train that morning before he put the rankings out—and thank God for that because he probably would've changed his mind. It was all she could think about during lunch, right through the afternoon workout in the gym and during dinner, that and the word Coach D'Amato had used during morning practice. *Inaccettabile.* That's what the tiny Italian coach called her footwork, and now, the day was almost over, but the word was still ringing in Indy's head. She was ranked fourth, even with her *inaccettabile* footwork.

Indy didn't speak Italian, but that word was easy enough to translate: unacceptable, not good enough, *weak.* That meant more practice. So after dinner she headed straight out to the junior practice courts to start addressing that weakness.

Tossing her racket bag against the fence, she leaned down and grabbed the small orange cones sitting on the ground. She'd start out simple. Moving to the middle of the court, she placed them about ten feet apart and stood in the center. One crossover step to the right and then back to the middle, another crossover to the left and retreat again. Over and over, keeping her feet moving and then faster and faster, like she'd seen Jasmine Randazzo do this morning at practice, like Penny Harrison did against Zina Lutrova. Time flew, and as the scuffing of her sneakers against the hard court sped up, so did her breathing, coming in short puffs. Her legs were tired after a long day of training, but that was all the more reason to push through. She couldn't just take a little break during a match if her legs got tired. Finally, she had to stop to catch her breath. She stood, hands on her knees, breathing deeply.

There were eyes on her. Indy could feel stares burning into her skin like white-hot laser beams, making the hair at the back of her neck, now sticky with sweat, stand up on end, sending a shiver down her spine.

"Some people, Addison, I swear. They just don't know their place," a sharp southern twang rang out from behind her.

"I totally agree, Lara."

Indy knew exactly who was standing there. Addison Quinn and Lara Cronin, the two girls who'd giggled when Jasmine snubbed her that morning. Lara was her future first-round opponent in the Classic and Addison was the girl who'd collapsed into sobs when she hadn't made the cut at all. Indy bit back a sharp retort and ignored them, hoping they'd go away. She started up her drill again, focusing more closely on keeping her footwork crisp and her strides long.

"I mean think about it," Lara continued, her voice rising with every syllable, clearly annoyed at Indy's lack of reaction, "we've been training here every day for four years, using this exact court, and then one day, someone else plants their prissy, overrated, no-talent ass at it like she owns it."

"It's just rude."

"So rude."

"Look," Indy said, sliding to a halt and whipping around, hoping to cut their little show short. They were standing at the baseline of the court, just a few feet behind her, hands on their hips looking ready for a fight. "I don't have time for this crap. It's a court, not your friggin' house. Get over it."

Addison huffed, but Lara's eyes narrowed. "You don't have any idea who you're dealing with, so you should just get your things and get out of here. Maybe go back to California while you're at it."

"And who exactly is going to make me?" Indy said, taking a step closer.

A stony silence was the only reply she got.

"That's what I thought," Indy said, turning back to her cones.

"It's not like you have any chance, anyway. I'm going to destroy you in the first round, bitch," Lara muttered.

"Is there a problem here ladies?" a voice called from the gate, getting closer with every word.

Indy whirled around again and stared at the guy the voice belonged to. She hadn't even seen him approach, but he was easily the best-looking guy she'd ever set eyes upon. Tall, dark and handsome didn't even begin to cover it, but it was a good start. He was built, not super skinny like some really tall guys tended to be, dressed in jeans and a crimson T-shirt with Harvard Tennis emblazoned across his chest—his very broad, very firm-looking chest, from what she could tell.

"Yeah, there's a problem," Lara spat out, flinging a hand out at Indy. "She's using our practice court, Jack."

His name was Jack, but…Jack what? He looked sort of familiar and as Indy tried to place his face he said, "Last time I checked there were over forty courts around here, girls. Why don't you go claim another one as your own before I bring Dom down here and tell him about this misunderstanding."

Lara's jaw dropped and it looked like she was about to say something else, but Jack crossed his arms over his chest, stretching his T-shirt over the muscle there, making Indy swallow hard. He was just too friggin' hot for words.

The other girls let out twin, long-suffering sighs and when Jack raised his eyebrow, probably daring them to protest, they marched away from the courts entirely, clearly having no intension of doing any practicing at all.

"Thanks," Indy said, pulling her gaze away from his body and up into his eyes, hopefully, before he noticed her staring. It wasn't a sacrifice. His eyes were bright green, an interesting shade considering his dark, textured hair and caramel-colored skin.

"No problem," he said, closing the gap between them with confident strides. "If there's one thing I can't stand, it's bullies."

Indy laughed. "I wouldn't exactly call them bullies. More like annoying little gnats."

He chuckled softly. "Glad to hear they didn't do any lasting damage."

"Nope, still in one piece," she said, smiling back at him.

"I don't think we've met before. I'm Jack Harrison," he held out his hand and she took it immediately, hoping hers wasn't too sweaty. His fingers wrapped completely around hers. It was like holding onto a mug of hot chocolate after coming in from the cold. Jack Harrison. That's why he looked familiar. He was Penny Harrison's older brother, agent and quasi-coach. She remembered seeing shots of him in the stands during the Madrid tournament, but her three-inch iPhone screen didn't do him justice.

"I'm…" She paused, her voice catching in her throat. "I'm Indiana Gaffney."

His smile widened. "Indiana. I like that."

Anyone else in the world and she would have corrected him. No one called her Indiana except her dad and it grated on her nerves whenever he did, but the way Jack said it, his voice soft and deep, she wanted to hear him say her name all day long. His hand released hers after a gentle squeeze.

"So, how have I not seen you around here before, Indiana?" He didn't step away, invading her space in the best way possible.

"Today's my first day."

"I didn't think I could miss someone like you." She blushed, but he nodded in the direction the terrible twosome had marched off. "And you've already made enemies. Impressive."

She shrugged, not being to help the grin spreading across her face. "They're just pissed because Dom ranked me ahead of them for the Classic."

Jack blinked at her and tilted his head in confusion. "The Classic? You're a junior?"

"Yeah, I mean, I was hoping Dom would think I was good enough, but I was shocked when he ranked me fourth. I've only been here a day. It probably wasn't the best way to make friends, but that's not really the point of training here, right?"

He took a step back and nodded, but Indy was pretty sure he hadn't heard a word of what she'd said. Then he spoke, "Well, I should really get going."

"Oh," Indy said, her brow furrowing, wondering if she'd said the wrong thing.

"Jack! There you are!"

Teddy Harrison strode toward them, hopping the fence with such ease Indy supposed he did it all the time. The resemblance between the brothers was astounding, though Jack was far more muscular.

"I've been waiting forever. You said you just had to…" He trailed off, as his eyes flashed to Indy. "But now it all makes sense. Hi again, New Girl."

"Teddy," she said.

"You two know each other?" Jack asked, looking back and forth between them.

"Indy was lost this morning and I was gentleman enough to show her the way."

"Yeah, after he snuck out of some poor girl's dorm room."

A silence hovered over them for a second. Finally Jack nodded, looking at the open gate as Teddy laughed outright at her calling him out.

"So what were you working on out here by yourself?" Teddy stepped into the space Jack had vacated beside her, but his closeness didn't quite have the same effect.

Indy felt her face flush. "My footwork," she said, nodding at the cones. "I was trying to…"

Teddy shook his head. "You aren't going to get anywhere with two cones and no one to watch you, right, Jack?"

"What?" Jack asked and Indy's eyes shot to the older brother, catching his gaze briefly before he looked away. Had he been looking at her? He'd definitely been looking at her.

"Focus, bro," Teddy scolded, but his smile was back in full force. "Don't you know some epic footwork drill we can show Indy?"

Jack shook his head, his mouth opening and then closing again, his shoulders stiffening, like he was preparing for battle. "I'm not sure if…"

Teddy shook his head as he picked up the cones she'd set out and tossed them to the side. "Yeah, you do. The insane one that Penny loves, what are they called?"

Indy felt her calf muscles spasm at the thought of another running drill. "Not Einsteins?"

An unexpected guffaw slipped out of Jack's throat.

"Do you want to show her or should I?" Teddy asked from the center of the court.

"I got this," Jack said, his eyes not leaving hers as he waved Teddy away. He stood in the center of the court, balanced on the balls of his feet for one moment and then he was off, a few crossover steps to his left and back, then to his right and back. Indy felt a small grin of satisfaction inch over her lips. She'd been on the right track with her own drills. Then her face fell as Jack's legs started covering more ground, pivoting at the corners of the service lines, sprinting to the net in diagonals and then back again.

"See, insane right?" Teddy said, from beside her as Jack literally ran circles around them.

He drew to a halt back where he started. "Got it?"

Indy bit her bottom lip and nodded. "I think so."

"Let's see it then," he said, moving out of the way for her.

She took the spot he'd vacated and set herself, but just as she started her crossover step, Jack's voice rang out. "No, no, stop."

"What?" she asked, spinning around to face him, hands landing on her hips.

"You're totally off balance. Come back here," he said, moving in closer. She complied. "Okay, now stand with your feet a little more than shoulder width apart—I said a little more, Indiana, not like the earth is tearing apart beneath you." He tapped the outside of her thigh and she jumped, or at least her heart did; she managed to keep her feet on the ground and slide them a little closer to each other.

"Good. Now keep your weight on the balls of your feet, not your toes. It's all about balance and staying in an athletic position, knees bent slightly, perfect, shoulders over your toes. That's it," he said as she followed his instructions. "And now the pièce de résistance, relax your joints. You're stiff as a board." His hands landed on her shoulders and the muscles there tightened reflexively. "Relax," he whispered. With a deep inhale and slow exhale, she tried to do just that, but it was nearly impossible with him standing so close. He must have sensed it because he stepped back and said it again. "Relax, stay loose."

"Okay," she said, allowing her shoulders to drop ever so slightly.

"Good. Now try it." Then he was gone, the warmth hovering behind her giving way to chilly solitude. It was like she was standing on stage all by herself and there was no one to give her a cue. With a deep breath, she began, her feet speeding through the exercise he'd demonstrated. Her stride was smoother, the flow of her feet easier.

"You feel that?" Jack's voice called out as she pivoted at the edge of the court and raced for the net.

"Yeah," she shouted back and finished the drill. It was like an Einstein on steroids, but she knew this stupid little drill was exactly what she needed as she prepped for the Classic.

"Hey, guys, are you ready?" a new voice joined them, one Indy recognized from TV immediately.

"Aw, Pen, you didn't have to wait for us," Teddy said as Penny Harrison stepped out onto the court and marched toward her twin brother, who'd been leaning against the net, watching the drill. She was showered and dressed in a mint green sundress dotted with wildflowers. Indy had never really pictured Penny as a sundress kind of person. Then again, she probably didn't wander around in tennis clothes all day.

"I wasn't waiting," Penny said. "You have my car keys and Jack has his, so cough 'em up, Ted." Her twin reached into his pocket and tossed her a set of keys. Then she turned the green eyes all three Harrison siblings shared to Indy. "Hey."

Indy's mouth went dry at finally being noticed. Friggin' Penny Harrison said hello to her. Praying she didn't make an idiot out of herself like she did in the morning with Jasmine, she said, "Hi, I'm Indy."

"Nice to meet you," Penny said, before looking over her shoulder at Jack who was standing just off to the side still as a mountain and silent.

"Indy's training for the Classic," Teddy said. "It's her first day today and Dom seeded her fourth."

One perfectly shaped eyebrow lifted and Penny pursed her lips. "So you're the girl they're all bitching about in the locker room?" Her eyes narrowed and she stared at Indy more intensely. Indy felt like an insect under the microscope of some scientist that was about to dissect it. The silence dragged on and Indy could practically feel something ridiculous building on the tip of her tongue when Penny said, "Good luck at the Classic."

A flush spread across her face. Penny Harrison had just wished her luck. So friggin' awesome. "Thanks."

With a nod, the other girl spun on her toe and strode off the court, totally ignoring her brothers as she left.

"I better go too," Indy said. "I've got a ton of homework to get done tonight."

"We were just going to get dinner," Teddy said. "Why don't you join us?"

"Ted, she just said she had a lot of work to do," Jack cut in. Indy felt like someone slapped her. Apparently, he didn't want her to go. Where was the guy who cheerfully rescued her just a few minutes ago from OBX's queen bitches?

"He's right. I really do have a ton of work, plus I already ate." She tried to ignore the clear relief that spread across his face at her words. "Thanks so much for your help. I'll see you guys around."

Indy left the court, trying to focus on the good. She had a great ranking for the Classic. That's what she'd come to OBX for, to win the Classic, but despite that, her thoughts kept drifting back to Jack Harrison and the way his voice sounded when he said her name.

~

The next morning pink slivers of light crept above waterline far in the distance, giving the beach an unearthly glow. Indy stretched her arms over her head, muscles suddenly so much heavier than they were the day before as she clomped down the wooden stairway leading from the OBX practice facilities down to the sand. Each step made every fiber of muscle in her legs throb. After just one day, her body was in shock. Her mind had forced her out of bed that morning knowing the sooner she moved, the less it would hurt— eventually.

Gingerly she reached the bottom of the stairs and landed in the sand, and suddenly, even standing still was painful as she tried to keep her balance on the soft surface.

"This was a friggin' stupid idea," she muttered to herself. She wanted to turn around and crawl back into bed. She could run tomorrow, when her body was more accustomed to OBX's training regimen.

She grasped the handrail of the stairs to pull herself back up them, but as she looked up, she saw Penny Harrison, long, dark hair piled at the top of her head and headphones plugged into her ears, jogging down the stairs.

Indy froze. It was one thing to be introduced to one of your idols, especially with two other people around as a nice buffer, but what the hell was she supposed to say now? Should she wait until Penny said something or just say hello to her like it was no big deal? She probably had people acting like crazed fans around her all the time and Dom had said not to bother her while she was training, but they knew each other now, so…

"Hey," Penny said, cutting into Indy's mental ramble as she jumped down the last couple of steps into the sand. She toed off her sneakers, then pulled off her socks and tucked them inside.

"Hi," Indy finally managed, and her resolve to limp back to bed crumbled. She came here to train at the academy that made Penny Harrison one of the best tennis players in the world. If that meant pushing through the soreness, then that's what she would do.

Penny raised her eyebrows and nodded down the beach. It was probably the closest thing to an invitation Indy was going to get, so she nodded and they set off, their pace even and measured.

The smell of the ocean air wafted up from the shore, filling Indy's senses, forcing the last traces of sleepiness from her. She quickened her pace just slightly as her muscles loosening and energy began to flow through her limbs.

"Easy does it," Penny cautioned from a step behind her. "You want to warm up, not tire yourself out for training later."

The sun finally burst out from the horizon, the ocean a sea of orange, purple and pink as the light reflected off the water. They ran for about ten minutes, turned at the edge of OBX property and followed their footsteps back toward the practice courts.

"Crap," Penny muttered as soon as they turned and saw a figure jogging in their direction.

"What?" Indy asked, squinting into the distance. The little part of her that would always be a tennis fan recognized the silhouette. Alex Russell was headed straight for them. Indy had no idea how that could be a bad thing, but she kept her mouth shut.

"Good morning, ladies," Alex said, flashing them a charming grin, his eyes twinkling at them, though after a brief glance in her direction, he focused on Penny. He wore a pair of long tennis shorts, but nothing else, the waistband just below his well-defined abs, the blue ink of a tattoo, words in a fancy script etched across his left ribcage. He was definitely hotter in person than he was on TV.

"Morning," Penny said and kept jogging. Indy followed her lead.

"Argh," Alex shouted from behind them and they both whirled around. He was lying in the sand a few feet away, clutching at his chest. "You wound me, right here, like a bloody arrow."

Indy snorted, trying to muffle her laugh and she glanced at Penny, whose eyes were focused at the sky, shifting now from the pinks and purples of the sunrise to a clear blue. Alex propped himself up on his elbows.

"See you at training, love."

Penny just shook her head and started running again, picking up the pace as she went. Alex winked at Indy before climbing to his feet and jogging in the opposite direction.

By the time Indy caught up to Penny, she was already at the bottom of the stairs, pulling her socks and sneakers back on.

"Are you okay?" Indy asked, not really sure what else to say.

"I'm fine," Penny snapped at her and then cringed. "Sorry."

"It's okay," Indy said.

"No it's not, but thanks."

Indy nodded and started up the steps. Her muscles weren't quite as sore anymore, thanks to the solid workout she'd just put in. Penny was right behind her. They walked in silence through the maze of practice courts, past the back doors to the atrium and they both turned left at the edge of the main building toward the entrance of Deuce.

Open twenty-four hours a day, Deuce served as a dining hall for the live-in students, staff and any tennis vacation guests, plus it was open to the public for lunch and dinner. With vaulted, wooden, whitewashed ceilings and contrasting dark-stained floors and tables, plus an outdoor eating area that overlooked the beach, it was the place people gathered before and after training, and that morning, it was bustling.

"Why is it so crowded?" Indy asked, looking around into a sea of faces she'd never seen before. It hadn't been nearly as packed during lunch and dinner yesterday.

"The Classic players started showing up last night and this morning. The players, coaches, families, it adds up to a lot of people at OBX for a couple of weeks," Penny said, leading the way to the breakfast buffet at the far end of the room.

They each grabbed some fruit and toast, and when Indy turned, she saw Jack and Teddy already sitting at a table waving them over. She hovered uncertainly at the empty chair between the Harrison twins for a moment, her eyes lingering on Jack, who was looking anywhere except in her direction, but then Penny looked up at her, eyebrows drawn together.

"Are you going to sit?"

"Oh, right," Indy said, putting her plate down and sliding into the chair.

Across the room, Lara and Addison were holding court with a few other OBX girls, including Jasmine Randazzo. If looks could kill, Indy knew she would've dropped dead as soon as Jasmine's eyes locked on her. All three Harrisons seemed oblivious to the attention, so Indy decided to ignore it. Having them with her was like a solid wall that could keep out any crap those girls probably wanted to throw at her.

"Got confirmation last night that Harold Hodges'll be here covering the Classic, Pen. He wants to do a feature with you and Alex, if that's okay?" Jack asked, dumping an insane amount of sugar into his coffee.

Penny's mouth twisted into a pout, but she nodded.

Teddy laughed and then using his fork for a microphone said, "You're like so famous, Pen. What's it like to be so awesome?" He nudged his sister with his elbow, making her drop the knife she was using to butter her toast, but Penny rolled her eyes and laughed with him.

It was weird. Indy hadn't really expected them to be so…normal.

"Indy!" Roy called out from the edge of the restaurant, approaching the table quickly. The entire restaurant, buzzing with activity just seconds before, fell into total silence. "Coach wants to see you. Come on with me back to his office."

"Oooh," Teddy said, chuckling as Indy's eyes widened in panic.

"Shut up, Ted," Jack said, glaring at his younger brother. She nodded to Penny, who smiled encouragingly as she stood and left with Roy. Her joints were stiff, her feet dragging like lead and her throat tightening against the panic that tore through her. Why the hell did Dom want to see her? It felt like being called to the principal's office, only a million times worse. Had she done anything wrong? He hadn't even coached one of her training sessions yet. Did he think she'd run into Penny this morning accidently on-purpose after he'd warned them to stay away? How would he have even known about it?

When they reached the atrium, Roy nodded at the staircase leading up to Dom's office and she scaled the steps slowly, only to find the office empty. Indy took a seat in front of his desk and waited. Her eyes focused on the clock and she watched the seconds tick by slowly. If he didn't show up soon, she might throw up. Her stomach grumbled, protesting that last thought. There wasn't actually anything to throw up. She wished she'd grabbed a slice of her toast before leaving Deuce with Roy, at least then she wouldn't be starving.

Then two sets of footsteps echoed on the stairs. Indy stood, wiping her sweaty palms against her shorts, then smoothed back her hair held up high in a ponytail.

Dom stepped into the room, followed closely by a tall blond woman in her mid-thirties.

"Indiana, good, you're here." Dom quickly strode away from the woman, frowning over his shoulder at her. His eyes darted around the room and his hand wiped over his entire face. Indy's stomach sank. That couldn't be a good sign. "I'd like to introduce you to Ms. Morneau."

The blonde smiled, showing off two rows of perfect, white teeth. She wore a white pencil skirt and a blush-colored, silk sleeveless blouse, cut high at the neck. "Caroline, please." She said her name in a soft French accent, like "Cah-row-lean" and Indy pictured her tilted slightly to the left, like that tower in Italy. Approaching Indy, she ignored her extended hand and bussed two faux kisses lightly on each cheek.

Indy pulled away sharply and looked back and forth between Dom and this odd woman who thought it was okay to kiss her.

"I take it your father didn't call you," Dom said, reading the confusion on her face.

Indy shook her head. "Dad doesn't have the time to call me. He's far too busy with work. You know, hedge funds don't manage themselves."

Dom cleared his throat. "Well Caroline will explain then. I'll just go."

Before Indy could ask him what the hell was going on, he was already out the door and down the stairs, leaving her alone with Caroline.

"Why don't we sit down?" Caroline motioned to the chairs in front of Dom's desk.

"I'm sorry," Indy said, ignoring the suggestion. "I don't mean to be rude, but who are you exactly?"

"Caroline Morneau. Your father has hired me as representation."

"Representation for what?"

"For you."

"I don't think I understand."

"I'm your agent, Indiana."

For the next twenty minutes, Caroline rattled on, but Indy barely heard a word. Only a few things stood out. Caroline worked for a company called Trinity Agency who specialized in representing athletes. They were a subsidiary of the law firm who represented her father, and as soon as Dom called with the news of her ranking, her father had put Caroline on a plane to North Carolina.

It was typical. Her dad was always doing things like this, barely speaking a word to her for months and then having a car delivered to her driveway for Christmas one year. Her mom used to say it was his way of showing affection. To Indy it just screamed of a guilty conscience. She wanted to go pro and sign with an agent, but hell would freeze over before she let her dad have anything to do with it.

"Indiana, are you listening to me?" Caroline finally asked, pulling her from her thoughts.

"No, I'm sorry."

"That's alright, I can start again."

"No, that's not what I mean. I'm sorry you wasted you time coming all this way. I haven't even gone pro yet, not officially, and anyway, when it's time, I'll pick my own agent."

Caroline smiled, a small rise of the corners of her mouth that made Indy feel like she was five years old. "Perhaps you should call your father."

"Perhaps," Indy agreed, but if he wanted to talk about this, he could pick up the phone. She had zero intention of telling her dad anything. "If you'll excuse me, I'm late for a training session."

"Of course," Caroline said. "Just take this with you. It is your contract. There is no need to make a decision today, but you father wishes to protect your interests."

"Sure." She took the papers and sped out of the office, down the stairs and back into the atrium.

"Everything okay, Indy?" Roy asked, laying aside his newspaper as she nearly flew past his desk.

She stopped dead and turned to him with a smile. If he knew her better, he probably would've been able to tell the smile was fake. "Do you have a recycle bin behind your desk?"

"Sure do."

"Could you throw this out for me?" she asked, holding out the contract.

"No problem," Roy said, taking it and glancing down at the cover page. "You sure you don't need this?"

"Positive."

CHAPTER 5

May 15th

Penny leaned over, hands on her knees, gasping for breath and glanced over at the sideline of the court where her coach was observing her training match. She was dying and she and Alex only been training for a little over an hour. They were playing a mock match and were supposed to be working on one of each other's weaknesses. Alex's was his tendency to go for a winner too early in a point, and hers was playing a more defensive game while dealing with the clay surface stripping some of the velocity from her groundstrokes. Instead, all they'd managed to do was exhaust each other.

Playing tennis with Alex Russell was almost exactly like having sex with him. No awkward fumbling of a first time or a short, unsatisfactory encounter some girls in the locker room whispered about, but the mind-blowing kind of sex most people dreamed of and very few actually had. It was intense and a constant struggle, a push and pull, every point a battle of wills, taking all of her physical and emotional strength, leaving her body suspended in a constant state of half pain, half pleasure.

Alex wasn't faring much better than she was. On the other side of the court, he was hunched over, each breath coming heavy and hard as he stared at her. His gaze was beyond unnerving. Not creepy, but not totally pleasant either. It was like he was looking deep inside of her into places she'd never let anyone see, not Jack, not Dom or even Teddy. Penny kept her eyes locked on his. Then he sent her a cheeky wink and quickly pursed his lips in a phantom kiss, before looking away.

"What the fuck is going on with you two?" Dom marched onto the court from the sideline, confident that they'd sucked in enough oxygen to catch their breaths and were ready to take a total tongue-lashing. His face was shifting from lightly tanned to bright red and the vein in his forehead was beginning to protrude. "P, why the hell are you letting him dictate the pace? Stop being hesitant and hit the fucking ball." She opened her mouth to respond, but Dom was on a roll. "And Alex, what is wrong with you? The way she's playing you should be thrashing her. What happened to the Alex Russell who would step on the neck of a player he had down? Just finish the point when she leaves you an opening! If either of you think this shit is going to fly in France, you've got another thing coming. We're going to have media crawling all over this place in the next few days for the Classic. You don't think they're going to sneak a look at your training sessions while they're here? Take a tour, clear your heads and come back ready to play."

Penny's legs were already carrying her to the gate, an instinctive response to orders issued by the man with total authority over her training regimen for years. A tour, as Dom put it, was a run around the entire OBX facility, through the maze of courts and then around the perimeter. She rolled her neck and broke into a jog, getting halfway down the pathway lining the practice courts before she heard Alex's long strides in a flat-out sprint as he tried to catch up with her. For half a second, she considered picking up her own pace and trying to lose him, but Dom would probably be pissed at her and make her do another tour.

Their strides matched, the rubber soles of their sneakers pounding the concrete in unison. She was perfectly happy to lead him around the complex in silence, and for a little while, it seemed he was too, but as they rounded the corner at the outer edge of the practice courts he broke it, "How much farther, love?"

"Done already?" she said, keeping her eyes trained ahead.

"Hardly, just making conversation."

"Well don't. I have nothing to say to you."

Alex chuckled, his stride breaking just a bit. "I don't know, I think we have a lot to say to each other. Last time we were really alone together we didn't exactly exchange a lot of words, though if I recall, my name was a favorite of yours."

Her nostrils flared as she tried to tamp down her reaction. They'd been operating under unspoken agreement for the last two days to just not talk about that night. Why the hell was he bringing it up now? "Just shut up and run."

"Hit a nerve did I?"

She didn't answer, but instead glanced up and sideways, taking in his profile, the strong jawline, a glittering blue eye, a nose slightly crooked, probably broken in a bar fight or something equally stupid.

"I wonder what Dom would think?"

That stopped her, both her mind and her feet. It was a few seconds before he stopped as well and jogged back to her. She wanted to scream, to blast him and let him know that night was the biggest mistake she'd ever made. But as he towered over her, his eyes softer than before, she couldn't.

"Please don't say anything to him," she said, avoiding his eyes. When he looked at her like that, it was so different than from before, back on the court.

He lifted a hand and ran it through his hair. "So he doesn't know?"

Penny shook her head. "No, I told him nothing happened."

Alex pursed his lips and a muscle in his jaw clenched. "And of course he believed you. No wonder he offered me a spot here. If he knew I'd shagged his star player…"

"Nice," she said with a snort, stepping around him and breaking into a measured run.

Again, he caught up with her in a matter of seconds. "Don't take offense, love. Despite what they say, I'm rather choosey, as I'm sure you are. And you can't deny we were fantastic together."

"You were fine," she said, a smile quirking up at the corner of her mouth. "I was fantastic."

Alex raised his eyebrows, but didn't take her bait. Instead, his eyes twinkled at her and for a moment she almost forgot she hated when he did that. "You were at that."

They fell back into silence, though a much more comfortable one than before as they approached the last and most difficult part of the tour, running on the sand. They were halfway across the beach when his pace started to slow. Penny glanced down out of the corner of her eye and saw his gate was a little labored, favoring his left leg.

She stopped and looked up at him as he did too, the sun light shining behind his head, making her squint. "Is your knee okay for this?" The sand was soft, much looser than their clay practice court or the low-impact rubberized paths they'd just run on. The unstable surface could be hell on a recovering joint, especially after all the work they'd just put in.

"Concerned? I'm touched."

"Purely selfish. I'll never be able to find another practice partner this close to the French."

"Right, of course," he muttered. "I told you, the knee is fine or do you need me to kick your ass on the court again to prove it? Let's go."

They ran together, his strides as smooth as her own. The practice courts came into view as they passed the last of the vacation homes attached to OBX property.

"Hang on a tick," Alex said, coming to a halt just as she was about to tackle the long wooden stairway that led up from the beach.

"What? We've already taken too long."

"C'mon, love, wait," he said, grabbing her arm. She froze and looked up at him.

"I asked you not to touch me."

"Right," he said, pulling his hand away, running it over the back of his neck. He shifted his weight back and forth, looking at her, but not quite meeting her eye. "I just wanted to tell you I won't say anything to Dom."

She stood stunned, not really sure what to say, so she settled for, "Thanks."

His eyes sparkled at her. What kind of cruel God would give a man like him the ability to make his eyes shine at her like she was the only woman in the world?

"Purely selfish," he said, throwing her words back at her and breaking the moment, "don't want him to kick me out on my arse."

Penny rolled her eyes and snorted out a breath. "Come on. Let's go."

They took the stairs together and then through unspoken agreement, sprinted the last twenty meters or so to their practice court. Dom was waiting for them, leaning up against the exterior fence. "You two ready to get back to work?"

"Let's do this," she said, heading out onto the court.

"What she said," Alex added.

"Excellent." Dom followed them through the gate and took a seat at center court. "Penny, you serve."

"Defensive game, right?" she asked, picking up her racket and taking a quick swig from her water bottle.

Dom shook his head. "Forget what I said earlier, both of you. You're thinking too much. Just play."

Penny furrowed her brow, but then shrugged. Dom was her coach, if he asked her to stand on her head, she would.

Alex stood on the opposite side of the court, lunging from side to side, and for a split second, she thought his face scrunched into a wince, but a moment later, it was gone. He twirled his racket in his hands and then nodded. He was ready.

She served out wide, hoping to catch him expecting her usual first serve down the center of the court, but his body reacted, instinctively, striding left and returning the ball back to her as she raced up to the net and put away his return with a short volley.

"Good job, P," Dom called. "Much better. You didn't force anything, even when he got that serve back. Good. Alex, let me see one from you."

Alex kicked at one of the balls at the back of the court, lifting it with his toe and popping it up into the air before catching it on his racket.

Penny rolled her eyes, but set herself. He stretched his neck back and around, before settling his feet, bouncing the ball into the clay. A quick inhale and he sprung into the serve, straight up the middle of the court.

She stuck out her racket and managed a return, taking a crossover step to the center of the court as he chased it down. They kept the rally going, neither of them backing down, not giving the other even the slightest opening. Penny hit a slice backhand over the net, hoping to catch him off balance, but instead, he ran around it and fired a forehand down the line, well out of her reach, for a winner.

"Damn good job, Al!" Dom yelled from the sideline. "Perfect shot selection and you waited for the right moment to strike. Okay, that's it. End on a good note. I'll see you two in the gym this afternoon."

Dom left the court with a spring in his step.

Alex leaned against the net. His hair, damp and darker with sweat, was longer than it'd been in Australia. Penny flexed her hand and then clenched a fist, digging her nails into her palm, trying to quash the urge to run her fingers through it. He smiled at her and asked, "So, you want to grab lunch?"

Penny smiled back and said, "No," before spinning on her toe and walking straight off the court, not having to look back to relish the look of shock on his face. She imagined he didn't hear that word very often.

Instead of heading for the locker room, she made a sharp left as she entered the atrium and made straight for one of the video rooms. Dom had satellite TV installed at OBX so they could screen matches of the players for everyone else still training at home, but with nearly everyone on campus right now, the room was empty. Penny turned on the television and quickly found the channel airing the matches from Rome. The tournament was in full swing and Zina Lutrova was making mince meat out of her opponents, looking a hell of a lot better than she had in Madrid.

The Russian star was up a set and two breaks on her opponent, Giselle Beauchamp of France, the eighth-ranked player in the world. Lutrova's famous high-pitched shriek echoed through the speakers as she powered a forehand past a lunging Beauchamp. Penny shook her head. Even on clay, Lutrova's forehand was super strong. It was why she could almost forgive Dom for bringing in Alex. He was the perfect practice partner if she wanted to take out the Russian on clay. Obviously, his shots were more powerful, but he was even more accurate than the women's number one player, forcing her level of play higher with every rally. If she could just get her head together, she would be fine. Easier said than done, though.

Her thoughts were cut short when the scent of melted cheese and pepperoni wafted into the room. Her mouth watered. She craned her neck backward and saw Jack standing in the doorway, a pizza box balanced against his hip.

"I hate you," she muttered, turning back to the screen. "Did you bring that in here just to torture me?" It was one of the last things she grasped about being a great player; you could train as hard as you liked, but if you filled your body with crap, it all pretty much went to hell.

"No you don't. You love me," Jack said, plopping down next to her seat and holding the pizza box in his lap. The smile plastered across his face bordered on stupidly big, his dimple popping out and his eyes nearly closed.

"Why's that?" she asked, keeping her eyes trained on the TV where Lutrova had three match points.

"Why don't you check out the pizza and you'll find out," he said, shoving the box into her hands.

"Fine, but it's not like I can actually eat any…" Her voice trailed off as she took in the pizza pie, pepperoni spread across the center spelling out the word, NIKE. She looked up at Jack then down to the pizza and then to Jack again. "Are you serious?"

"Got the phone call a half hour ago. They've upped their offer and totally blew away everyone else's. It's exactly what we've been hoping for, Pen. They want you to be the new face of their tennis line. They're calling you America's Sweetheart, and if you fulfill even just a few of the incentives in this contract, it'll be worth close to fifty million dollars."

It took a moment for Jack's words to sink in. Nike wanted her and they were willing to invest a huge amount of money to get her. Suddenly Alex Russell and his twinkling eyes and Zina Lutrova and her powerful groundstrokes didn't matter.

"This is... I can't..." She trailed off, tears starting to burn at the corners of her eyes. This deal wasn't only about her; it was about her family too. If she was careful and invested wisely, that kind of money would ensure her children's grandchildren would never have a financial worry a day of their lives and Teddy could have whatever kind of car he wanted. "Thank you, Jack. Thank you so much!"

"Don't thank me, Pen. This is all you," he said, picking out a piece of pepperoni from the pie and smirking at her as he chewed.

"Oh shut up," Penny said, grabbing him into a huge bear hug, the pizza forgotten as it slid off her lap and onto the floor.

CHAPTER 6

May 16th

The junior practice courts echoed with the sound of balls hitting rackets, feet scrambling to set up a shot and Dom's voice as he paced back and forth, shouting corrections at each and every girl. The sun was setting and a cool breeze came in off the water, a little relief from the heat they'd been working in all day. The muscles in Jasmine's forearm quivered as she hit yet another forehand. She watched as across the practice court, Indiana set herself for a backhand and returned the ball over the net.

"Better, Indy, better," Dom called from the sideline of the practice court and Jasmine felt his focus shift to her as Indy's shot traveled toward her. "Now, Jasmine, step into this one."

Another forehand. That was the point of this drill, forcing them to use their worst strokes, fine-tuning them until their weaknesses became strengths. That was the idea anyway, but mostly it was just a struggle. Jasmine crossed over and attacked the ball, but her shot felt the same as the last, a little uncomfortable and not nearly as powerful as she wanted it to be, even against someone whose footwork was as bad at Indy's.

Jasmine frowned as the other girl took a crossover step and lined up another backhand. Okay, so her footwork wasn't quite the mess it was a few days before, but it was still miles from where it should be.

"Don't drop your shoulder, Indiana!" Dom yelled as Indy's shot landed well short of where it should have. "Come on now, Jas. Don't let her get away with that shot."

Jasmine took three small steps forward, keeping her shoulders aligned with her hips and hit a cross-court forehand past the tall blond girl.

"Nice job, ladies," Dom said and then raised his voice over the shuffling feet and racket thwacks echoing from the attached practice courts where the other junior girls were performing the same drill. "That's all, girls. Hit the showers, and don't forget—the Classic Coaches and Players

Reception is tomorrow night. I expect everyone to be there by seven sharp to greet our guests."

Jasmine spun away from the court and went straight for her bag. It had been a long, grueling day and she was glad it was over.

"Great shot, Jasmine," Addison said as she jogged over from her court and started digging through her bag. Lara was right behind her.

"Thanks, I really feel like my forehand is getting there."

"It totally is and we're going to kill at Classic," Lara said, holding out her fist for Jasmine to bump.

They knocked knuckles and Jasmine glanced quickly at Addison. The other girl had a pinched look on her face, but just shrugged when Jasmine met her eye.

"Just kick Gaffney's ass off the court," Addison said to Lara, who'd be facing Indiana in the first round.

"Don't worry. She's not going to know what hit her," Lara promised. They looked over to the other side of the court where Dom was talking to Indy about something.

"Have you been working on your returns during free session?" Jasmine asked. Lara was a good player, but it wouldn't matter how good she was if she couldn't get Indy's serve back.

Lara opened her mouth and was about to answer when Dom called out from across the court. "Jasmine, hang out for a minute, okay?"

She nodded. The other girls gathered their things and left. Jasmine hitched her bag over her shoulder and approached Dom and Indy.

"The footwork is getting there, but you need to keep at it. Do you understand what I mean, Indiana?" Dom was asking as Jasmine approached.

"Yeah, I get it," Indy said, but stopped talking as soon as Jasmine got closer.

"So what's up?" Jasmine asked, looking up at Dom.

"Harold Hodges from *Athlete Weekly* is here to do a feature on Alex and Penny. He's going to cover the Classic too and he's agreed to interview the both of you."

Jasmine's mouth dropped open and she looked back and forth between her coach and Indiana. "Both of us?"

"Yep, he wants to paint a picture of the rising talent in American tennis. He wasn't sure if it would fit into the schedule, but he's got Penny and Alex down at the beach for a photo shoot right now, so he's got time to talk to you two." Dom rocked back on his heels.

Her mouth was suddenly dry and Jasmine swallowed quickly, trying to understand what was happening. Dom wanted Harold Hodges to talk to her...*and Indiana?*

Dom led them from the practice courts and down to the beach where a photo shoot was in full swing. Wind kicked up from off the water, swirling sand around the two objects of the photographer's lens, Penny Harrison and Alex Russell. The photographer's angle was obvious. Penny was in an all white tennis dress with a gold Nike swoosh logo across her chest. Alex stood right beside her in a black T-shirt and black tennis short, no logos, no sponsors, just himself.

Standing at the bottom of the stairs was Caroline Morneau, one of the top agents in the world. Jasmine recognized her from parties her parents used to drag her to when she was little.

"Dominic, you did not even let them shower?" Caroline asked now, shaking her head.

Dom just ignored her and turned to them, "Stay here, girls." Then he strode down the beach a little further closer to the photo shoot.

Caroline began digging through her large bag. "Men, they never think of these things." She pulled a hairbrush out of her bag and handed it to Indiana. "Fix your hair so you do not look like a crazy woman for your first big interview. Just think of all the buzz this will create. Everyone will be talking about you!" Then she left them as well, kicking off her stiletto heels and carrying them down the beach with her, heading straight for Dom.

Jasmine took a deep breath and then turned to Indiana. "Is Caroline Morneau your agent?" she snapped.

Indy yanked her hair out of her ratty, sweaty ponytail and shrugged. "She thinks she is."

Jasmine tried to keep her reaction off her face, clenching her back teeth. One of the best agents in the world wanted to rep this girl with the terrible footwork and zero track record. Meanwhile, her parents wouldn't even let her hire an agent. They kept saying she should keep her amateur status, just in case. In case of what, she had no idea.

"That's great," Jasmine managed to choke out.

"Yeah, well, we'll see," Indy said, her eyes focused down the beach as she pulled her new ponytail tight. Jasmine followed the direction of her stare and it landed on Jack Harrison, who was watching the photo shoot intently, like he did everything in his little sister's career.

"You want Jack Harrison instead?" Jasmine asked, more to herself than to Indy, but then she turned back to the other girl.

"What?" Indy asked, turning to her with her eyes wide.

"You want Jack Harrison?" Jasmine repeated herself.

"To be my agent? No." Indy's nose wrinkled. "I think Dom's calling us."

Dom was waving from down the beach, standing next to a short, balding middle-aged man in a golf shirt and khakis, Harold Hodges, who had Caroline at his other arm, listening to her intently.

There were lots of people around, makeup artists, the photographer's assistants and they all seemed really busy, but it all barely registered for Jasmine. Her mind was still reeling. Nothing had ever blown her mind quite like this before, except maybe when Teddy kissed her. No, even that paled in comparison. Her whole life, her entire tennis career had been leading up to these next few days when she'd take on the best the world had to offer and now, suddenly, she had to share it.

"Okay, I think that's it," the photographer shouted, drawing her from her thoughts.

Penny marched away from Alex without a word, straight up the beach. Alex watched her go for a moment, and then with a shake of his head, turned and walked toward Caroline Morneau.

"Hey, they've got you doing this too?" Penny asked when she finally reached them, but she was still looking at Alex.

It took Jasmine a second to realize that Penny wasn't talking to her, at least not *only* her. Then she remembered breakfast yesterday. Indy showed up with Penny and then sat with the other Harrisons. Obviously they were friends, though she had no idea how. Except Teddy knew Indy from her first day, so of course the new girl would use that angle to get in cozy with OBX's best player. She'd reeked of ambition from the moment she stepped on the practice court just a week before the OBX Classic. Trying to buddy up with Penny Harrison definitely wasn't beneath her.

"How was shooting with him?" Indy asked, a smirk lifting up at the side of her mouth.

Penny rolled her eyes and groaned. "He's just... He thinks he's God's gift to women. He pretty much just latches on to anything female in his line of sight." She waved her hand back down the beach where Alex was leaning into Caroline Morneau and smiling widely as they headed away from OBX. "Case in point. I'm gonna get going before the photographers suck me back in. See you guys later," she said as she started up the stairs.

"Penny, hold up!" Jack called, as he, Dom and the man Jasmine recognized as Harold Hodges finally walked away from the photographer and toward them. "Girls." Jack nodded to them both, but followed straight after his sister.

Jack followed Penny up the stairs, but Dom stopped in front of them with the reporter. "Jasmine, Indiana, this is Harold Hodges." Then he stepped back, giving them some room to talk.

"It's a pleasure to meet you, Mr. Hodges. I love your column," Indy said, shaking his hand.

"Thank you, Indiana, and, Jasmine, we've met before, though I doubt you remember it. I did a profile on your father during his last year on the tour. You were just a baby at the time."

Jasmine smiled tightly.

"Well, girls, it's all going to be very straightforward. Just a few questions, nothing too difficult, I promise." Jasmine rarely took reporters at their word, but Hodges's reputation was pretty solid. "Let's get started, shall we?" Hodges took out his phone and started up a recording app.

"Both of you have a real shot to make a splash on tour next season. Why don't you tell me a little about how you got to where you are? Jasmine?"

"It's been a long hard road. I sprained my ankle at last year's US Open juniors, but I just got back from Madrid, my first tour-level event, and that was super exciting and now we're prepping for the Classic and the French Open." She'd learned the pivot technique from her dad. It was best to give answers that didn't really answer the question. It kept reporters from putting together whatever narrative they wanted to write and forced them to write what you wanted.

"And Indiana?"

"The last few days have been so crazy I don't even know where to start. A month ago, I was trying to figure everything out, decide whether to go to college or stick with tennis. Now I'm seeded fourth at the OBX Classic and how did you put it? I have a chance to make a splash on tour next year. It blows my mind."

"Who are your inspirations?" Hodges asked, moving his phone back to Jasmine.

"Definitely my parents." Short, sweet and to the point. There would be no way for Harold to take it out of context, but instead of moving on, his eyes lit up. She cringed inwardly. She'd opened the door to questions about her parents.

"Do you feel extra pressure to perform well given the high standard your parents set, particularly your father, during their pro careers?"

Jasmine shook her head and smiled. "No," she said from between her clenched teeth. "I'm not them."

"And what are your goals this year? Your mother won the French Open when she was your age," he asked, as if she needed reminding. The trophy was in her living room for Pete's sake.

"My goals are to play my best. That's the only thing I can control."

Hodges nodded and then turned to Indy. Jasmine let her smile fall.

"And you, Indiana, who is your inspiration?"

"Tennis inspiration or just plain old awesome inspiration?" Indy asked, twirling the bottom of her ponytail around her finger.

Hodges tilted his head. "Whichever you prefer."

"My mom then. This was always our dream. She inspires me every time I walk out onto the court."

"And where's your mother now?"

"She passed away about a year ago from cancer."

Jasmine's stomach sank. She hadn't expected that.

"I'm so sorry to hear that," Hodges said. "Is that why you've put off playing at a higher level until now?"

"Partly," Indy said. "If you don't mind, I don't really like talking about it."

"I'm sure she'd be very proud to see how far you've come in such a short time. Why don't you tell me about training at OBX, the best thing and the worst thing."

"The worst thing is that I was in such terrible shape before I got here, so the conditioning's been pretty rough, but the best thing by far has been working with Dom and the other coaches here. It's a whole new level for me, but they've been really supportive."

"I spoke to your coach, Dom Kingston," Hodges said, glancing behind him to where Dom was still standing, "and he said and I'll quote, 'Indiana Gaffney has the most natural talent I've seen in a player since Penny Harrison.' What's your reaction to that?"

Jasmine felt her knees buckle, like someone had come up from behind her and slammed them with a baseball bat. That was an insane comparison. Penny was one of the best players in the world. She turned to Dom, wide eyed, but he wasn't looking at her. He was focused on Indiana, who was just standing there, staring at the reporter. If that was true, if that's what he really thought, then where did that leave her?

Finally, Indy found her voice, "I'm not sure I have a reaction, being compared to Penny is an honor I hope I can live up to someday."

Jasmine's stomach twisted and she felt a lump slide up into her throat. She could see the article in her mind already. Penny Harrison, the star. Indy Gaffney, the one to watch. And Jasmine Randazzo, the daughter of two tennis legends. That was just great.

"Thank you, that's wonderful," Harold said, fiddling with his phone before pocketing it. "I think that about covers it, ladies. Thanks so much for your time. I know you probably have practice to get to. Good luck in the tournament to you both."

"I'll walk you back," Dom said to Hodges, and they went back to the photographer, who was nearly finished clearing up his equipment.

"I guess I'll see you tomorrow at training," Indy said, as she began walking away, back up the beach.

"Yeah," Jasmine said, still staring at the men as they walked away. Had that really just happened?

She heard Indy climbing the stairs, leaving her behind and she couldn't just let her leave.

"Hey, Indy," Jasmine called. The other girl stopped. "Do me a favor?"

Indy turned. "Yeah?"

"Kick Lara's ass in the first round, okay?"

Indy titled her head, a small grin tugging up at one corner of her mouth. "I plan on it."

A swell of courage roared through Jasmine's body. "Good, then I'll have the pleasure of beating the hell out of you in the final."

"We'll see, won't we?" Indy shouted back.

"Damn straight we will," Jasmine said to herself, "damn straight."

CHAPTER 7

May 17th

Dumping the last bucket of ice into the tub, Indy slid out of her training clothes with as little movement as possible. She let them fall to the training room floor. Bending down to pick them up wasn't an option; it would hurt way too much. It didn't matter though. She had her dress for the Outer Banks Classic Players and Coaches Reception hanging in her locker.

Her body protested with a violent jolt, joints unbending, as she lifted one leg then the other, her calves spasming in protest as she lowered herself into the tub of icy water. Huffing out a breath, her entire body tensed as the frigid water saturated her skin, shocking her muscles into submission.

Less than a week at OBX and she was in constant agony. Every workout was harder than the last, every mistake magnified and dissected by her new coaches. Her strengths were twisted into weaknesses; her limitations were highlighted at every opportunity.

She knew going in it would be hard. She just never imagined it would be *this* hard. Then again, she wasn't sure what exactly she imagined. Whatever it was it definitely hadn't included ice baths.

Groaning as her head fell back against the edge of the tub, she tried to force her mind to think about anything other than the numbing cold surrounding her body. It would get better soon. It had to get better soon or she was going to crack.

Fifteen minutes later, she lifted herself out of the tub, teeth chattering and gooseflesh spreading over her skin. She wrapped herself in a towel and moved into the main locker room.

Friendly chatter was common in the OBX locker room. It wasn't so different from her locker room at school, except back in California, Indy had friends. As soon as she passed each row of lockers, the girls there dissolved into whispers and stares. She turned into her row and across the aisle, Lara and Addison were putting the finishing touches on their outfits for the night, Addison pinning her long red hair into a bun at the top of her head and Lara sliding bangle bracelets onto her wrists. Both girls ignored her, which was an improvement as far as Indy was concerned.

"Hey," Penny said, emerging from the other end of the row wrapped in a towel as well. "Enjoy your ice bath?"

"Shut up," Indy said, her teeth still chattering as she spun through her locker combination. The shivers outweighed any nervousness she still felt in front of OBX's star player.

"You'll get used to it." Penny pulled on a pretty, pale yellow sundress, clearly not what she was planning to wear to the party, which was a formal affair held every year just prior to the beginning of the Classic. OBX students were supposed to mingle with the press and sponsors, and welcome the other players. The only welcome Indy wanted to give her competition was a serve into the body, but it was a mandatory event for all OBX players and staff, Dom's orders.

"Doubtful," Indy replied. She pushed the metal clamp up on her locker and opened the door. She stood a moment, blinking at her empty locker: the garment bag with her dress in it was gone.

"Did you bring your dress here?" Penny peered into the locker too.

"I thought I did." Indy leaned in, as if searching the empty space would somehow make it appear again. "What the hell? It was right here when I went out to practice."

Penny frowned and glanced across the row to Addison and Lara, who were putting on a badly acted show of indifference, but glancing at Indy every few seconds. "I think I know."

Indy closed her eyes. Those bitches. "I'm going to kill them. Both of them."

"No," Penny said, grabbing her arm. "Put on whatever clean clothes you have and come to my house. I have way more dresses than I know what to do with and we're close to the same size. We can find you something."

"I can't just let them get away with this," Indiana whispered through gritted teeth

"Yeah, you can," Penny said and then lowered her voice. "They're only doing this because they're terrified of you. The tournament starts tomorrow and you're going to kick Lara Cronin's ass all over the court in front of everyone. That is so much better than cat fighting her in the locker room."

Indy took a deep breath and nodded. "You're right."

"Of course I'm right," Penny said. "Get dressed."

Five minutes later, they walked shoulder to shoulder out of the locker room, pointedly ignoring the giggles and whispers of the girls surrounding them.

~

Indy didn't know what she expected from the Harrison home, but the pretty, blue-shingled house with the basketball net in the driveway and two SUVs with Harvard and Duke magnets on the back bumpers definitely wasn't it.

Penny led her inside, dropping her car keys on a table next to the front door. Indy followed her past a comfortable-looking living room and up a flight of stairs, lined with photos of the Harrison kids are various ages. It was all so friggin' normal. Indy's eyes caught on the last picture. It looked pretty recent, maybe last Christmas, if the brightly lit tree in the background was any indication. All three Harrison kids were standing beside their parents, the perfect family.

"Come on," Penny said from the doorway to what Indy assumed was her bedroom. "We don't have a lot of time."

"Sorry, I was just…" Indy trailed off, following her into the room, her words failing her as the idea of being inside Penny Harrison's bedroom hit her full force. They were only separated by a few months in age, but Penny had accomplished so much of what Indy wanted for herself. She'd thought that maybe the room would be lined with trophies and ribbons, evidence of her ridiculously successful career, but the walls were painted a soft lavender, a patchwork quilt rested across her bed and the only indication that the room's occupant wasn't a normal girl was the end post of her bed where dozens upon dozens of tournament player passes hung. It looked like Penny had kept every single one.

"Okay, I'm wearing this one," Penny said, from her closet, pulling out a hanger with a gold silk dress, "but take your pick from the rest."

Indy hesitated. "Why?" she asked, suddenly not quite sure this was for real.

"Why what?"

"Why are you doing this? You barely know me."

Penny raised an eyebrow. "You think you're the first girl to show up at OBX and piss people off just by walking on the court?"

"Oh," Indy said, feeling awful for questioning Penny's motives.

"Now pick something out," Penny said, letting her off the hook.

"Seriously?" Indy asked, approaching and staring into the closet in awe. "Where did all these dresses come from?"

"Sponsors and events. There's a red carpet at all the big tournaments and designers will give you a dress for free if you get your picture taken in it."

Indy snorted. "You mean they'll give *you* a dress for free."

"Whatever. Just pick one out."

"Penny, this is a friggin' Versace," Indy said, pulling out a silver strapless mini-dress, intricately designed with crystal patterns across every inch of the fabric.

"Oh," Penny said. "Yeah, I wore that one in Australia this year." Indy bit her lip, wondering if that meant she couldn't wear it, but Penny shook her head. "Go for it. It'll probably look better on you than it did on me. I left my eyeliner in the bathroom, I'll be right back."

As soon as the door clicked shut, Indy shimmied out of her shorts and yanked her tank top over her head. Carefully, she stepped into the Versace and slid it up over her hips. It fit perfectly, hugging her like a second skin. She moved in front of Penny's mirror and smoothed down the satin against her thighs.

"Penny, let's go. We're...Indiana."

In the mirror, she could see Jack standing in the door staring at her.

"Hi," she said, not turning around, but keeping her eyes locked on his through her reflection.

"Where's..." Jack cleared his throat. "Where's my sister?" He took a step into the room.

"Penny's in the bathroom."

He moved closer until he was right behind her. Reaching forward, his hands ghosted over her shoulders before sliding down to the line of fabric across her back.

"What are you..." she started to ask, but stopped as the dress tightened across her breasts. She breathed deeply at the brush of his fingertips against her skin and shivered. His eyes still held fast to hers even as his hands fell away. This wasn't the same man who'd practically ignored her on the beach during the *Athlete Weekly* interview and at breakfast the other day. It couldn't be, not with how he was looking at her.

His eyes wrenched away from hers suddenly and stumbled back a step. "You missed a clasp," he rasped, shoving his hands into the pockets of his dress pants.

She turned to face him. "Jack," she said.

"Wow, Indy, you look great," Penny said from the door, dressed for the party. She looked like Belle from *Beauty and Beast*, if Disney let the artists cut her hemline at mid-thigh and drop the back of her dress into a deep V, ending at the small of her back.

Jack's eyes widened in panic, but Indy stepped around him and smiled at his sister. "Right? Thanks for the loan."

"No problem," Penny said and then turned to her brother. "You ready to go?"

"Absolutely," Jack said, storming out of the room.

Penny raised her eyebrows, but Indy just shrugged. "Come on, let's finish up and go before Dom has us running Einstein's in stilettos."

Deuce was already packed with people when they arrived. The tables were gone and a small band played in the corner, leaving the large room open for mingling and dancing. Jack immediately stalked off to the bar, but Indy scanned the crowd, recognizing some of the best coaches from around the world, their pupils at their sides. She'd been there for five seconds and this was easily the best party she'd ever been too.

Jasmine Randazzo was at the opposite end of the dance floor with her parents. She wore a bright pink strapless dress, cinched in at the waist and flowing down to just above her knees. Harold Hodges chatted with Mr. Randazzo, while his daughter, looking incredibly bored, crossed her arms over her chest. Just a few feet away, Alex Russell stood surrounded by a crowd of girls. Looking closer, Indy saw Caroline beside him, hand resting on his arm, dominating the conversation. The other girls looked happy enough to simply stand near him, ignoring Dom's edict to stay away while he was at OBX. Then her coach made a beeline for the group and several of the girls scattered, including Caroline, who sidestepped him lightly and disappeared into the crowd.

Indy laughed and looked to Penny, hoping she'd seen it as well. The other girl's eyes were still trained in that direction, but they were wide and her hand shot out and gripped Indy's wrist tightly. "Do not leave me."

Indy looked back and saw Alex stalking across the dance floor straight for them, a tumbler of amber liquid in his hand.

"Ladies," he said, but he never even looked at Indiana. He wore a black suit that hung perfectly on his tall frame, probably made for him, but no tie and the top button of his sky blue dress shirt was undone. His ever-present five o'clock shadow was gone in favor of a close shave.

After Penny just stared at him in silence, he finally glanced at Indy. "That's a beautiful dress, darling," he said, smiling at her, though it didn't quite reach his eyes. "I think I've seen it before. It has a tricky little clasp at the back, if I recall."

Finally, Penny let go of Indy's arm, though her nails had left half-moon shaped marks in her skin. "Alex, don't do this, okay?"

His eyes softened at her voice and he swayed in place, the glass in his hand clearly not his first. "You sure about that, love?" he said, taking a large sip from the glass, swallowing it cleanly.

Penny narrowed her eyes, taking a step closer and inhaling softly. She wrinkled her nose. "Positive."

"Shame," he said, with a casual shrug of his shoulders, but one look into his eyes and Indy knew that the rejection stung.

Penny just shook her head and turned to Indy. "Let's go."

"Why was he talking about my dress?" Indy muttered as they walked away. She glanced back over her shoulder, but Alex was gone. It didn't take a genius to figure out that the only way he'd know about the hidden clasp at the top of the dress's zipper was if he'd undone it himself, but Indy wasn't going to push, not with the way the color had drained out of Penny's face.

"I'm sorry. I shouldn't have let you wear it. Just trust me. It wasn't about you, okay? You look great."

"Okay," Indy said, wanting to say more, but having no idea where to even start.

"Indiana!" a voice carried over the crowd. She spotted Caroline across the room talking with an older man in a finely tailored suit. The agent, wearing a pale pink sheath dress, fixed at the waist with a large black patent-leather belt, waved her over with just a flick of her fingers.

"I'm being summoned," Indy said, rolling her eyes at Penny who smiled. "Whatever, it's not like she's actually my agent." In fact, Indy thought she'd made it pretty clear to Caroline that she wasn't interested after ignoring every call and text she'd sent over the last few days.

Penny snorted. "Looks like she thinks she is."

Indy turned and saw Caroline stalking toward them, the man matching her stride. She groaned.

"Indiana." Caroline air-kissed her cheeks when they arrived, totally ignoring Penny, then gestured to the man. "I'd like you to meet Mr. Edward Franklin. He's from Solaris Beachwear."

"I'll leave you guys to it then," Penny said, nodding to Mr. Franklin, but looking straight past Caroline and then grinned a farewell to Indy.

"It's very nice to meet you," Indiana said.

Mr. Franklin drew his eyes away from Penny's retreating back and shook Indy's hand. "I'm really looking forward to watching you play this week."

"Thank you."

"Caroline was just telling me about the feature *Athlete Weekly* did on you."

Indy felt her face flush a little. "Well, it was on few of us…"

"Modest too. Here's my card." The man passed it over to her. "Good luck in the tournament, Indiana. Caroline, I look forward to hearing from you."

He excused himself and Indy turned to Caroline with an eyebrow raised. "Solaris Beachwear?"

"It's not Nike, but you haven't actually won anything yet. Then again, neither has Penelope Harrison, a big tournament yes, but certainly not a major."

"And you think Nike is going to want me?"

"I speak, as I find. You win something, Indiana, like this tournament and Solaris Beachwear won't be the only one knocking on our door."

"We'll see," Indy said. "I still haven't gone pro."

Caroline's smile grew wide like she knew something Indy didn't. There was something in that smile that didn't sit quite right with her.

Just as Caroline opened her mouth to speak again, Indy saw Teddy Harrison pushing through the crowd in her direction. Jacket and tie nowhere in sight, the sleeves of his burgundy dress shirt were already rolled up to his elbows.

"Sorry, Caroline, gotta go," she said and met him halfway. "Dance with me?"

"Did you really want to dance or did you just want to get away from her?" Teddy asked, laughing, as they moved through the dancing couples, the band playing a slow jazz tune.

"Sorry," she said, shrugging. "I know I need an agent, but there's something about her. She's just…"

"She's a shark, at least that's what Jack says and he's usually right."

"Is he?" Indy said, but Teddy didn't answer, as she wrapped her arm around his neck and looked out over his shoulder. In the corner of the room, Jasmine, Lara and Addison, along with a bunch of other OBX junior girls were twittering away and staring at them, not even pretending they weren't.

"We have an audience," Indy whispered.

Teddy shoulders tensed under her hands and he swallowed thickly. "Do you mind if I…" He trailed off, but nodded in that direction.

Indy glanced over his shoulder again and the daggers flying out of Jasmine's eyes could've shredded her to ribbons. "Go," she said and Teddy smiled tightly before leaving her on the dance floor and walking over to Jasmine.

Indy watched as he stuffed his hands in the pockets of his dress pants and rocked back on his feet. He nodded out to the dance floor, but Jasmine shook her head and marched away, the other girls trailing behind her.

Indy made sure to stay clear of their path as she made her way to the bar. She had enough enemies at OBX, mostly because of things totally out of her control. She didn't need to earn any more by going after Jasmine's best friend.

"Seltzer please," she asked the bartender and then turned, leaning back against the bar with the glass in her hand.

"Jack and coke," a voice next to her ordered and she glanced sideways to see Jack Harrison. Earlier, she'd been so focused on the feel of his hands against her skin, there hadn't been enough time to admire just how well he filled out his navy blue suit.

"You haven't seen my sister anywhere, have you?"

"Oh, um, she's…." She nodded to the other end of the bar where Penny's eyes were glued to the television mounted high on the wall where a replay of a match in Rome was airing. Zina Lutrova was soundly beating the world's number three player, Jin Jun Huang.

"Great, torturing herself."

"I don't know. If I were an agent, I'd be thrilled if my client wanted to win as much as she does."

"As an agent, I am thrilled. As a brother, sometimes I wish she could relax a little bit. I wasn't like that when I played."

"No? What were you like?" she asked, relieved he was just as willing as she was to push past any lingering awkwardness from that moment in Penny's room.

Jack huffed out a short laugh. "Relaxed. Tennis was just something I did for fun."

"At Harvard right?" He tilted his head leaving his question unasked. "The day we met you were wearing a Harvard tennis shirt," she explained, leaving out the part that she Googled him and found an old Harvard roster from three years before with his name on it.

"Right, well yeah, three years at Harvard, before law school."

"Law school?" He was only twenty-three, another nugget she'd dug up during her internet stalking session and he'd already graduated from law school. "Impressive."

He laughed again, his eyes crinkling as he did. "What? Not, 'why didn't you go pro, Jack?'"

Indy smiled and shrugged. "I assume you weren't good enough."

Jaw dropping, but the smile not leaving his eyes, he nodded. "You're right. I wasn't." Then slowly his laughter faded and with it so did the ease surrounding them. His shoulders straighten and his entire body stiffened as he looked away, out over her head. "I...I better go. Good luck tomorrow. I know you're going to do well."

"Thank you," she whispered.

He finished his drink and placed the glass back down on the bar. Then he leaned down and brushed a kiss against her cheek. "Good night."

~

Sitting in the locker room the next day, Indy twirled her racket in hand, a twist of her wrist had it spinning around fully before coming to rest in her palm again. This was it, her first match at the Classic. Indy's leg bounced up and down, her toes curling and uncurling in her sneakers.

"How's that?" the trainer asked, tapping Indy's wrapped wrist, drawing her from her thoughts. "Range of motion good?"

She flexed her wrist back and forth, the wrap just there for some extra support. "Perfect."

"Have a good match," the trainer said as she left the room.

Once she was alone, her stomach clenched and her throat tightened. There were the nerves. It was actually comforting to feel them. It had been a year since she'd been out on a court for a real elite-level match. Plus, this was the first time she'd be out on the court without her mom in the stands. Anyone would be a little jittery. Indy checked her racket, bouncing the heel of her hand against the crisscrossed strings. The tension was perfect, not too tight and not too loose, allowing both power and control.

Taking a slow, steady breath, she packed her racket into her bag and mentally ran through the match. Lara Cronin, the one who tried to bully her off a practice court and most likely the evil bitch who stole her dress for the reception, had a solid overall game. They'd played against each other a little bit during training. Good backhand, better forehead, could move well, but not well enough. The plan was to stick to the power game. Lara definitely wouldn't be able to handle her serve. Indy was prepared. Now all she had to do was execute.

"You ready to go, Indy?" a deep southern-drawl asked from just outside the doorway.

Slinging her bag onto her shoulder, Indy nodded to Roy. "I'm ready."

They walked down the long corridor, past the Title Wall, and through another hallway that led to the OBX main court. The door was braced open. She could hear the buzz of the crowd and the hard rock music blasting through the speakers. Lara was already standing at the door, waiting. Indy was the higher seed and thus had the honor of entering the court last.

The radio clipped to Roy's belt crackled. "Two minutes."

"Hang on right here, ladies," Roy said, pausing at the door.

She bounced on the balls of her feet to stay warm and burn off the extra energy she felt flowing through her veins. She'd never felt anything quite like this before, a buzzing through her entire body, almost making her vibrate.

To her right, held in a glass case, was the Classic Trophy. It was an old-school brass cup, about the same height as a desk lamp with two large handles. The tournament was in its fifth year, but only had two winners.

The names of the previous champions were engraved on the cup.

Amy Fitzpatrick
Penelope Harrison
Penelope Harrison
Penelope Harrison

By the end of the week, her name could be cut into the brass just below Penny's; by the end of the week, she could be the Outer Banks Classic Champion.

The radio crackled again. "Okay, we're a go."

Lara entered the court first, the crowd applauding for her. Roy held his hand up, holding Indy back and her eyes grew wide. It was really loud out there, definitely the loudest she'd ever heard a crowd for one of her matches, not that she'd really had a crowd before—ever.

"Good luck," he said, his hand squeezing her shoulder before he waved her through.

Empty, the OBX main court didn't seem that big. Compared to the huge stadiums at the Grand Slams, it was actually very small, but standing on the court with every seat taken, music blaring in the background, and the din of people chattering in their seats, to Indy, it might as well have been Centre Court at Wimbledon. All of these people were here to watch her play, to watch her win or lose.

Indy's heart began pounding in her chest, mimicking the harsh bass echoing through the speakers. The music was meant to pump up everyone up in the stands, but it was sending her pulse rate through the roof.

Glancing into the crowd, she saw Caroline courtside next to the rep from Solaris Beachwear. A few rows back, Penny sat with Dom and Jack. Teddy was just behind them next to Jasmine. Her match had been earlier that morning. She'd won easily.

Indy looked away. She had to take it one match at a time. There wouldn't be a chance to face down Jasmine unless she won this one and two after it.

Sitting down in her chair, she pulled the laces of her sneakers tight and took several deep breaths, trying to block out the noise, but it was almost impossible.

"Players to the center of the court," the chair umpire said, standing next to the net. A coin flip would decide who served first.

"Heads," Lara said.

"The call is heads," the umpire said, and flipped it onto the court. The coin bounced once, spun and then rattled flat onto the ground. "It is tails. Miss Gaffney?"

"I'll serve."

Lara's face went pale and Indy's nerves faded. Her opponent was afraid and there was nothing more crippling for an athlete than fear.

As they warmed up, Indy made sure to unleash her serve at maximum velocity, paying little attention to where it went. She wanted to nurture the fear, not give Lara the chance to overcome it.

Finally, the chair umpire said, "Play."

The tennis balls were brand new. They would fly hard and fast.

Across the net Lara was lined up far behind the baseline, shifting her weight back and forth, waiting. Indy didn't make her wait any longer.

The serve was perfect, down the center of the court, skidding off the white painted line and past Lara, who flinched, but had no chance to return it. Indy smiled, feeling her entire body relax, the rush of adrenaline settling into a comfortable ease. The match was over before it had even begun.

CHAPTER 8

May 19th

"Game. Set. Match. Gaffney."

Penny stood, applauding Indy's win, her third in three days. It was a decisive victory and she could remember what that felt like; just a few years ago, she was down on that court, winning her first Classic semi-final. Long before there were sponsorships and British bad boys, there had just been tennis and her simple love for the sport. She still loved it, of course, but everything was just so complicated now.

Indy and her opponent met at the net and shook hands to end the match and Penny turned to leave. She had a training session with Dom in fifteen minutes. Coming down the stairs out of the OBX stadium with the rest of the crowd, Penny felt him before she saw him. It was like that in Australia too. She felt his eyes on her long before he'd approached her. She tried to disappear into the throng of people, but he stood head and shoulders above nearly everyone. If he wanted to find her, he would. She'd managed to avoid being alone with him since he'd sauntered over to her at the reception a few days before. Dom was always at training as a buffer and it was easy enough to avoid him during her off time.

"Penny," Alex said, suddenly beside her. The people around them shifted, and she was forced closer to him, her nose nearly pressing into his chest. "Come on. We need to talk." His hand landed on her shoulder and slid down to her elbow, his grip firm. Despite that, she knew he wouldn't force her to come with him even though she knew he could. Maybe it was biological. It definitely wasn't rational, but she found it extremely attractive. "Please, love."

"What do you want, Alex?" she asked, acutely aware of the eyes that followed them as they started down the path leading away from the stadium.

"I want to talk to you," he said. He drew to a halt near their practice court.

"I don't have anything I want to say to you."

"Yeah see, I don't believe you," he said, a smug grin tugging at his lips, waving his hands around at the empty practice courts.

She shrugged. "Believe what you like."

"I get it. You're hacked off at me. You've been hacked off at me for months, since that night at the Aussie."

Penny blinked at him and shook her head in disbelief. "Seriously? You really think now is the time to talk about this?"

"I meant to the day I arrived, but you kind of put up this force field, love, so I put it off and then the other night I worked up some courage."

"You mean you drank until you weren't scared of me anymore."

"Right, that and you just shot me down."

"You were drunk and you didn't just want to talk." She arched an eyebrow at him and he shrugged unapologetically.

"I'm not drunk now and while I'd much rather *not talk*, I think maybe we should."

"We can't. We have a training session. Dom'll be here in…" Her phone buzzed in her pocket, cutting her off. Alex's phone buzzed as well. Only one person would be texting them at the same time.

"Dom's not coming," he said, reading off his screen. "He's got press to do with Jasmine and Indiana for the final tomorrow."

"Of course he does. I'm out of here."

In two strides he leapt out in front of her, blocking her path. "Oy, where are you going? We've got to train."

Penny looked up at the sky, a dusky blue color as a few dark wispy clouds gathered high in the heavens. Maybe if she were really lucky, lightning would strike and put her out of her misery. "First you want to talk, and now you want to train?"

"We can't do both?"

"Train first," she said, "then talk." Of course she had no intention of sticking around once they finished their session. He'd just have to get over it.

They stretched out on their practice court in silence, like they had every day since he arrived, but even without words, the connection between them was practically tangible. Every time he shifted, her body wanted to mimic the motion. She fought it, trying desperately to focus on her own stretching regime.

What was it about him? Aside from the mind-blowing sex, of course. It was getting harder and harder to brush aside the memories of that night. She'd never experienced anything like it. Their bodies were made for each other and though her mind was set against him, her body refused to let her forget.

"Okay?" he asked, pulling her from her thoughts, but not enough to make her forget the last time he'd asked that question, leaning over her, one hand gripping her thigh, the other holding himself up against the mattress, his body cradled by her hips, slick with sweat, straining with the effort of holding back, waiting for her permission.

"Penny?" She pushed herself out of the fog of the past and stood up, brushing the clay from her shorts.

"Let's just do a short warm-up," she suggested, hoping he'd agree.

"Yeah," he said, a wicked grin blooming across his face. "Then let's play."

A few practice serves, forehands, backhands and some net work later and they were both geared up for a set.

"Go on then," Alex said, "let's see what you got." He chucked a ball at her from across the net and she plucked it neatly out of the air.

Bouncing the ball down at her feet, Penny let her weight fall back and then explode forward through the ball, sending a flat bee-bee down the center of the court. He blocked it back, but she raced forward, putting away a short volley, totally out of his reach.

"15-Love."

And so on and on it went, trading point and after point, breaking serve, breaking back, forcing deuce and losing at love, their level of play rising with every stroke of the racket for nearly an hour. They stopped keeping score early in, recognizing the need to just *play.*

"Next point wins," Alex called out finally as they caught their breath between points.

"Tired?" she challenged.

"Nah, I've got somewhere to be and you owe me a bit of a chat."

"Fine, next point."

It was his serve. He stood tall then coiled his body down, his back bending as he lifted the ball up into the heavens. Then, like lightning, he sprang, the ball a missile, but she was ready, pouncing on it, returning it deep into his side of the court.

"Out!"

"Bull shit," she called back at him, jogging around the net. It was a clay court; there would be a mark where the ball landed. He met her there, pointing to the skid just past the white line with his racket head.

"Out," he repeated. "Shame you refuse to take me at my word, love."

Penny's head snapped up. "And why should I trust you?"

"Have I ever given you reason not to?"

It was a fair question, she admitted to herself, not that she'd ever tell him that, so she just shrugged. It's not like it mattered. Whether she could trust him or not wasn't the issue. She couldn't trust herself to keep her focus if she was with him. If it happened in Australia, it could happen again and Penny wasn't willing to take that risk.

"I think I know what the problem is. You don't know me."

"I know you as well as I ever want to." She made for the edge of the court, sliding her racket back into its bag, zipping it up.

He waved away her response and kept talking. "I mean it. I like training here. I like working with Dom and God help me, I actually like training with you, but if we don't figure out some of the shit between us, it's not going to work, not long term."

"Yeah, you not around to torture me, that would be tragic."

He ignored the sarcasm and nodded. "Indeed it would, so come here and lie down on the court with me."

Penny squinted at him, the request coming out of nowhere. "What? No."

"This will help your game."

She shook her head, unconvinced, lifting her bag over her shoulder, ready to leave.

"Jesus, do you fight everyone like this or is it just me?"

If only he knew it was only him. No one had ever made her feel the way he did. "I'm not lying down."

"Do you want to win the bloody French Open or not?"

Did she want to win the French Open? Of course she did. So she put her racket bag back down. "Sounds too good to be true," she said and watched him as he reclined back on the court. "Was this what you were doing on your first day here?"

"Yes. It was something I hadn't done for a long time, but if you'll trust me for half a second, I promise it'll work. Now get down here."

She kneeled down, the dirt shifting beneath her and sticking to her sweaty knees. Then she rolled over onto her back, careful to keep a body width of distance between them. "Okay, now what?"

"Now close your eyes and just let your mind go blank."

"That's not possible. I'll just be thinking about not thinking."

"Penny," he said, reaching out, his fingers wrapping lightly around her wrist. She wanted to pull away, but something about the way he said her name, a desperate note in his voice she hadn't heard before, kept her still. "Just close your eyes and breathe."

He inhaled deeply and she followed him, matching his breathing pattern. A soft pressure on the inside of her wrist kept time for them, back and forth, his calloused thumb stroking against the sensitive skin.

"Do you really hate me?"

The question startled her so much, she actually answered, "No." She didn't have to open her eyes to know he was smiling. "I don't hate you."

"Then why did you leave?"

"What?"

"That morning, I woke up and you were gone."

It was so much easier to talk with her eyes closed, when she couldn't see him, it was almost like no one could see her, it was so easy she decided not to be pissed off at him for tricking her into talking. "I was embarrassed."

"Of me?"

Penny shook her head, feeling the clay beneath her pasting itself into her hair. "No, not you, of me. I don't do things like that, one-night stands."

"Oh," he said simply.

"And then you grabbed the nearest supermodel, got drunk and crashed your bike," she said, the dots finally connecting in her head. Had he gone out and gotten himself drunk because she left? Had he wanted her to stay?

"Something like that."

"So it's my fault. It happened because I left."

"No," he said. The soft feel of his thumb disappeared, replaced quickly by her entire hand being wrapped up in the warmth of his. "That was all me. I was spiraling."

"You've been doing really well here."

"Like I said, you don't really know me."

Penny laughed softly. "Sure I do. The youngest man to ever win Wimbledon, the first

British man to do it since 1936, youngest man to ever win the career Grand Slam..."

"All that's missing is the Olympic gold," Alex filled in for her.

"Well, the Olympics are only three years away."

"Yeah, in Rio. Great city. Brazilians know how to party."

"Is that really all you think about?"

"No," he said, "I think about you a lot."

"Alex," she warned, but it didn't stop him.

"First time I saw you, it was in Australia."

"Yeah and look how that turned out."

"Not this year. Last year, when you won the junior tournament."

"Oh."

"I thought you were the most incredible-looking girl I'd ever clapped eyes on, and Christ, you could play too. You reminded me so much of me, of who I used to be, focused, driven, not letting anything or anyone stand in my way."

"You can still be like that. You've been like that since you got here," she said, growing more and more uncomfortable with each sweet word that spilled from his lips. It was like a confession, one she shouldn't be privy to even though he was talking about her.

"We'll see, but we're not here to talk about me. This is about you."

"I hate when things are about me."

His fingers laced between hers and he squeezed. "You put on a good show then."

"I guess I'm used to it, but it doesn't mean I have to like it."

Alex grunted. "Speaking of not liking things and getting back to my original question, you may not hate me, what exactly don't you like about me?"

"You're…" She hesitated.

"Just say it, love."

He was probably the last person in the world she would choose to say these words to, but maybe he was the only person in the world who would truly understand.

"You said I remind you of yourself. I guess I know what you mean and the truth is, you're what I'm afraid of becoming. I almost…I wanted to be with you that night. I wasn't thinking. I didn't want to think, at all, for once in my life. I could've been on that motorcycle with you and then maybe everything I'd ever worked for would have been gone in an instant and you made me feel like…"

"Like what?"

"Forget it," she said, ready to jump up and leave if he pushed her to say it. That she'd never felt so alive as she had when she was in his arms, not even on a tennis court. "It's not important. I was acting like an irresponsible idiot. I lost control for one night and it won't happen again." It had practically become her mantra over the last few months.

"You can't be in control all the time. It's okay to let go, love."

"No, it's not," she said, pulling her hand free from his and scrambling to her feet. She was halfway to the gate when she heard him call her name.

"It wouldn't have been you."

She froze, but didn't respond.

"I would have got you home safe. It wouldn't have been you." His voice was soft, but firm, just like his touch when he took her hand, like he was trying to convince himself that he spoke the truth. For her part, she wasn't so sure.

"I…" Her voice caught in her throat. "I've got to go."

"So that's it?"

"Yes, that's it." She didn't owe him an explanation. She didn't owe him anything at all.

"You're a terrible liar, love. I want you. You know I do and that scares you, but the only thing that scares you more is that you want me too," Alex rasped, his voice deep and husky.

Penny's pulse thrummed in her throat and she closed her eyes, trying to keep herself steady. He was moving closer her. She could hear his sneakers against the clay and when she opened her eyes again, he was standing right in front of her. He stepped closer, cupping her cheek, tilting her face up to his. He leaned in, his nose brushing against hers before following the path of his fingertips.

"Alex," Penny said, her eyes drifting closed as she leaned into the touch. "Wait." She pressed her hands against his chest, though she didn't push him away. "I'm sorry."

"Penny…" He leaned down, resting his forehead against hers, his hands dropping to her waist, pulling her closer.

"This isn't who I am," she said, twisting her fingers into the cotton of his shirt. "I just can't… I can't do this."

"Can't or won't?"

"Won't," Penny whispered.

Alex stumbled backward like he'd been sucker punched. "Fine. If that's what you want, fine."

"Alex? Are you finished? We have a reservation."

Penny looked up and saw Caroline Morneau at the gate. The agent's timing was as impeccable as she looked. Her blond hair was elegantly arranged in a twist at the back of her neck, a sharp suit jacket and pencil skirt, giving her an air of sophistication and grace that made Penny feel like an underdressed little kid, especially since she had clay sticking to the backs of her legs and rubbed into her hair and clothes. Then she remembered, he had somewhere he had to be and apparently wherever that was, Caroline Morneau was going with him.

"I've gotta go," she mumbled, nodding to Caroline as she passed her, careful not to get any dirt on the woman's designer clothes.

As soon as Penny stepped through the door of her house, she caught sight of Jack pacing back and forth in the living room, his cell phone glued to his ear.

"Who is that?" she mouthed, but he just shook his head. She moved into the living room and plopped down on the couch, waiting for him to finish up.

"Thank you, Frank. I'll be in touch tomorrow and her schedule will be in your inbox as soon as we hang up. Alright, have a good night," Jack said and ended the call.

"Who's getting my schedule?"

"Frank Granholm from Nike Tennis." He nodded at a stack of papers at the center of the coffee table, brightly colored tabs protruding out of the pile. "They sent over your contract."

It was the perfect distraction, dozens of pages to sift through that would take her mind off Alex and everything that just happened while they lay side by side on her practice court. They had almost kissed. She wanted him to kiss her and she felt like a total idiot, especially in those last few seconds while Caroline Morneau bugged him about their date or whatever it was. It wasn't jealousy. There was nothing to be jealous about. Maybe they were having a business meeting; maybe Alex was looking to sign with Caroline or maybe he just wanted to screw her. It didn't matter. Despite what he'd said, about how beautiful he thought she was, he'd probably thought that Aussie supermodel was beautiful too and Caroline was undeniably gorgeous. Besides, Alex could go out with anyone he liked, why should it make any difference to her?

The contract required her signature in several places and there were three copies, one for Jack, one for herself and one to send back to Nike, and each time she signed it, the small sparks of everything she'd felt for Alex since that night in Australia were pushed aside and eventually, she hoped, they'd be gone for good.

CHAPTER 9

May 20th

For as long as Jasmine could remember, her dad would give her a last-minute pep talk before a match. It was hard for him, after so many years of playing, to sit in the stands and watch with very little control over the outcome. So he would create a strategy for every match. Most of the time it was helpful, especially if she didn't know much about her opponent's strengths and weaknesses. At most tournaments she was too busy playing to scout out the competition, but she watched Indy every day at training and all week during the lead up to the final. She knew what she had to do. Of course, that didn't stop her dad from giving his traditional pep talk in the locker room just minutes before she had to be out on the court.

"Just keep your feet moving and don't give an inch on her serve," John Randazzo said as Jasmine packed her racket bag. "On change-over have a banana, and then after the first set, an electrolyte chew." He handed her a plastic bag with the items already packed.

"Thanks."

"If she plays a baseline game, make her move and force an error. She's got power, but she's sloppy. Be patient like always and you shouldn't have any problems."

"I know, Dad," she said, trying to hide her exasperation. It was everything she'd observed about Indiana all week and yet, Dom was still gaga over the girl. Jasmine planned to put a stop to that today.

Her mom saw through it right away. "Okay, John. That's enough, let's go get our seats."

"What?" her dad asked, looking at his wife and then back to Jasmine. "Okay. Good luck, Jas. You'll do fine. Just stick to the game plan."

"Thanks, Dad."

Jasmine sent a silent thank you to her mom as she led her dad from the locker room.

She let out a sigh of relief and then checked the clock. Her ankle was wrapped up tight. She'd sprained it a few months ago and the wrap was just a precaution, plus it gave her a little bit of extra stability. Her rackets were ready and her bags were packed. Just fifteen more minutes until it was time to step out on the court and win her first Classic trophy. A thrill shot through her body at the thought.

Shaking out her arms and then her legs, she tried to stay warm, but it was impossible. The air conditioning was pumping at full throttle as the temperature outside climbed into the mid-nineties, high for May in the Outer Banks. Jasmine was counting on that as well. She was in better physical condition than Indy and the heat would expose it. She planned to make the other girl run, blocking back her shots, tiring her out. That would help weaken her serve and whatever advantage it gave her.

She checked the clock again, ten more minutes. A run in the hallway wouldn't hurt, just a light jog to keep loose. The hall was empty and she could hear the crowd echoing down from the main court through the door at the end of the tunnel. The steady thrum of her heartbeat spiked, the pre-match adrenaline starting to flow. She jogged in the opposite direction, swinging her arms around, trying to keep warm and her nerves under control.

"Hey, Randazzo."

She turned to see Teddy striding down the hallway from the door to Indy's changing room. Of course he'd go talk to the other girl first, just one more girl on Teddy's list of potential conquests. She knew it was mean, but it would just make beating Indy that much sweeter.

"Hey," she said, avoiding his eye and moving back toward the locker room to grab her bag.

"You don't call. You don't write," Teddy said, rubbing at the back of his neck. "Did you get any of my messages?"

Jasmine bit her lip, a small bubble of guilt building in her stomach. She got his messages, all ten of them, and ignored every single one. It was just too hard to pretend to be his friend when she wanted so much more.

"I just wanted to wish you good luck," he said, hovering in the doorway as she slung her racket bag over her shoulder.

Jasmine's heart clenched in frustration. He was smiling like nothing was wrong, like he hadn't just come from wishing Indy good luck and like he hadn't crushed her heart into a million pieces with one stupid kiss. "Right," she said, trying to push down the hurt. "Thanks."

"What's the matter?"

She used to find his obliviousness charming. Now it grated on her nerves. The hurt wrapped around her frustration creating a knot of anger.

"You really have no idea, do you?"

"No," he said, shrugging. "Want to fill me in?"

"Don't be an idiot, Teddy. I know you like Indy."

He gaped at her, his mouth opening and closing, before finding his voice. "I barely know her. It's not like that. Plus, even if it was, why do you care?"

"I don't care," Jasmine scoffed, her anger skyrocketing. "I know you don't give a shit about it, but do you get how big of a deal this tournament is for me? Whoever wins is a shoo-in for major wildcards. If I win I won't just be playing juniors at the French Open, I'll be in the main draw. Indiana is my competition, Teddy. She's the one standing in my way."

"I was just being nice."

"Right, *nice* and if she wasn't gorgeous and blond, would you still have been nice?"

"She was having a hard time. Most of the girls in this place have been acting like real bitches to her. Nice of you to step in."

Jasmine pursed her lips, glaring at him. "I don't control what those girls do."

"Please, one word from you and they would've stopped. What did you think? If you let them bully her, it would improve your chances to win this thing?"

The truth was she hadn't even thought about it, but she was too angry to defend herself.

"Screw you. You're supposed to be my friend. That's what we said, that we're better as friends."

His cheeks flushed red and his jaw muscles clenched as he crossed his arms over his chest. There was no sign of his easy smile now. "We are—"

"Some friend, trying to hook up with my competition," she said, trying not to let the bitterness seep into her voice. She was unsuccessful.

He opened his mouth to speak and then closed it again as Roy appeared in the doorway, walkie-talkie crackling at his hip. Jasmine's shoulders sagged as the argument came to an abrupt end. She didn't want to know what he would've said next.

"Jasmine?" Roy glared at Teddy, who shrunk back against the wall. She didn't know how much the old man heard, but it made Jasmine feel a little better to know he was on her side. "You ready to go?"

"I'm all set, Roy."

Five minutes ago, she was ready, mentally prepared and focused. Now, she was a mess of anger and frustration, her heart racing and her blood at a boil. She had to get herself under control. She pushed past Teddy, leaving him in the locker room and followed Roy down the hallway. Indy was already waiting at the door to her changing room, eyes wide, fists clenched against the straps of her racket bag, knuckles white.

Though it felt like hours ago, her father's advice from just minutes earlier popped into her head. *Indy's got power, but she's sloppy. Be patient like always and you shouldn't have any problems.* If Indy was nervous then she'd be even more careless than usual. The more controlled and conservative Jasmine played, the more likely Indy would be to overplay and make an error.

Jasmine inhaled through her nose, feeling the anger flow out of her body as her game plan took hold. Then she let the air spill out from her lungs and her nerves with it. She didn't have time for nerves right now; she could worry about everything later, like after her victory party.

The radio crackled again as Dom's voice came through. "Let's get this show on the road."

"Alright, ladies, if y'all are ready, let's get goin'."

The hum of the crowd swirled around them like a tornado building to a roar. The stands were full, coaches and players, sponsors and the media, all parties eager to catch a glimpse of the future of tennis. There were cameras surrounding the court from every angle. The match was being streamed live over OBX's website.

Her eyes flew over the stands, finding Harold Hodges sitting beside her father, notebook at the ready. The tournament would be a huge part of the *Athlete Weekly* feature. She found her dad and he gave her a thumbs up.

Just a few rows away, Teddy was walking down an aisle toward his brother. His face was drawn and serious. Jack said something to him;

Teddy shrugged, then threw himself into his seat, arms crossed over his chest.

Since she'd known him, Teddy was always on her side. He was always a voice in the crowd cheering her on, supporting her. Now their friendship was torn to pieces and she wasn't sure if they could repair it or if she even wanted to. Was it worth it? Would she be able to stand watching him go back to his old ways, jumping from girl to girl or worse, committing to someone else?

"Welcome, ladies and gentlemen, to the final of the Outer Banks Classic." Dom's voice, enhanced by the microphone he held in the center of the court, broke through her thoughts. "Today's Girls' Final features two athletes from right here at OBX, Indiana Gaffney and Jasmine Randazzo. Ladies, please approach the net for the coin toss."

Jasmine tore her eyes from the crowd and pushed all thoughts of Teddy Harrison out of her mind. She glanced over at Indy and if it was possible, the blonde looked even more nervous than she did in the tunnel. There was no way to predict how a player would respond to the pressure of an important match. Some players, like Penny, were immune to it. Others battled with the nerves until they learned how to deal with them, and some players, no matter how talented, never overcame the fear of the big moment.

It was time to prove to the world—and Dom—what kind of player she was and while she was at it, show Indiana Gaffney she was in way over her head.

~

"Out!" the line judge called, arm shooting out wide.

"Game, Miss Randazzo," the chair umpire said.

Across the court, Indy stood, hands on her hips, staring at the ground beneath her feet. Her shoulders rose and fell with every breath, coming hard and heavy as they neared the end of the first set in the best of three set match.

Jasmine spent the days leading up to this match shortening her reaction time and prepping her return game in anticipation of facing Indy's killer serve. So far, all that preparation was proving unnecessary. She was playing well, but her 5-1 lead in the first set was due more to Indy self-destructing than anything Jasmine was doing. Indy's serve was all over the place and the rest of her game was just as inconsistent, spraying forehands and backhands with plenty of power, but no accuracy, and planting herself behind the baseline, leaving the front court wide open.

Indy was playing right into her hands as Jasmine forced her to scramble all over the court. The weather was cooperating too. The sun was beating down on them and slowly, but surely, the velocity of Indy's serve was dropping, giving Jasmine an even larger advantage.

She checked the clock in the corner of the court. The match was only twenty minutes old. Jasmine was serving and after she won this game, she would take the first set.

"Quiet, please," the chair umpire said, admonishing the crowd, most of who had lost interest in the one-sided match and started conversations.

Jasmine approached the baseline and waited for Indy to do the same. She had the mental edge in the match and she wasn't about to relinquish it. Solid shots, nothing too crazy, allowing Indy to make the mistakes and the first set would belong to her.

Finally, Indy stepped up to the baseline, bending at the waist, racket held out in front of her as she shifted her weight left to right.

Jasmine tossed the ball into the air, then, instead of hammering through the back of the ball, she hit through the side. It was a subtle adjustment, no more than a millimeter or two, creating a slice spin on her serve and forcing Indy to lunge out wide.

Indy got there just in time, blocking the ball back. Jasmine charged the net, taking a swing on the run and smacking the weak return into the opposite corner, giving Indy no chance to retrieve it.

"15-Love," the chair umpire said.

The crowd applauded politely.

Jasmine pulled a ball from the hidden pocket under her tennis skirt and compared it to the offering from the ball girl. She returned the fluffier of the two and looked to Indy, once again bent at the middle, physically ready to receive the serve, but mentally all over the place.

This time Jasmine stuck to her flat serve. She didn't have a ton of power, but what she lacked in velocity, she made up for in control. The serve drew Indy to the center of the court, allowing her to return it, but opening up the corners. Jasmine shifted her feet, angling her body as she hit a forehand. Then as Indy's momentum carried her across the court, she moved up again, taking the next shot off Indy's racket and burying it deep into the opposite corner.

"30-Love."

Jasmine couldn't hold in her smile as Indy chucked her racket against the ground in frustration. Tennis, at the highest levels, was more a mental game than anything else. If a player couldn't keep her head, she didn't have a chance against one who could.

She served again, a measured, solid serve right down the middle of the court. It was even slower than her last. Indy's body buckled as she misjudged the velocity. She stepped into the forehand, a harsh grunt forcing its way out of her lungs as she sent the ball sailing long and deep across the court.

Jasmine stepped out of the way, letting the ball fly by her.

"Out," the line judge shouted.

"40-Love."

She had three set points, three chances to close out this set and be halfway to the championship.

Across the court, Indy stood flat-footed, racket ready, but her shoulders slumped and back stiff. She looked beaten. Jasmine fired a serve as hard as she could down the middle of the court, but Indy didn't even react. She just turned and moved back to her chair at the side of the court.

Jasmine pumped her fist. Looking up into the crowd, she found her dad, applauding like a madman, a large, silly grin spread across his face. One more set. All she had to do was keep steady for one more set. Defense, patience and a cool head, that's all it would take.

"Game," the chair umpire said. "Miss Randazzo leads, one set to love."

CHAPTER 10

May 20th

Pathetic, totally pathetic. Indy fell into her chair and took her towel from the ball girl. She buried her face into it, muffling a scream, before tossing it over her head, trying to create some shelter from the blistering sun; the heat and humidity were teaming up to torture her.

She rubbed at her eyes, trying to clear her head, before sitting up and letting the towel fall around her shoulders. Reaching into her bag, she pulled out a sports drink. She needed to replenish the electrolytes she lost in the last—she glanced at the match clock in the corner of the court—

twenty-three minutes. Twenty-three pathetic minutes and she was already down a set. It was the nerves; she just couldn't shake them.

It began in the locker room. Teddy stopped by and wished her luck as she got her wrist taped. After he left, followed by the trainer, the pre-match jitters showed up, just butterflies in her stomach, anticipation, not anxiety.

Then she heard the voices carrying down the tunnel from the locker room across the hall, Teddy and Jasmine's voices. They were fighting about their friendship and a hookup and *her*. Everything made sense; Jasmine was in love with Teddy.

Indy refused to blame herself. She wasn't interested in Teddy and it wasn't her problem that Jasmine liked him. Yet, she couldn't help feeling a little guilty and that just jangled her nerves more. Then Roy was at the door and they were walking onto the court, louder than earlier in the week, the heavy bass of the music pounding out from the speakers, pulsing through her chest and the crowd buzzing with excitement. This match wasn't just about beating Jasmine Randazzo or winning the Classic; it was about proving to herself that she belonged here. She caught sight of Caroline and Mr. Franklin from Solaris Beachwear in the stands. When Dom called her and Jasmine to the center of the court for the coin toss, her hands started to shake.

They were still sitting together now, but Solaris Beachwear wouldn't want anything to do with her after this performance. Maybe Caroline wouldn't either and that would be the only positive thing about her performance so far.

Nothing was working. Her serve was a mess and her rally strokes were out of control. Also, there was no denying it. Jasmine Randazzo was flat-out awesome. She could track down almost any shot, her quick feet eating up the court like a roadrunner. She also had the uncanny ability to force mistakes. Indy didn't know how she did it. The point would be rolling along and then out of nowhere her ball would find the net or spin wide.

Indy's grip on her racket tightened, the urge to slam it into the ground rushing through her as she sat, leg bouncing, waiting for the second set to begin. She held in the frustration and closed her eyes.

She had to stop being stupid. Dom wouldn't have brought her to OBX if he didn't think she could hack it. He wouldn't have ranked her fourth if he didn't think she could win. Her leg stopped shaking and the tightness in her neck and shoulders ebbed away.

Forcing her eyes open, she stared at the scoreboard. The match was best of three. She still had time to fix this. She would serve to start the second set. Goal one, win that first game. The question was, how?

She had to change it up. Like Coach D'Amato taught her on her first day with her Einsteins, doing the same thing over and over and expecting a different result was insane. It was time to try something new.

Maybe serve and volley. She'd been focusing on her footwork since she got to OBX, but despite that, she still wasn't totally comfortable up at the net, where footwork was the most important thing. The idea did have one major advantage though. It would shock the hell out of her opponent. What was the worst that could happen? She was already losing, halfway to a crushing defeat. Anything was better than what she suffered through in the first set.

"Time," the chair umpire said through his microphone, calling an end to their break.

Indy glanced over at Jasmine, who was digging through her bag, probably confident she'd already won the match, maybe thinking about the party her parents would throw to celebrate the victory.

She leapt to her feet. This set would be better than the first and that started with better body language. Sometimes standing up tall and lifting your chin could help make a long, uphill battle seem just a little easier.

Jasmine took her time, examining her racket as she walked to her side of the court. Indy was ready and waiting at the baseline.

Finally, the other girl was ready to receive, twirling her racket in her hands, bent at the waist just a few steps into the backcourt.

Indy slammed a serve and as it left her racket, she raced forward, careful not to get too close to the net. Jasmine blocked it back easily, but Indy was right there waiting. The ball touched the strings at the perfect angle and with a quick flick of her wrist she hit a short volley winner, while Jasmine stood stunned behind the baseline.

"15-Love."

Indy turned to the ball girl, signaling for her towel. The heat was still crushing the court. Wiping her face and her arms, she didn't look back. She didn't need to see Jasmine's face. She could imagine the expression, mouth agape, holding her racket down at her knees, one hand propped on her hip, wondering where the hell that came from.

A murmur spread through the crowd. Indy had their attention. Now she had to get them on her side. Everyone loved an underdog and right now, the rich girl from Beverly Hills was an underdog. The universe was totally weird sometimes.

She'd confused Jasmine with the last point. Tennis was a game of adjustments, but it was tough to adjust on the fly. If she piggybacked that serve and volley with another one, attack the same way, Jasmine probably wouldn't be ready for it.

Firing a bullet up the T again, Jasmine returned it the same way and again, Indy raced up the court to meet it, slicing another volley beyond Jasmine's reach.

"Yes," she said, her voice echoing through the court, as the crowd was still quiet, respectful of the silence necessary to play the game.

"30-Love."

Her eyes met Jasmine's and she almost smiled at the hard expression on the other girl's face.

Now it was time to switch it up. Jasmine would think she knew what was coming. She'd be ready to attack Indy's serve and volley, the same way she attacked her power game in the first set. Indy fired a serve and Jasmine returned it, but this time she stayed back at the baseline as Jasmine took a few hesitant steps in anticipating a volley. Instead, Indy wound up and shot a forehand past her, skimming it off the white line for a clean winner.

"40-Love."

The crowd cheered the point, not just indifferent, polite applause, but loud voices engaging in the match. They were rooting for her, acknowledging her making an effort after such an awful showing in the first set. Tennis fans were all alike, and what they wanted was very simple: more tennis. If Indy won this set, the match would go to a deciding third set and that's what they wanted to see.

"Quiet please," the chair umpire said. The crowd noise faded to a soft hum, but the buzz was there, like electricity flowing through the air. As she ran her towel over her forehead, she let that energy wash over her, drawing it into her. She looked back over the net. Jasmine was ready, but the confusion was written across her face. She had her. Now all she had to do was execute.

Confidence flowed through Indy's veins. Her serve felt good for the first time all match and she was ready to unleash it. She rocked forward and then back, her body coiling powerfully as her racket swung down and then up, whistling through the air and launching the ball as hard as she could. A split second later, the ball ricocheted off the wall behind Jasmine.

"Come on!" Indy shouted, pumping her fist and then looking up into the crowd. They responded, the noise growing to a roar. Her adrenaline spiked, drawing energy off them, despite the heat and the mountain she still had to climb.

"Game, Miss Gaffney."

~

| #1 Randazzo, Jasmine (USA) | 6 | 5 | 7 (5) |
| #4 Gaffney, Indiana (USA) | 1 | 7 | 7 (5) |

The second set was close, really close. As soon as Indy jumped to a lead, Jasmine came storming back, adjusting to the new style of play. The third set was even closer. They were locked at five points all in the third set tiebreaker. The match could bounce either way, both of them two points from a win. One way or another, it was almost over.

The crowd rose to their feet, giving them a standing ovation, showing their appreciation for such a hard-fought match, regardless of who won or lost.

Indy moved to the other side of the court. She checked the match clock in the corner of the court—2hr 45min—definitely not pathetic, more than respectable, bordering on epic. There were no announcers, no ESPN crew sitting in a box high above the court, analyzing the match, but she could hear their voices in her head, talking about how her power serve was a major advantage in a tiebreak, but that Jasmine's better conditioning might cancel it out.

Blissfully, cloud cover and a soft breeze swept in off the water. The cooler air was a relief against her skin after baking under the sun for nearly three hours. Indy looked up into the sky. Just a few more minutes, she pleaded with the clouds. She needed just a few more minutes of shade. She couldn't last for much longer; it was time to take a risk, go for a line and hope it landed in.

Jasmine stood on the other side of the court, readying to serve. It was the weakest part of her game, and the longer the match went on, the weaker it got. Indy was ready to expose that weakness one more time. Jasmine leaned back, then pushed up and out, the ball hitting her racket with a soft thwack.

The serve was slow and flat, bouncing up at the perfect height for Indy's forehand. She stepped into the shot and rifled a forehand up the line for a winner.

The crowd erupted, people leaping to their feet, screaming and cheering, applauding like crazy, but it wasn't over yet.

"Miss Gaffney leads the tiebreaker, six points to five."

Indy tried to ignore the wall of sound crashing down onto the court; it was almost as oppressive as the heat. Match point.

"Thank you, players are ready," the chair umpire said. "Thank you." The crowd quieted, though not entirely, the energy still reverberating through the court, waiting to ignite again.

In a tiebreak, the players alternated serves and it was Indy's turn. She had enough energy in her tank for one more. It was time to end this. She took her time, making sure her rhythm was perfect. Her muscles bunched and then snapped up and through the air, sending a low-lying missile across the court. Then with a final burst of energy, she sprinted forward, meeting Jasmine's return with a sharp-swinging volley. The ball hit the blue hard court just inside the line. Jasmine's sneakers squeaked against the ground as her quick feet raced forward to get to the ball, but before she could reach it, it bounced again.

"Game, set and match, Miss Gaffney."

~

Indy sat on the trainer's table in the center of the room trying to slow everything down, but her head was still spinning. Showered and dressed, she was ready for the party at Deuce about to be held in her honor. She had brought a dress with her, just in case, along with a pair of sweats and T-shirt she would wear back to the dorms had she lost.

It was all a blur after that last point. She remembered shaking hands with Jasmine and the chair umpire, then moving back onto the court and applauding the crowd, clapping her racket against the heel of her hand, thanking them for their support. Dom brought the trophy out to her, congratulating her on the win, and he hadn't seemed all that surprised at the result. Then she floated back to the locker room, the trophy held tightly to her chest, arms wrapped around it.

She won. It was one thing to wish it or to imagine it, but it was totally different to have done it. She beat Jasmine Randazzo and a handful of the best junior players in the world. That made her one of the best, right? No, that made her *the* best. This was everything she and her mom had dreamed about, and now, it was real. A prickling of tears edged out of the corner of her eyes, and for the first time in a long time, she let them fall. Just a week ago, she was sitting in physics, getting a detention, and now she was at the top of the junior tennis world, a major steppingstone toward a professional career.

"You're going to freak everyone out if you show up at the party sobbing," Penny said from the doorway.

Indy wiped at her eyes quickly. "Sorry, I just, it's a lot to take in."

Penny pulled a tissue from the container on the trainer's table, holding it out for her. "Don't try. You might hurt yourself. After all, you are pretty thickheaded. It took you an entire set before you figured out you had to go serve and volley."

Indy took the tissue, dabbing under her eyes and laughed. "You coming to the party?"

"Uh, no, sorry, tonight's about you."

"It's okay. I get it," Indy said, standing up and smoothing down the skirt of her dress. If Penny went to the party, she'd be a distraction to the sponsors and media.

"Anyway, I just wanted to be the first to congratulate you," she said, opening her arms and Indy fell into the hug gratefully. "You should get up to Deuce. Everyone's waiting for you." She stepped away and turned to leave, but paused at the door. "Oh and, Indy? Good luck."

"What do you mean?"

"You'll see. Welcome to the big time."

Penny's meaning was crystal clear as soon as Indy stepped through the doors at Deuce.

A group of fellow OBX juniors rushed her, pulling her in for hugs and congratulating her.

"You were awesome, Indy," Addison said, hugging her tightly.

"Beyond amazing," a girl whose name she didn't know said, grasping her hand and squeezing it. She even saw Lara standing at the edge of the crowd, though she wasn't quite brave enough to join in. Could they be any more superficial? She was suddenly grateful for the way they acted when she first arrived. There wouldn't be a struggle to weed out the genuine people from the fakes.

"Thanks, guys," she said, pulling away from them, only to be intercepted by Dom. Her coach's arm came around her shoulders as he led her to a group of gentlemen, the rep from Solaris Beachwear among them. Jack was there, chatting with a man she didn't recognize and just a step or two away, Caroline stood all smiles next to Harold Hodges, chatting with her hands flying around her as the reporter nodded along with whatever she was rambling about.

After more handshakes than she could count and hearing more names than she'd ever be able to remember, Indy was practically swaying on her feet. She had no idea where Dom had vanished to, but she was caught in a sea of well-wishers, all of whom seemed desperate to congratulate her.

"Indy, what a win," yet another man in a suit said. She had no idea who he was, but that was par for the course. She had to get used to people she didn't know knowing who she was, "I'd love to talk to you about representation." Apparently he was an agent. He held out a business card. Indy took it, but before she could even glance at the name, a hand snatched it from her grip.

"Now, now, Mark, you know better than that," Jack Harrison said, shoving the card back at the man, whose mouth turn down into a scowl, but then he nodded sharply and walked away.

Indy looked up at Jack, brow furrowed, but before she could speak, his hand cupped her elbow and with the gentlest of pressure, he steered her away from the group.

"Sorry about that," he said when they reached an empty corner of the room. He stood in front of her, blocking her from view. "Mark D'Angelis is the worst kind of agent. He runs his clients into the ground, sucking every dollar from them and then drops them as soon as their play suffers. Signing with Caroline Morneau is one thing. She's a shark, but she wants what's best for her clients. D'Angelis is just a snake."

"Oh," she said, the tension that had been building in her shoulders since she arrived at the party suddenly loosening when she realized no one could see her. "Thanks for getting me out of there. I was… This is just so…"

"Overwhelming? You looked like you were about to keel over," Jack said. "All this can be difficult at first."

She laughed a little. "Yeah, I think Penny tried to warn me, but I wasn't expecting…I don't, I guess I wasn't expecting anyone to care."

"Of course they care. You won. Congratulations, by the way."

Shrugging, she said, "It doesn't seem real. I can't believe it yet."

Jack laughed, his green eyes sparkling at her, hypnotizing in their intensity. "I can." The soft tone of his voice sent her back to the night before the tournament. Just thinking about the kiss on the cheek he gave her made her toes curl. It was so innocent. If his lips against her cheek felt like that, what would it feel like to really kiss him?

"What are you doing here anyway?" she asked, trying to keep him talking, hoping he wouldn't shut down on her again.

"There were a couple of sponsors I had to firm things up with before they left town *and* I wanted to congratulate you."

"Indiana!" Caroline's voice carried into their corner, even past Jack's broad back.

She groaned, not thinking and leaned forward, her forehead landing against Jack's chest. He stiffened for a moment before a large, warm hand came up to rest against her back, not quite an embrace, but close enough for Indy to pretend. She let herself relish the closeness for a second and then she stood, taking a deep breath and straightening her shoulders.

"Ah, there you are," Caroline said, reaching out to drag her away again, but Indy pulled back.

"Just a second," Indy said and Caroline stepped back a few feet, keeping her eyes locked on Indy.

Jack cleared his throat. "I should get going." He hesitated for a moment before he stepped closer, pressing his lips against her cheek. Indy tried to fight the instinct to tilt her head just a fraction of an inch and end this torturous game he insisted on playing. It was a losing battle. Just as he began to draw away she turned, letting her lips brush against the corner of his mouth.

Instantaneous electricity snapped through her veins at the ghost of a touch, her entire body reacting to him.

He pulled back and stared at her wide-eyed, mouth opening and closing, but not uttering a word. Then after a few silent, tense moments, he nodded a farewell, turned and left.

Indy watched him go, pressing her fingers against her still-tingling lips.

"He is very handsome," Caroline said.

"Yes, he is," Indy agreed.

"He is Penny Harrison's brother and agent as well, no?" Her tone was casual, too casual to truly be so. Caroline was a shark. Jack was right. Of course he was right. He was brilliant and she'd kissed him—kind of.

"Indiana?" Caroline said, looking at her expectantly.

"Sorry, were you saying something?"

"Yes, I was congratulating you again on a wonderful performance out on the court today. Simply fantastique."

"Thank you."

"I have been speaking to several sponsors tonight. I do not have to tell you that you are very interesting to them. Your looks and the potential they see, it is an excellent combination. I will be speaking to Dominic. This win, it will mean wildcards, Indiana, and wildcards will put you on the biggest stage in the world. These companies will be willing to pay to see their brand showcased on that stage, but my hands are tied until you make your decision."

Caroline gestured out into the party where men and women in business attire were working the room. Tennis was a high-end sport and its sponsors leaned toward the ritzy side of the market. Which companies were interested in her? Rolex? Longines? Nike? Lacoste?

She bit her lip, suddenly feeling guilty. Caroline had been working on her behalf without any guarantee that Indy would forgo her NCAA eligibility, drop her amateur status and pursue tennis professionally. She was a shark, but maybe in a world where people treated you like shit one minute and then smothered you with attention the next, maybe she needed a shark.

"Okay."

Caroline tilted her head. "Okay?"

"Okay, I'm in. Where do I sign?"

The agent's smile was as wide as her stiletto heels were tall. She pulled a file folder from her large clutch purse and then offered Indy a pen.

"Your signature here, below your father's."

She signed her name beneath her dad's bold, confident scrawl and smiled.

"Magnifique," Caroline said, adding her own signature. "You will not regret this decision, Indiana. You are talented, very talented, more so than you even realize, I think."

"I think I'm starting to understand."

CHAPTER 11

May 20th

Rivulets of sweat dripped from her forehead as Penny attacked the ball. Air pushed through her lungs, she grunted with the effort of playing the ricochets off the wall. She counted in her head, ninety-eight, ninety-nine, one hundred backhands. She let the ball fly by her after the last stroke, her eyes slipping closed as she tried to regain her breath.

Her hands fell to her hips. "Damn it."

With the rhythm of each solid shot against the wall, she could hear Alex calling her "love," his voice in that half-sarcastic lilt, the smallest touch setting her entire body on fire, then that other way he spoke sometimes, the earnest, deep tones telling her she was the most incredible-looking girl he'd ever seen. They hadn't even spoken since their almost kiss, not even during training. She wasn't sure if he was avoiding her or the other way around, maybe both. Pushing herself to near exhaustion just wasn't working. No matter how hard she went at it, it was impossible to clear her mind. It was like Australia all over again and she couldn't let that happen. They left for Paris in five days.

She tossed her racket against the fence surrounding the small half-court used for groundstroke drills and grabbed a towel from her bag, wiping the sweat from her forehead, down her arms and across her midriff. Her sports bra and shorts were soaked through.

Her breath came back to her and she took a small swig of water before picking up her racket again—one hundred forehands and then she'd call it a day.

~

Wandering to the locker room, muscles aching pleasantly after her long workout, Penny hesitated at the door. She didn't want to go home. She turned around and walked down the path, away from the locker rooms and toward the beach. Glancing up at the sky, the sun was just beginning to set. She could get in a quick run on the sand before it got too dark.

Her thoughts turned into a complete mess as her feet pushed through the sand. She stayed close to the water where the ground was firmer, but her calves still burned with the effort. Her focus needed to be completely on tennis and not on Alex Russell or his stupid meditation exercises or their almost kiss or why he was almost kissing her if he was going to dinner with Caroline Morneau or how four months after their night together she could still feel a thrill surge through her body at the mere thought of those moments in his arms.

Up ahead, she saw a dark lump sitting in the sand, the setting sun reflecting off something next to it.

Jogging closer, the lump took human shape, a man hunched over, knees up, and a glass bottle wedged into the sand beside him. It was Alex. He caught sight of her as she drew near and he held the bottle aloft, saluting her, before taking a long draught from it.

"What are you doing here?" she asked, stopping a few feet away.

"I live here," he said, jerking his thumb back to the house a few yards up the beach. "What are you doing here? Come back for that kiss, did you?"

She ignored the biting tone in his voice. "Just trying to clear my head."

"Well, we wouldn't want that head of yours foggy, would we? You might do something stupid like give me the time of day."

"You're drunk."

"A little," he admitted, standing up and dusting off his jeans. "This is how I clear my head, love. You know, when the meditation doesn't quite do the job."

"It's a stupid way," she said, though she was vastly tempted to throw herself onto the sand, steal the bottle and just drown her problems in alcohol.

"You run until you're so tired you pass out. I drink until I pass out. Don't see there's much of a difference."

The conversation was going nowhere fast. "Fine. Enjoy your bottle." She wanted to turn around and keep running, but there was this inexplicable need inside of her to be near him. When he wasn't around, it was a tiny ache, a constant reminder that something was missing. Now that he was there, standing just inches away, close enough to reach out and touch, it was so much worse.

"Penny?"

"Yeah?"

"You're still here."

"Yeah, um," she said, her mind racing to come up with an excuse.

He reached out a hand and she stared at it for a split second, hesitating as if it might burn her. She pressed her hand into his and shivered as the calloused tips of his fingers slid across her skin. Looking up, she saw he'd moved closer, close enough to bend his head to hers, if he wanted, close enough to—

"Penny," he murmured, his warm breath ghosting over her lips. He slanted his mouth over hers, deepening the kiss immediately. She could taste the alcohol on his tongue, but it barely registered as she pushed up onto her toes, winding an arm over his shoulders, hooking a finger into the belt loop of his jeans, anchoring herself to him. His stubble scratched against her cheeks and his hands fell to her hips, pulling her body into his, their hips colliding, before one slid up to her neck and the other down over her backside. A jolt surged through her as a low moan escaped the back of her throat.

He broke away then and trailed his hot, open mouth across her jawline and over her neck. Penny shivered in his arms as his lips hovered over her pulse point.

"Stay with me," he mumbled, his teeth scraping lightly against her skin.

"What?" she asked, trying to force her mind to focus on his words and not the feeling of his fingertips slipping beneath the hem of her running jacket, brushing against the skin of her waist.

"The house I'm letting, it's right there. Stay with me tonight," he whispered, cupping her cheek and pressing a soft kiss to her lips again. His eyes softened. "Penny," he started again, but she stepped away from him, cutting him off. He was drunk. Who knew if he would even remember this in the morning?

"I'm sorry."

~

Awkward. That was the only way Penny could describe the heavy silence that hung over Dom's office the next morning as they waited for their coach to arrive. There were only inches separating the two chairs in front of her coach's desk and that meant she was sitting only inches away from Alex, after a text message from their coach had summoned them both there instead of where they should be, out on the training court.

What the hell was taking Dom so long? It was seven o'clock in the morning. Nothing else was going on at OBX except breakfast, and so help her, if she was sitting in the most painfully awkward situation of her life while he was enjoying his morning coffee, coach or not, she was going to let him have it. Her fingers started tapping against the wooden arm of the chair.

Granted, she'd still have to be near Alex, but at least they'd have something else to do, a distraction from how good it had felt to give in, to finally close the space between them. Penny had never been kissed like that, like she was the only thing holding him together, like he needed her.

She glanced to her right and had to suppress a sigh. He looked like hell—dark, purple circles under his eyes, drawn expression, shoulders slumped. He was probably hung-over.

Suddenly, a warm hand landed on top of hers, ceasing the tapping. "Please stop," Alex rasped. Her hand stiffened under his and she nodded. Their eyes met for the first time since she'd walked into the room to find him sitting there, slumped down in the chair, head hanging back, legs extended out in front of him, crossed at the ankles.

"Ah, good, you're both here," Dom said, jogging up the last few steps into his office. They turned toward him together and Alex's hand shot away from hers, but not before Dom saw it and raised his eyebrows. He pushed on, however. "Sorry about the wait," he said, but didn't offer an explanation. He stepped behind his desk and sat down, picking up a thick envelope and fiddling with the flap.

"So," he said, looking back and forth between them, "do you want the good news or the bad news?"

"Bad," Alex muttered.

"Good," Penny said right over him.

Dom snorted and shook his head. "The draw is out for Paris."

Penny sat up straight, but Alex didn't move.

"Funnily enough, you're ranked the same, twenty-five."

"Lovely," Alex said through a grunt.

"Damn it," Penny said. She knew her ranking might drop after not playing in Rome, but she'd hoped to stay in the top twenty. "When would I get Lutrova?"

"Third round," Dom said, winking at her. "So the end of week one, just about."

"Gotta win two matches first, love," Alex quipped, his posture unchanged.

Penny rolled her eyes and then turned to Dom. "Wait, was that the good news or the bad news?"

Dom grimaced, opening the envelope. "That was the good news." He stood, pulling out two packets of paper and handing one to each of them. It was a print out of the *Athlete Weekly* website and there, front and center, was a collage of pictures from the past week and every single one was of her and Alex. The photo in the center was from their photo shoot, but it was surrounded by candid shots. The first was from the Classic Reception, Alex towering over her, a tumbler in his hand while she glared up at him. The next was of them arguing over a point on the practice court; another of them on that same court, lying down, hands entwined and the last from that same night, him leaning in, his mouth hovering just over hers, her fingers curled around the cotton of his T-shirt.

"Now look," Dom said, "what either of you does off the court is none of my business, but…"

"You're right," Alex cut him off. "This is none of your damn business."

Dom raised his hands up in surrender. "Easy there, Al. I'm not the enemy here. I was on the phone with Hodges already this morning, but he claims he didn't take these pictures. He says they were sent in anonymously and when his editor saw them, he was forced to run them."

"Dom, this isn't what it looks like," Penny said, scanning through the article quickly. From what she could tell, they were creating their own narrative, starting with Australia—she and Alex leaving the Nike party together, then the motorcycle accident with another woman, filling in the blanks with whatever garbage they thought would sell the most magazines and whatever Hodges observed while he was at OBX. Apparently, she and Alex Russell had a rocky on-again, off-again, relationship, which she didn't want to commit to because he was bad for her public image, and with that, Penny stopped reading and crumpled up the papers. "None of this is true."

"I don't know," Alex said, finally sitting up, as he read through the article. "Some of it they nailed right on the head."

Penny turned, ready to blast him, but Dom said. "Look, like I said, this is none of my business, but what do you want me to say once the phone calls start pouring in?"

"No comment," they said together.

Penny laughed, though there was absolutely no humor in it. At least that was one thing they could agree on.

CHAPTER 12

May 21ˢᵗ

Jasmine rolled over and buried her face into her pillow. She wasn't ready to face the day. Groaning, she pulled the covers over her head. It didn't help; she could still hear it in her mind, like a song on infinite repeat for two days. The chair umpire's voice amplified by the microphone as the crowd roared, "Game, set and match, Gaffney."

Sleep was impossible. She tossed and turned late into the night, body exhausted, but replaying the match over and over again. Then the expression on her father's face when he saw her after the match would swim behind her eyes, part disappointment and part disbelief. She'd let him down and that hurt even more than the loss itself.

"Jasmine!" Her mother's voice carried up the stairs, followed by the pounding of footsteps. "Jasmine, wake up!" Her mom, bracelets jangling, burst through her door and grabbed her duvet cover, yanking it away.

"Mom," she grumbled. "Go away."

"You have to get up, *mija*. You gave yourself a day to wallow. You lost. It happens from time to time, but today you must go back to training. The OBX Classic is over and the French Open begins. Simple as cake."

"Pie. Simple as pie." Even after nearly twenty years in the States, her mom tended to mix up her idioms.

"Cake, pie, I love both. Now, get up." She felt a soft tap against her backside and then her curtains and windows were thrown wide open, the morning air blowing in and the sunlight blinding her.

Jasmine rolled over, sitting up and her stomach lurched. She couldn't go in to OBX and face everyone, not after that loss and not after what the *Athlete Weekly* article wrote about her.

Dom probably went nuts on Hodges for focusing his article on Penny and Alex's off-the-court relationship in what was supposed to be a serious sports publication, but it wasn't the tabloid crap that worried Jasmine. It was a separate section entirely, one that focused on the results of the Classic.

Mental toughness is a necessary quality in any champion. Both John and Lisa Randazzo had it in spades, along with far superior athleticism and instinct, but the same can't be said for their daughter, who folded under the pressure in the tournament's final after coasting through a relatively weak field...

There, in black and white was an analysis of what happened during the final match that hit far too close to home. Athleticism, instinct, mental toughness, things necessary to succeed as top athlete in any sport, qualities Harold Hodges, a tennis expert, didn't think she possessed.

That's why the loss was eating away at her. She'd lost big matches before and they were always disappointing, but this one was different. It was a match she should've been able to win but didn't. The competition at the OBX Classic was good, but at the end of the day, it was still a junior tournament and a great junior player didn't necessarily become a great tour player. Indiana was very good, but she had a week of elite-level coaching under her belt and managed to beat her. It shouldn't have happened and yet, it did.

"What if he's right? What if I'm not good enough?"

"*Mija*, he is one man." Her mom sat down beside her on the bed and wrapped her arm around her shoulders. "He is one man who watched you play for one week. He is not God. He is not the final word."

"He's one of the best tennis reporters in the world." She slipped out from under the embrace and stood, crossing her arms over her chest.

"It's his opinion. He doesn't know you and the article is such trash."

It didn't make her feel any better, but she knew her mom wouldn't stop, so she plastered a grin on her face and nodded.

"Fine, you're right. He's one man and he doesn't know me."

"Good, get dressed. I'll make you breakfast before training." Sometimes her mom saw what she wanted to see and not what was right in front of her.

Jasmine eyed the crumpled printout of the article sitting on her nightstand next to her phone, which had finally stopped beeping at her after she ignored Teddy's tenth message. Harold Hodges was one man, a man who didn't know her game beyond what he saw last week. Her parents were great, but they couldn't be objective. And Teddy, he was the last person she wanted to talk to about anything. There was only one person she knew who would be brutally honest.

~

The atrium was empty when she arrived at OBX, aside from Roy, his nose buried in his paper as usual. Jasmine made a beeline for the stairs to Dom's office, knowing he usually set aside mornings for paperwork. As she climbed the stairs, she had to move aside for Penny, who nodded at her quickly, and Alex Russell trailing just behind, his eyes boring into the back of Penny's head.

"Jasmine," Dom said from behind his desk as she emerged from the stairs into his office, motioning to the chair before it, inviting her to take a seat, "what can I do for you?"

She ignored him. "You know why I'm here."

Dom pinched at the bridge of his nose. "That damn article. I wish I never agreed to it."

She nodded, but Dom's regrets were the least of her worries.

"Was he right?" she asked.

He leaned forward rubbing his face with both hands before looking at her again. "Jasmine, you've got to understand, Hodges wasn't writing about how you performed in the tournament, at least not entirely. You did a great job against your competition, and that final match, well no one saw that coming."

"Then what was he writing about?"

Dom opened his mouth to speak and then closed it again, pulling his lips into a thin line.

Jasmine felt her knees shake and she let herself sink into a chair across from him. "You agree with him."

"No." There was no hesitation and Jasmine felt a little better, but he still hadn't given her a straight answer. "I think his analysis was shortsighted at best."

"Then what? Either I have what it takes or I don't."

"It's not that simple. The tennis world isn't black and white. You've worked so hard all these years to try and measure up to your parents." She opened her mouth to protest, but Dom kept talking. "Don't deny it. I've known you since you were seven years old. I know you want to prove to the world that you're every bit the tennis player the daughter of Lisa Vega and John Randazzo should be."

"But I'm not," she finished for him. "Is that what you're saying? That I'm not as good as my parents?"

"I'm saying that not everyone is Top Ten material, Jasmine. Not everyone is going to win Grand Slams and Olympic medals."

"Not me, you mean."

"Not you, at least, not yet. You're only eighteen years old. You have to give yourself some time. You can still have a very good career. You've got a great head for the game and you're a hard worker."

His words didn't have much meaning in that moment. The whole world expected greatness from her. Good, in the face of those expectations, just wasn't good enough.

"Thanks," she said, leaping up from her seat and striding to the stairs.

"Jasmine," Dom called, but she didn't turn back. She didn't need Dom to see her cry. It would just be another thing to add to the list of her faults as a player: emotional basket case.

She raced down the stairs and flew through the atrium toward the women's locker room. There was a maintenance man standing at the end of the hallway, a small power drill pressed into the wall. The shrill whirring of the drill-bit securing Indy's victory plaque into the Title Wall was worse than nails on a chalkboard, setting her teeth on edge. She swiped under her eyes, forcing the tears back. Stalking past him into the locker room, she changed into her training clothes and marched out to the practice courts. OBX was in full swing, practice courts packed with players and coaches.

"*Bene*, Indiana, keep your feet moving. No hesitation. *Bene*," Coach D'Amato said as Jasmine stepped onto the training court where Indiana Gaffney and the rest of the Junior Elite Girls were training on an agility course meant to increase stamina and improve footwork. Jasmine felt her stomach clench. The OBX Champion was getting better, doing what she needed to do to win again.

"Nice job, Indy," Lara called from the line of girls at the baseline.

Indy skidded to a halt as she finished her agility run, then turned and nodded, but didn't say anything as she went to the back of the line.

"Ah, Jasmine. *Eccellente.*" Coach D'Amato greeted her with a sharp nod. "I will be right back and then you girls will play a set."

Jasmine blinked in total confusion as her coach left. She was late, but D'Amato hadn't said anything about Einsteins. Did they really think she was that much of a lost cause? No sense in making her run because it wouldn't make her any better? She turned to Indy whose mouth twisted into a pout, but obviously, Indy couldn't come up with anything to say, so she just shrugged. Later, Jasmine wouldn't be able to explain what happened, but with that shrug of Indy's shoulders, something inside of her just snapped.

"You," she barked, stomping out onto the court, getting right up into Indy's face, looking her dead in the eye. "This is all your fucking fault. Everything was just fine before you showed up."

"What are you talking about?" Indy asked, taking a step back.

"This was supposed to be my year. And then you came out of nowhere and stole it."

"That's not..." Indy started.

"Come on, Jasmine," Lara said, standing just a few feet away.

"Stay the hell out of this, you little hypocrite," she snapped and then whirled to Indiana again, "And don't pretend like you don't know what I'm talking about. You waltzed in here like you owned the damn place. You've been here two seconds. I've been training my whole life, and in one week, you took it all from me."

People were wandering over to the court, the Junior Elite Boys group from the adjacent court, Jack Harrison who'd been working with them and dozens of others drawn by Jasmine's raised voice, but the rage boiling through her veins couldn't be cooled, not even by embarrassment. She had to get away before she did something really stupid, like burst into tears in front of everyone. She turned and started to run off the court, but her retreat was interrupted.

"No," Indy yelled at her back.

"No?" Jasmine repeated, wheeling around so fast her ponytail whipped her in the face. "What the hell do you mean, no?"

Indy stalked forward, coming straight at her, her hands clenched into fists. "No, you're not going to dump all your shit on me. I beat you fair and square. It's just that simple. I beat you. You want to blame someone? Take a look in the mirror. Maybe next time you won't fold under the pressure."

Those were the exact words Hodges had used in the article and hearing them spill from the lips of her biggest rival was just too much for her.

"You don't know shit about me," Jasmine screeched and launched herself forward. Her hand got there first, her open palm striking skin with all the force she could manage. Indy reeled, clutching her face, thrown off balance from the blow, but

Jasmine wasn't done. She was inches from tackling the bitch, ready to scratch her blue eyes out of her head, but her forward momentum stopped as an arm snaked around her waist and held her back.

"Easy there, Jasmine," Jack Harrison's voice rumbled through his chest and into her back. She struggled against him for a moment, but his grip was like iron. He lifted her off the ground easily enough and carried her off the court. She thought about kicking him in the shins, but figured maiming him probably wasn't a great idea. Finally, just outside the gate, he let her down. She pushed her way out of his arms and whirled around to run away, but was suddenly face to face with Coach D'Amato.

Jasmine felt herself deflate, the reality of what just happened, what she'd just done sinking in. "Shit."

CHAPTER 13

May 21ˢᵗ

Indy slumped in the chair across from Dom's desk and propped her elbow on the armrest. Her cheek was still stinging and she winced as she leaned against the ice pack in her hand. Just inches away, Jasmine sat rigid in her seat, staring out of the floor-to-ceiling windows in Dom's office, looking over the OBX grounds and the beach in the distance. Her day had started off great—a really tough training session with Coach D'Amato, pushing herself through agility workouts that just a couple of weeks ago would've been impossible for her. Then Jasmine showed up.

If Indy's face didn't hurt so damn much, she would chuck the ice pack at the other girl and finish off the fight Jack interrupted. She was bent over, clutching her face when she saw eldest Harrison emerge from the crowd that gathered around the court, spring over the fence and pull Jasmine away from her. She almost wished he hadn't gotten there in time. Then her face would still hurt, but she would at least have gotten in a shot or two.

Heavy footsteps on the stairs drew her attention and she lifted her head gingerly as Dom stomped into his office, glaring at them. Indy glared right back. Jasmine could spin the story however she wanted. Indy knew it wasn't her fault.

"As if this day weren't already a shit show, now I have to deal with the two of you," Dom snapped as he moved in front of them. "Do you have anything to say for yourselves?"

"Yeah, I'd really like to know why I'm sitting here," Indy fired back. "I was minding my own business at practice when she storms up, freaks out, and then when I gave her a little back, she attacked me."

"I was told exactly what happened, Indiana," Dom said, frowning down at her, "including what you said."

Jasmine made a soft noise in the back of her throat, but it was enough to draw Dom's attention. "As I said, I know *exactly* what happened. Violence is unacceptable, Jasmine. You're done training for the rest of the day and I'll be calling your parents."

"What? You can't."

"I can," Dom said.

Indy rolled her eyes. The day off and a call to Mommy and Daddy. What a friggin' slap on the wrist. She'd bet every dime she had that if the roles were reversed that punishment would be just the tip of the iceberg. No wonder Jasmine couldn't handle losing, consequences were just a totally foreign concept.

"Can I go?" Indy asked, starting to stand.

"No. Sit down." She fell back into the chair and winced when her elbow bounced off the armrest, jarring her body and making the entire side of her face ache. "What happened today is my fault. I didn't realize the rivalry between you two had progressed to this level, but that stops today. From now on you two, as our top rising juniors, will train together, as a doubles team."

"Are you insane? I can't train with—"

"You've got to be kidding me. There's…"

"Shut up, the both of you. This is how it's going to be. If you don't like it, you're free to seek out a different coaching situation." His jaw was set, his brow furrowed and his shoulders held high, body language Indy recognized even after such a short time at OBX. He was dead serious. Silence reined in the office as Dom looked at Jasmine, then back to her. He pursed his lips and then his posture relaxed, just slightly. "I've been in contact with the tournament officials in Paris. There's a spot in the women's doubles draw opening up. If you two can prove to me that you can work as a team, it's yours."

Indy felt Jasmine's eyes on her, but she wasn't going to look back. "Fine," Indy said, her patience wearing thin. "Now can I go?"

"Go."

She stood, careful not to press the ice pack too hard against her cheek. Not that it mattered much; the side of her face was almost numb and the ice was melting. Frowning, she tossed the damp bag wrapped in a towel to Dom, who caught it. "I'll see you tomorrow."

Jasmine stood too, but Dom shook his head. "You, sit. We're not done yet."

Indy bolted out of his office and down the stairs, but not before she heard Dom's sharp, "What were you thinking?" though she didn't hear Jasmine's reply.

The atrium, usually empty during morning practice sessions, was buzzing with players and even a couple of coaches. Most were at least pretending like they had a reason to be there, chatting with Roy or digging through their racket bags, but some were just staring up at the windows to Dom's office, obviously trying to figure out what was happening behind the glass. The room held the unnatural silence of too many people trying not to make a sound, and when she emerged from the stairwell, every eye focused on her.

"What?" she shouted and a visible jolt went through the crowd, sending them scattering.

As the large room emptied out, Indy caught sight of Caroline stepping through the atrium's front doors and checking in with Roy.

"Indiana," she called out, striding toward her quickly. "I just heard what happened, are you okay?"

"I'm fine," Indy said. "Wait. How did you find out what happened?"

"Dom called your father and your father called me to take care of this."

Indy rolled her eyes. Her dad found out she was in a fight and his first call was to her agent. Why didn't that surprise her?

"It's already taken care of."

Caroline's eyes narrowed. "How has it been taken care of?"

"We have to train together now. He wants us to play women's doubles at the French Open, which would be amazing, if we don't kill each other first."

The agent snorted and tossed her head like an agitated racehorse. "That is unacceptable."

"What's unacceptable?" Indy asked, but Caroline was already gone, the click-clack of her heels echoing through the atrium as she marched toward the stairs to Dom's office. "Caroline, what the hell?"

"He is allowing his ego to cloud his judgment and I will not allow it," Caroline said as Indy caught up with her. "Dominic!"

"He's in there with Jasmine," Indy said, just as Jasmine raced down the stairs, and without lifting her eyes from the floor, took off for the locker room. "Or not." Caroline was halfway up the steps by the time Indy caught up again. "I really don't think this is a good idea," she managed to whisper before they reached the top.

"Ms. Morneau," Dom said from his desk, letting his head drop back, talking to the ceiling instead. "To what do I owe this pleasure?"

"I heard you're punishing assault with an afternoon off and a trip to Paris," Caroline said, stomping right up to the front of his desk.

Dom's head snapped back up to face them. "As always, I determine how my players are disciplined."

"And that this player's father is the owner of this facility has nothing to do with this so-called punishment?"

"Dismissal for the day is standard practice in an altercation like what happened today, but besides that, I don't believe this is any of your business, Ms. Morneau."

Caroline pressed her flat against Dom's desk and leaned over it. "Indiana is my client and she is my business. That girl physically assaulted another athlete and you give her the chance to play doubles at the French Open."

"You'll note your client is included in that chance."

Caroline waved her hand in the air, dismissing his point. "Yes, but why doubles? Why not an entry to the French Open junior girls tournament? Or better than that, the women's singles? When Penny Harrison won the Classic, that is where she went next, no?"

"Penny had already won the junior Australian Open and she'd have been given a spot either way, Caroline. You know that."

Caroline sniffed, clearly unimpressed. "Still, I wonder that you did not inquire?"

Dom stood up, resting his hands against his desk for support, his face close to Caroline's. "Of course I inquired. I think the doubles will be a better experience for her, definitely more worthwhile than the junior tournament. A little less pressure and a chance to acclimate herself to the tour." He shook his head. "I don't even know why I'm explaining this to you. I'm her coach."

Caroline's nostrils flared. "I am her agent. It is my job to look out for her best interest and I wonder what is your motivation for these decisions?"

Dom threw up his hands. "Here we go. You ever need a good conspiracy theory, Indiana, go straight to your agent. She's spectacular at making mountains out of molehills."

"Do not make this about me. This is not about the girls. This is about you."

"Yeah, how do you figure?" Dom shot back.

"What are you even talking about?" Indy chimed in.

"Do you not understand, Indiana? Dom coaches a great men's player and perhaps the best woman's player if Penny wins in Paris. Now he wishes to create a great doubles team. This experiment with you and the Randazzo girl, it is all about his reputation as a coach. He wishes to dominate all parts of the game."

Dom groaned, throwing himself back into his chair. "You're insane, do you know that? Totally insane. I knew it was a bad idea to let you in here. I should've kicked you out the day you showed up, just like I did five years ago."

"You have a broken memory. You did not kick me out. I kicked you out."

Indy exhaled in disbelief. Suddenly this entire argument made sense. It wasn't even about her. It was about them. "Oh my God, you two used to be at thing?"

They both stopped yelling and faced her, gaping like they'd forgotten she was standing there.

Dom sighed. "It was a long time ago."

"A very long time ago," Caroline added, crossing her arms over her chest.

Indy shook her head. "Whatever. So since this thing," she said, waving her hands at them, "clearly isn't about me, how about we settle it like this: Dom's my coach, so he makes the tennis decisions. Caroline, you work with whatever Dom sets up."

"Sounds like how things are supposed to work," Dom said, a smug grin spreading across his face as he looked back at Caroline.

"Right, okay, I'm going now," Indy said, spinning on her toe and racing out of the office. Her mind was still reeling. Her coach and her agent, she tried to think back and she remembered things being a little tense between Dom and Caroline, but she never would've guessed they were a couple.

She went back to the practice court, but morning sessions were over. She could grab lunch at Deuce, but that would mean seeing everyone who just watched her get bitch slapped by Jasmine Randazzo and she wasn't quite up for that yet, so she turned and headed back to her dorm. As she walked, with every step what happened that morning started to hit home. She got into a fight, her coach yelled at her, her agent yelled at her coach and apparently they had a long history that had absolutely nothing to do with her, but none of that really mattered because, in the middle of all that, she'd also been invited to the French Open.

For half a second, as she unlocked her door and tossed her bag inside, she thought about calling her dad, but as soon as the thought fully registered, she dismissed it. She'd probably get his voicemail, and then in a few hours, his secretary would email her or worse, Caroline would stop by since it seemed she was his new go-between.

Indy sat down on her bed and kicked off her sneakers before lying back and staring up at the ceiling. She was going to a Grand Slam, the first of many if she had her way. A surge of energy flowed through her body. She punched her hands into the air and kicked her legs out, letting a small shriek escape her throat. Popping up onto her feet, she bounced on her mattress for a moment before throwing herself back down, laughter bubbling up into her throat. Holy friggin' shit. She was going to the French Open.

CHAPTER 14

May 21st

One of the great things about being a professional athlete in the 21st century was that even when practice was done for the day, there were hundreds of other ways to train. For Penny, that often meant sitting in the cool, dark video analysis room, studying match tapes of herself and her potential opponents, breaking down strengths and weaknesses. Usually, her attention was fully focused, pulling her into a zone not unlike what happened when she was actually in the middle of a match.

However, as she stared at the screen, trying to establish a pattern in Zina Lutrova's shot selection, her mind drifted. Rolling her eyes, she paused the video, pulled her phone from her pocket and thumbed through the pictures *Athlete Weekly* had used in their article.

A pictorial review of the biggest mistake she'd ever made and the constant distraction Alex had proved to be since then. His physical presence every single day was the sweetest torture, like nothing she'd ever felt before. So what was stopping her?

Then someone flipped the light switch, blinding her for a second.

"What are you still doing here?" Dom frowned at her from the doorway.

"Just some vid-analysis."

"Yeah, I can see that." He nodded at the paused screen that she obviously hadn't been even looking at, let alone analyzing. "Go home, get some rest. We've got a long road ahead of us once we get to Paris and an even longer season after that."

"Right," Penny said, putting her phone back in her pocket and standing.

"Pen, don't let this press bother you, okay? None of it means anything."

Smiling tightly at her coach, she nodded. "You know me, Dom. Nothing to worry about."

Before he could respond, she hustled out of the room, down the hallway and into the atrium. It was empty at this time of night. She took a step toward the front entrance, and then stopped. She didn't want to go home where she'd have to face her family and talk about that stupid article and Alex and everything. She just needed some peace.

She didn't even realize where her feet were taking her until she found herself standing just outside her practice court. She stepped out onto the empty court and inhaled deeply. A breeze swirled up from the water and the salty air invaded her senses, but her shoulders were still tense, her mind still full of everything that happened that day – hell everything that happened since she found Alex in this exact spot just a few weeks ago.

Maybe he was on to something. She lay down and closed her eyes. She was close enough to the water to hear the waves rumbling against the shore, a sound that was overshadowed during the day by voices and match noise and the general OBX buzz. A deep breath in and a slow exhale out and then another, but it wasn't having the calming effect he promised her.

"This was a stupid idea," she mumbled to herself, sitting up.

"It's not stupid. You're just doing it wrong."

Her back teeth clenched together at the distinct British accent that rang out over the soft roar of the ocean. He was standing just outside the court, leaning on the top rail of the fence.

"Didn't ask you, did I?" she shot back, standing up and dusting off her shorts.

Alex raised an eyebrow at her, a smug smirk tugging at his mouth. "Then what are you doing here?"

"I don't know. I... Fine. Tell me what I'm doing wrong," she said, hoping that if he got in whatever shot he wanted to take, she could escape with at least some of her pride intact.

He hopped the fence, the chain link jangling against the frame, and approached her slowly. "You're thinking too much. That's your problem, Penny. You think too bloody much."

She refused to meet his eye as he drew closer. "So I should be like you? No thinking, no worries, just do whatever the hell I want, to hell with the consequences."

Alex bit out a laugh. "Consequences? What consequences? A silly article that everyone will forget about in a week?"

"Forget it. Obviously none of it matters to you."

Spinning on her toe, she started to walk away.

"That's right," he called out, "run away. Don't worry your pretty little head about any of this, and in a day or two, it'll be like none of it ever happened."

She wanted to keep walking, but her feet stayed rooted to the spot.

He was right behind her now, hovering just inches away. She wanted to lean back into him, collapse against his chest and let him hold her, give in to what she'd craved since the moment they met.

Instead, she whirled around, her hair whipping out, making him lean away. "You don't know what you're talking about."

His eyes narrowed, his gaze moving from hers down to her mouth and back again. "You sure about that?"

"Yes," she lied, not giving an inch as he moved closer.

"Liar," he murmured, before lowering his mouth to hers.

~

"How do you feel?" Alex's voice rumbled in her ear. She lay draped across his chest, their bodies entwined together in the center of his bed. His fingertips traced mindless patterns over the skin of her back, making her shiver despite the heat they generated together.

The sun rose behind the water in the distance, reflecting in through the floor-to-ceiling windows of his bedroom, a spectacular sight to wake up to. She stretched against him and brushed a kiss against the sharp cut of his collarbone, trailing kisses up over his neck, his stubble scratching against her lips until her mouth hovered just above his.

"Incredible," she said, letting her lips move against his. It felt so good to just give in, to stop fighting against what her body had been pleading for since he'd arrived. The battle against her own will had been exhausting.

"Incredible sounds about right," he said, as her mouth moved down his jawline again. He drew her face to his and pressed his mouth to hers in a short, sweet kiss. "Good morning."

"Morning."

She wasn't even sure how they made it back to his house. In a tangle of limbs, neither willing to surrender the other's lips for longer than a moment or two, they'd stumbled off OBX property and across the beach, falling to the sand more than once. She remembered him carrying her some of the way and barely making it into the bedroom before their clothes littered the floor.

"You fell asleep on me," he accused playfully, running his knuckles over the curve of her hip, then opening his hand and sliding it over her waist, pulling her even closer. "I was ready to go another round."

"It's been a long couple of days. I was tired," she said, tracing a line of freckles that dotted his chest with her fingertip and watched, fascinated as gooseflesh broke out over his skin.

"Hmm, sleepiness is weakness of character." His hand crept down over her thigh, the calloused tips of his fingers stroking lightly over the back of her knee, sending a shiver through her entire body.

Laughing, she snuggled closer. "You stole that."

"Doesn't make it any less true," he teased, sitting up and letting her head fall onto his pillow, before rolling away. He reached onto his nightstand, brushing aside the two empty condom wrappers, and picked up an orange plastic bottle. He shook two pills into the palm of his hand and swallowed them dry.

"What's that?" she asked, propping herself up on elbows.

"Just some anti-inflammatories."

She raised an eyebrow. "Prescription strength. Your knee?"

Alex smirked, and before she could react, he was leaning over her, his lips brushing against hers as he said, "I had you up against that wall last night, love. Did it seem like my knee was hurt?"

She could still feel the wall against her back, his hands supporting her at the thighs and the feeling that she was going to burst out of her skin. "No, but…"

"No buts." He cut her off and the mattress shifted as he stood. In seconds he had on a pair of basketball shorts and was digging around in his dresser for a shirt.

Feeling a little exposed, Penny pulled a sheet over her body.

He turned, mouth open, ready to say something, but stopped himself. For a moment he just stared, his eyes scorching her skin the way his hands and mouth had just hours before.

"What?" she asked, feeling heat rising in her cheeks. It seemed so natural to let him look at her during their frenzy the night, but in the light of day, it was different, more personal.

He shook his head. "You feel like a run? Unless I wore you out completely…" He trailed off. Then, unbidden, a soft growl echoed up from her stomach.

Penny bit her lip. "Breakfast first?"

"As the lady wishes," he said, his gaze raking over her again, before turning abruptly and leaving the room.

Penny slipped out from beneath the sheet and gathered her clothes. Stepping into her shorts and sliding her shirt over her head, then sat back down on the bed, trying to tame her hair into a ponytail as reality set in. She'd done exactly what she promised herself she wouldn't do and now what? Had she woken up to a happily ever after or a walk of shame? It felt more like limbo, like their fate was entirely in their own hands, but that the slightest misstep could shatter everything.

She wandered out of the bedroom and down the hallway toward the kitchen. A small pang fluttered through her chest when she saw his luggage leaning against the wall. They weren't leaving for another three days and he didn't strike her as the type to pack way in advance.

"You're already packed for France?" she asked, leaning against the archway that opened to the kitchen.

Alex was leaning against the island at the center of the room, flipping through a newspaper. "Nah, heading to London tomorrow to see my mum before the tournament."

"Does Dom know?" It stung a little that she hadn't known, but then again, why would he have told her?

"Yeah, had it planned for a while now."

"Oh," she said, moving to him. Her bare feet cold against the tile floor, she stepped up behind him, wrapping her arms around his torso, pressing her cheek against his warm back.

"I would have told you, but—honestly, love—I didn't think you'd care."

She sighed against his skin. He was right, she wouldn't have cared or at least she would have pretended she didn't.

Blinking up at him, she shrugged. "It's okay. I'll just have to recruit Jack to hit with me until we leave."

Narrowing his eyes, he leaned in close. He was about to kiss her, but her stomach growled again.

"I believe I promised you breakfast," he said, motioning to the counter behind him, where two tall pink smoothies were waiting. "Strawberry banana."

Her favorite. "Did you Google me?"

Smirking, he shrugged. "Maybe. Drink up," he said, handing her a straw, "and then we run. Gotta keep our legs under us if we're going to kick ass in France."

They drank in a comfortable silence and when they finished, Penny took their glasses and washed them out in the sink.

"Let me just grab my trainers and we'll go."

"No," she said, drying her hands on a towel. She grasped his hand and led him toward the glass doors that opened to the beach. "Barefoot."

"Barefoot, in the sand?"

"Barefoot," she confirmed as she released him and took off across the beach, sand kicking up around her legs. He caught up easily enough and they ran in silence, their strides matching remarkably well for two people separated by almost a foot in height.

The rhythm of their steps set a beat behind her thoughts as she ran to the edge of the inlet. Past the jetty, she could see the edge of her neighborhood. She was really just a few blocks from home, could run there if she wanted. Her parents' faces swam in her head. They probably thought she spent the night at the OBX dorms. She did that sometimes when training ran late. What would they think about this? About Alex? She shook her head. She couldn't worry about what they would think, especially since she hadn't figured him out for herself yet.

Penny stopped and it took a few strides for Alex to realize she was no longer beside him. He jogged back, his breathing harsh.

"What's wrong?"

She didn't know how to put it into words. How could she possibly explain that she wanted him to be a part of her life, but she didn't know if it was possible?

"I..." she began, but stopped, shaking her head and looking up into the sky for answers.

"I swear to God, love, you're scaring me. Whatever it is, just come out with it."

"I don't know what this is, you and me," she said in one breath.

He brought a hand up, rubbing his palm against the back of his neck. "Christ, is that all? I thought..."

"What did you think?" She opened her eyes and met his.

"I thought you were..." He hesitated, waving a hand in the air, searching for the right word, "I don't know, regretting it, like in Australia."

Shaking her head, she stepped closer. "Should I? Regret it, I mean?"

Alex stepped forward, his hands reaching for her, settling against her cheeks, his thumbs brushing gently over her skin. "Penny, I've never— I don't know how to describe how I feel about you, but I know I've never felt it before and I've spent every moment since I got here scared shitless that you wouldn't want anything to do with me. For a while there, I thought I'd have to live with that, and trust me when I say, it wasn't pretty."

He was one of the most confident men she'd ever met. She couldn't imagine what he just said was even possible, let alone how he actually felt.

"I don't believe you," she said with a laugh, pulling away, the seriousness in his voice was a little scary.

Alex shook his head, reaching out for her hand. "Maybe we ought to have a little more faith in each other. Can you do that? Can you have faith in me?"

Penny pushed up on her tiptoes and pressed a kiss to his lips, hoping he wouldn't notice she didn't answer. The truth was she wasn't sure if she could, at least not yet.

A few moments later, she pulled away breathlessly. "As much as I'd love to stay here all day just like this, we better get going."

"Relax, love. It's early still."

"It's not that early. Dom'll be waiting for us. Come on."

~

Dom stood on their practice court, arms crossed over his chest, clearly unimpressed that they'd arrived ten minutes after six, the time he'd asked them to be there, an early start time to help them acclimate to the time change once they arrived in Paris. He raised an eyebrow, clearly expecting an explanation, but Alex beat her to it.

"My fault," he said. "I asked her to wait for me."

Their coach's mouth twisted into a frown. "Alright. You know the drill. Ten minutes, ten Einsteins. Stretch out and then get going."

Alex groaned beside her, but Penny just laughed. "I told you so," she said, as they ran through their stretching regime, starting with the toes and working their way up the body. Then they ran side by side, sprinting from line to line, pushing each other with every stride. They ran through the last line after their tenth circuit, and as they pulled up, his shoulder bumped hers. She caught herself easily and brushed against him as she turned back toward the court.

"All right, enough messing around," Dom barked, pushing off the fence where he'd been watching them run. "I'm not going to have another fight on my hands, am I?"

Penny shook her head and glanced up at Alex who'd sidled up to her, leaning over her shoulder. A day ago she would have pulled away, but now she reveled in having him close. If she was truly going to surrender to this, to stop fighting, she had to go all in and try to maintain a balance between those feelings and what she wanted to accomplish on the court.

"Good," Dom said. "I want the both of you at the top of your game in Paris."

He tossed Alex a ball. "You serve first."

They fell into the routine they'd established over the last few weeks of training as they warmed up. The tension from their previous sessions was gone, replaced by a comfortable rhythm, controlled and precise.

When they were both ready, Alex tossed a ball high in the air and fired a laser beam down the centerline, a perfect ace, impossible for anyone to return.

"Wow," Penny called out across the court, but her eyes narrowed when she saw a flash of pain flit across his face. She wasn't the only one who noticed.

"Al, you okay?" Dom asked, rising from his seat on the sidelines and ignoring the wave of dismissal from the younger man.

"I'm fine," Alex protested when Penny jogged to the other side of the court.

"You're not fine," Dom said. "It's your knee right?"

"Left, actually, and it's fine, just a twinge."

"But you took meds this morning, you shouldn't have any pain at all," Penny said, but as the words flew from her mouth she knew they were the wrong ones. Dom's eyes widened and Alex's closed in resignation.

"You're on pain medication? You told me that knee was fine."

"It is fine," Alex bit out. "I wouldn't even call it pain, like I said, just a twinge now and again."

"Bullshit. Go get it looked at in the trainers' room and we're going to get an MRI done before you leave for London."

"If I say I'm fine, I'm fine, Dom," Alex snapped. "I'm not one of your students. I don't jump when you snap your fingers."

"Alex, maybe you should get it looked at," Penny said, her brow furrowing as she studied his knee.

"Don't be a bull head about this, Al. We're just asking you to have it checked," Dom said, his tone softening.

Alex wasn't having any of it. "And I'm asking you to trust me, but apparently there isn't a lot of that around here."

He said the words to Dom, but Penny felt them deep her in her chest and as she watched him walk off the court, his stride confident and steady—no hint of a limp at all—she knew they were meant for her.

CHAPTER 15

May 22nd

Jasmine tiptoed down the stairs, glided across the tiled kitchen floor then slid through the French doors at the back of her house. She held her breath as she braced the door against her palm, letting it shut with a soft *click*. Sighing in relief, she sprinted across the patio and down the wooden walkway that led to the beach. She felt like a criminal escaping after a heist, her heart pounding in her chest as she started down the beach toward OBX.

Dom made good on his threat to call her parents and she spent the last twenty-four hours suffocating beneath the weight of their expectations for her, not as a tennis player, but as a person. She could barely look either of them in the eye and couldn't wait to get back to training, leaving behind the heavy cloud of disappointment.

It was easier to get to OBX in the mornings by crossing the private beaches that sat between her house and the training center. She could avoid the crush of cars in the parking lot, the dozens of younger athletes who would want her attention— oh who was she kidding? She was sneaking in to avoid the stares and gossip in the locker room.

The lights were still out and the usually bustling space was empty, no voices echoing off the tiled floor and metal lockers. The fluorescent lights that lined the ceiling flickered to life as she made her way to her locker, hoping to dress and grab her equipment long before anyone else arrived. As she pulled her hair into a ponytail and clipped back her bangs, her luck ran out.

"I wonder if she'll even show her face." Lara Cronin's voice echoed against the lockers, dripping with ill-concealed glee.

A laugh, high-pitched, bordering on the edge of a screech, responded. That was Addison. "I know. I mean *everyone* saw what happened."

The girls giggled together.

"Really, though, how pathetic can you get?"

"Please, she's so overrated. The only reason Dom lets her train here is because of her parents."

Jasmine slammed her locker shut and stepped out into the main walkway. The same girls who'd made Indy's life miserable when she first arrived at OBX stared in shock, then small, cruel smiles slipped over their features. Spinning on her heel, Jasmine didn't give them the satisfaction of eye contact even as she heard one of them say, "Oh my God," before they dissolved into uncontrolled cackles.

That was what Indy felt like, those first days, with everyone against her. It must have been awful and Jasmine could have put a stop to it, but she didn't, just like Teddy said. A knot of regret twisted in her stomach. Exhaling a harsh breath, she adjusted her bag over her shoulder and marched toward the courts. Those girls didn't matter and she could only hope that the people who did would forgive her.

First, she had to talk to Dom. She had to set things right with him. He was her coach, but while she lay in bed, avoiding her parents the day before, she realized something else. He was right about her game. He knew her strengths and weaknesses better than anyone.

Jasmine mumbled to herself. "Dom, I'm so sorry. What I did was awful and I'm grateful you're giving me a second chance." That sounded about right. She nodded and pushed through the gate, catching sight of her coach setting up the ball machine.

"Dom," she began, but her voice caught when Indy stepped into her vision, dumping a basket of tennis balls into the machine's feeder.

Practice started at eight and it was a quarter to the hour. What was Indy already doing here?

"Jasmine," Dom said, waving her in, "welcome back."

His words said one thing, but his eyes, trained on her like a hawk, said another. He only meant welcome back if what happened over the weekend would never happen again. Taking a deep breath, she opened her mouth to assure him it wouldn't, but he cut her off.

"Warm up, then we can get started. I mean now."

She nodded and started her stretching routine. She would apologize the first chance she got, probably after he got whatever training torture he had in mind out of his system.

She and Indy stretched together. Jasmine kept her eyes glued to the fence at the end of the court, but felt Indy watching her. Her stomach twisted again, like in the locker room, only worse. She still couldn't stand the bitch, but a sharp sliver of empathy cut against her conscience.

"Ladies, are you ready?" Dom called, striding toward them. They stood and Jasmine glanced quickly at Indy, but she was looking at their coach now. "Today we're going to start with some light conditioning." There was something in his voice that drew Jasmine's attention. She turned to him and saw a sadistic glint in his eyes. He nodded at the doubles line. "Einsteins."

"How many?" Jasmine asked.

"Until I tell you to stop."

The trick with Einsteins was to not think about how awful you felt, to just clear your mind of the burn in your legs and the shortness of breath and to try to focus on something else. Dom was leaning against the fence, watching them to make sure they ran to each line and not just short of it. Jasmine didn't count as their feet pounded down upon the hard court; she focused on Dom and ran her apology over and over again in her mind like a penance for her sins.

Sorry, grateful, second chance. Sorry, grateful, second chance.

The words were like a mantra to the thuds of her sneakers.

Sorry, grateful, second chance. Sorry, grateful, second chance.

"Okay, girls, grab some water," Dom called and they skidded to a stop. Jasmine glanced at Indy. She wasn't huffing and puffing, not like she did on her first day. Still, her breath came hard and quick, while Jasmine wasn't all that winded. They both grabbed their water bottles and stood together, sipping slowly.

"What's he doing here?" Indy said as Alex Russell strode up to the court and waved Dom over. The two men spoke for a few moments, keeping their voices low, then Alex shook Dom's hand and left.

"All right, ladies, footwork drills, on the service line, no rackets," their coach said, ignoring the curious looks they were both shooting him.

The drill was pretty straightforward. They stood where the service boxes met, halfway between the net and the baseline while Dom stood opposite them with a ball in his hand. Moving his arm left and right, they would mirror the action with their footwork, until he released the ball. Without a racket, they were expected to catch it before the ball could bounce twice. Jasmine loved this drill. It played to her strengths, quick feet and quicker reactions.

She felt Indy's eyes on her and she met the other girl's gaze for the first time all morning. Jasmine motioned out to the court, "After you."

Dom kept Indy's feet moving, short, quick steps against the clay court, before he tossed her the ball and she lunged to her left and caught in with the tips of her fingers. Indy stood, tossing the ball back to Dom.

"Beat that," Indy muttered.

"Game on," Jasmine mumbled back as they switched places.

"What was that?" Dom asked.

"Nothing," Jasmine said, setting her feet shoulder-width apart and waiting for Dom's first cue.

Twenty minutes later, they were both dripping with sweat, but neither had dropped a single ball.

"Okay girls, take ten."

"No," Indy protested, dragging her wrist across her forehead, then over her knee that she scraped when she laid out for one ball.

"Not yet," Jasmine agreed, hands on her hips, bent slightly at the waist to try and regain her breath.

Dom laughed at them outright, clearly satisfied with their performance. "Take ten and rehydrate."

He began to walk away and Jasmine saw her opportunity. "Dom, hang on a second," she said, jogging to catch up with him. "I just wanted to—"

"I know what you want to say, Jasmine, but I don't want to hear you're sorry. I want you to *show* me you're sorry."

The laughter and smile from just seconds before were gone, replaced by a stern glare and a set jaw.

"I will. I promise."

"Good. Now try not to start another fight while I'm gone."

After Dom walked away, Indiana and Jasmine made eye contact for a second, but the other girl looked away first. Indy bent and dug through her racket bag, pulling her cell phone out and shooting off a rapid text.

"So Dom's been pretty tough so far, huh?" Jasmine said, swallowing back her pride.

It was lame, but it was the best she could do and, hell, at least she was trying.

Indy looked up from her cell phone, disbelief written across her face. "Yeah, I guess." The phone *binged* in her hand and drew her attention.

Jasmine watched as Indy wandered to the opposite end of the court, tapping away at her phone screen. "Or we could just not talk."

"Hey, Randazzo."

Her shoulders stiffened as an involuntary shiver slid pleasantly through her body. It was so annoying that Teddy could still do that to her, even when she was pissed as hell at him. He stood just outside the fence, smiling at her. A sense of déjà vu niggled at the back of her mind; they'd been here before, just after they kissed.

"Isn't it a little early for you?" she glanced over her shoulder at Indy, who was still focused on her phone.

Teddy shrugged. "We need to talk and I knew you'd be here."

"I don't want to talk to you."

She thought she'd made that pretty clear right before the Classic final, and if that hadn't done it, she'd ignored every single text and voicemail he'd sent since. When was he going to get the point? Why couldn't he just accept that things would never be the same between them?

"You don't have to talk. You can just listen." His eyes crinkled at the corners, the damned dimple appearing alongside his easy smile, and then he hopped the fence. "Or you can stand there and pretend like you're not listening while I talk."

"You're such a stubborn ass, you know that?" Jasmine avoided his eyes. If she looked into his eyes she'd be lost, just like the night they kissed.

"So, how's it going?" he asked, a hand gesturing at the court.

Her patience was already gone. "Seriously, that's what you're leading with? 'How's it going?' Did you actually want to talk to me or are you just wasting my time?"

"Not well then, huh?"

"Teddy—"

"Fine, look, I wanted to talk to you because…" He trailed off, losing his momentum. Jasmine had enough of his hesitation and stepped forward, pushing past him, but he caught her arm. "Because I feel terrible about what I said to you. You were right. I was being a shitty friend."

"Come on," Jasmine said, shooting a hesitant glance toward Indy, who was still focused on her phone. The last thing she needed was for Indiana Gaffney to know what an idiot she made out of herself with Teddy. She led him through the gate and around the corner back behind the courts where they would have some privacy.

"You wanted to talk, so talk." She crossed her arms over her chest and waited.

"Don't look at me like that, Jas. We both said some crappy things to each other. And look, you were right, about Indy. I wasn't helping her just to be nice. I—"

"You always did have a thing for blondes." She cut him off, pushing the hurt down as best she could. "If you like her, you should go for it. Ask her out, I mean."

"Maybe," he said, shrugging.

Jasmine looked away, studying the twisted chain-link fence intently and avoiding his gaze. "I shouldn't have let those girls be horrible to her. I could've put a stop to it and I didn't."

Teddy sighed. "We shouldn't have done a lot of things, huh?"

Like getting drunk and kissing and nearly destroying their friendship. "You got that right."

They lapsed into a comfortable silence for a moment, and then Teddy looked down, before shooting her a boyish grin, that dimple reappearing, making it impossible for her not to smile back.

"So, how is it going, really? Penny told me Dom paired you guys up at as a doubles team."

"We haven't done much yet."

"I think you two would make great partners."

"You would," Jasmine drawled.

"Not like that. Your games, they're complementary." He shrugged, waving a hand in the air. "It's like pairing up Sampras and Agassi, power and precision with speed and hustle. Her weaknesses are your strengths and vice versa. A perfect match and Dom's a genius for thinking of it."

"Yeah, he's a real Einstein." The muscles in her calves twitched at the mere mention of the word. "Besides, that's not the worst of it."

He stood there, silently, waiting for her to continue, but the words caught in her throat. The girls she thought were her friends clearly weren't, and she definitely couldn't tell her parents. She didn't have anyone else to talk to and Teddy used to be the person she'd trust with anything, but she couldn't anymore. She couldn't tell him about how Dom agreed with Hodges about her game and how he didn't think she had it in her to be in the Top Ten. That she wouldn't win Grand Slams or Olympic medals or live up to her parents' legacy and that everything she worked for all these years was just a stupid dream, one that they all let her believe in for way too long. So, instead, she let the dam inside her break, a lump in her throat choking her as the tears burned in her eyes and fell in streams down her cheeks.

Somehow, even after all the crap they'd been through, he knew exactly what she needed. She needed him to just be there. Teddy didn't love her, not the way she wanted him to, but in that moment, as his arms tightened around her and he hushed her lightly, Jasmine knew she would never find a better friend and maybe one day that would be enough.

CHAPTER 16

May 24th

"You know staring at your phone isn't going to make a text magically appear, right?" Indy stood in her closet, positive nothing inside of it was appropriate for Paris. "And you're supposed to be helping me pack."

On their last day before leaving for the French Open, she and Penny were spending their lunch break in her dorm, digging through her wardrobe for the clothes she'd need, plus a dress for the Player's Gala before the tournament began. The dress had to be elegant and sexy and strike Jack Harrison speechless. Not that it would be much of an accomplishment. He hadn't uttered so much as a word to her since the day she won the Classic. Even when he'd jumped in to stop Jasmine from tackling her on their practice court, he'd barely spared her a glance.

Penny sat down on Indy's bed, laying her phone done beside her.

"I'm sorry. It's just things were so weird when Alex left for London. We barely had a night together and then he was so mad when I spilled about that medication. It's just… It's making it almost impossible to focus at training. And Jack's an okay hitting partner, but he's not even close to the same level of play."

Indy sighed, sitting down next to her. At least Penny had someone who wanted her or would admit that he wanted her or whatever. "He's busy. He's probably got a lot on his plate, and besides that, he's got to train."

"I know," Penny said, flopping back on the bed. "I know you're right, but everything just happened so fast."

"Like you wanted to rip Alex's clothes off the second you met him," she said, leaning over her friend with a wicked smile.

Penny grabbed a small pillow and smacked her in the head with it. "Like, I barely had time to catch my breath after we hooked up, and now it feels like none of it happened, like it was some insane, amazing dream."

"You could always go online and check out what the gossip sites are saying about you if you need proof." Penny chucked the pillow at her this time, but Indy caught it before it could hit her. "You're leaving for Paris tomorrow. You'll see him there, and after you kick Zina Lutrova's ass in the final, you two can figure things out."

"Third round," Penny corrected. "If we play, it'll be in the third round."

"Third round then," Indy said and just as she did, Penny's phone vibrated against the bed. Indy grabbed it and held it just out of Penny's reach. "You don't get to talk to him unless you promise you're not going to turn into one of those mopey girls every time you guys are apart. If that's going to happen, we so cannot be friends."

"I promise," Penny said, a little too quickly.

"Pinky swear?" Indy held out her little finger.

Penny looked longingly at the phone. "You're kidding?" It buzzed again. "Fine, fine, I pinky swear." She hooked their pinkies together.

Indy handed the phone back to her desperate friend. "Here."

Penny's thumb raced over the screen and her shoulders slumped as she read the text message. "He says he'll see me in Paris. That's it, nothing else."

"You will see him in Paris, *tomorrow*. Now come on, you promised, no moping."

"You're right and we've got to get back to training. Forget the dress. Jack's going to have some sent over to the hotel, you could just wear one of those."

"Ah, you're the best!" Indy called to her friend's back as Penny sped through the door.

She dumped the clothes she wasn't taking back into her closet before trudging outside for another uncomfortable practice session with Jasmine and Dom. Okay, that wasn't totally fair. It was awkward, but they were training hard and Dom's idea of them being doubles partners probably wasn't as crazy as she thought at first. Their styles were totally different and that was a huge advantage.

"Indy, glad you're back," Dom said, waving her over to where he and Jasmine stood, just outside the training courts. "I was just about to tell Jasmine, your draw has been confirmed and it looks like you'll be playing Lutrova and Grishina in the first round."

"Wow, that's—" Jasmine started, but Indy cut her off.

"Scary as hell." Indy looked at her doubles partner and smiled. She could see Jasmine fight it for a moment, but then a bright smile spread over her face as well.

"Go big or go home, ladies. Now let's get started," Dom said, grinning from ear to ear.

~

"Indiana, I am glad I have found you," Caroline's voice ricocheted off the metal of the lockers and the tile floor of the locker room.

"Yep, this is usually where I am after practice," Indy said, tightening the towel around her. "Could you turn around? I have to get dressed."

Caroline waved off the request and Indy shrugged, dropping the towel and grabbing her clothes. If her agent didn't mind, then neither did she.

"I have fantastic news," Caroline said.

"You're a little late," Indy said, pulling her OBX T-shirt over her head and then buttoning her white jean shorts. "I know it's really exciting, Caroline, but we did already kind of knew this was going to happen."

Caroline breathed a dismissive sound through her lips. "You are speaking of the doubles tournament?"

"Of course. What else would I be talking about?"

Her agent smiled. "An old friend of mine is the assistant tournament director."

"Old friend?" Indy asked, raising her eyebrows. "The same way Dom is an old friend?"

"No," Caroline said, examining the clear sheen painted on her nails, which made Indy believe she'd hit the nail right on the head. "He was a friend of my father's."

"Sure, okay, what about him?"

"He has managed to procure you an entry into the junior girls' singles tournament. Dom was unfortunately correct about your lack of experience hindering a spot in the main draw, but this is most certainly the next best thing. I expect, after how you destroyed those other girls in the Classic, that you will have no problem winning this tournament as well. There are sponsors who will be very interested to see these results."

Indy pulled her hair into a ponytail and tried to keep her excitement down. The truth was she was beyond ecstatic at this news. It was a solid next step and it made so much more sense than playing doubles with a girl she could barely stand. Dom probably wouldn't see it that way though.

"Dom is supposed to be making all the tennis decisions."

"He will be thrilled of course. This will bring more exposure for both you and the Academy," Caroline said, spinning away on her stiletto heels. Indy followed slowly, dreading the explosion her agent was about to ignite.

~

"Absolutely not," Dom said, leaping up from the bench just outside a practice court, making the tiny ten-year-old boy he was coaching literally jump in terror. "Didn't we just have this conversation Caroline? It's not your place to go looking for tournaments for my athletes."

Caroline laughed off the reprimand. "Do not be ridiculous. Of course she will play."

"She'll play the junior tournament or doubles, but not both. And frankly, I prefer the doubles."

"You are just angry because you were unable to give her this yourself."

"How do you know that?" Dom asked, hands crossing over his chest. "She doesn't have the endurance to do both yet."

"She is more than capable. Professional players do this all the time, Dominic. You know this."

"She isn't a professional player yet."

"*She* is right here," Indy cut in, "or should I just leave?"

Dom turned to her, his face apologetic, or at least as close as it ever got. "Indy, it isn't as simple as your agent would have you believe. Your game is up to scratch, and I have no doubt that you would do well, but your endurance level simply isn't where it needs to be for your first pro singles tournament, and certainly not your first Grand Slam, even if it is at the junior level."

"*C'est des conneries!*" Caroline said, moving closer and nearly bumping chests with him.

"It is not bullshit, Caroline, and you know it. You're just so desperate to find the next big star you're willing to put this girl's career on the line."

The volume of their argument grew with every insult, and Indy rolled her eyes. She hated when adults acted like children, which was a lot more often than any of them would ever admit.

"You two let me know when you've worked it out."

Her words went unacknowledged and she spun away from the court, practically running down the pathway to get away from the shouting. It was like she was seven years old again and her parents were screaming at each other over whatever stupid nothing they were always fighting about.

She made it into the atrium, leaned against the wall, and slid to the floor. Roy sent her an encouraging smile from his desk and Indy managed a grimace in return, despite how pissed off she was. This should be one of the most exciting days of her career. She was going to the French Open tomorrow. She'd be playing on the famous clay courts of Roland Garros like so many legendary athletes before her. This wasn't how she imagined feeling. She should be ecstatic and nervous and maybe even a little scared, but not annoyed. She let her head fall to her knees.

"Well, this can't be good."

Her head shot up at the sound of Jack's voice. He was standing over her in a sweaty T-shirt and shorts, racket still in hand.

"Hey," she said, feeling a flush creep up over her cheeks. The last time they'd spoken she'd thrown caution to the wind and kissed him—sort of.

"You okay?"

"Peachy."

"Want to talk about it?"

"No," she said, resting her head against her knees again, hoping he'd take the hint.

"Okay then," Jack mumbled and the sound of his footfalls began to move away. She raised her head an inch to watch him go, his broad back moving to the far end of the atrium near the entrance to the locker rooms.

"Wait," she called out, leaping to her feet and racing to catch up to him. He was part agent, part coach and regardless of what was—or wasn't—going on between them, probably the best person to ask about the argument probably still raging out on the practice court.

He stopped without warning just outside the door to the men's locker room and Indy crashed into his back. He whirled around, probably to try to catch her before she fell, but as he did, his elbow collided with the side of her head.

Stars exploded in front of her eyes and a sharp pain began to radiate from the point of impact.

"Shit, Indy, I'm sorry."

"I'm okay," she said, her eyes squeezed shut. She pressed her hand against her temple, only to pull away with a hiss when the ache increased with the pressure.

"Come on," he said, his warm hands cupping her face. "Open your eyes and look at me."

His tone was so authoritative she obeyed without question, meeting his gaze. "Any blurriness?"

"No." She could see every fleck of green and gold in his eyes and small brown ring around his pupils that she'd never been able to truly appreciate before.

"Ringing in your ears? Are you dizzy?"

"Nope," she said, shaking her head. "I'm okay."

"Good," he said and she could actually see his concern melt away and his mask of indifference fall back into place. She hated when he did that, when his personality just shut down like he was afraid if he was nice to her for more than two seconds she'd try to rip his clothes off or something. It was just so frustrating. "Tell me what's got you so upset. I'd like to help, if I can."

Indy sighed in defeat, the adrenaline spike fading with his words, so instead of calling him out on it, she explained the power struggle going on between Dom and Caroline on the practice courts.

Jack looked thoughtful for a moment and then shook his head. "That's an easy fix. Caroline must have Dom really tied up in knots if he didn't figure this out right away."

"Yeah?" she asked.

"You accept both invitations and you wait it out. The junior girls don't start until later into the tournament. You'd have to at least get to the third round of the women's doubles draw before you'd play your first-round singles match. If you have to drop one after that, so be it, but there's no reason to worry about that until it actually happens, if it actually happens. Once those two calm down enough to think clearly, they'll figure it out on their own. No sense in you worrying about it."

Indy smiled and she felt all the stress of the last few minutes completely disappear. "I should have hired you to be my agent."

Jack shrugged, his expression blank again. "I don't know about that."

Her smile dropped. "Well, thanks. I've gotta get going. I'm sure rumors are flying around here about me dropping doubles by now. I better talk to Jasmine before she has a total breakdown and decides to slap me again."

~

The Randazzo house was easy enough to spot as she drove down Ocean Trail. It was the biggest structure around, aside from the OBX buildings.

The gates to the large stone driveway were propped open, saving her the embarrassment of explaining "Hi, I'm the girl who beat Jasmine at the Classic. Can I come in?" That would go over really well.

Indy took a deep breath, reached out and rang the doorbell. Moments later, she heard shuffling on the other side of the door, then it was opened by a woman who looked exactly like she imagined Jasmine would in about twenty years.

Lisa Vega-Randazzo, a legend in the tennis world for her talent and for giving it all up to start a family. Indy tried not to be intimidated, but it wasn't easy.

"Hi, Mrs. Randazzo, I'm...."

"I know who you are, come in, come in," she said, waving her inside. "Jasmine!" she shouted up into the house, her voice echoing in the large entryway.

"What, Mom?" Jasmine shouted from somewhere on the second floor, before she appeared on the landing. "Oh, it's you."

"Jasmine, there's some fresh lemonade in the kitchen. Why don't you and Indiana go in there and talk?" It sounded like a suggestion, but Mrs. Randazzo was sending her daughter a piercing look that Indy remembered well. It was the same one her mom used when she had to do something...or else.

A minute later, she was sitting at the table in the Randazzo's kitchen, a full glass of lemonade in front of her. Jasmine was silent as she marched across the polished wood floor, replacing the glass pitcher of lemonade and slamming the stainless steel door closed. The silence was just too friggin' awkward so Indy took a large gulp of her drink.

"I heard you got an entry into the French Open Juniors. Congrats," Jasmine said, joining her at the table.

Indy swallowed quickly. "Thanks. Look, I know there are rumors probably flying around right now that I'm dropping doubles, and I came here to tell you that's not true."

Jasmine twisted her mouth and nodded. "I might have gotten a text or two about it."

"Well like I said, it's not true. I'm going to accept both invitations and then see what happens from there."

"See what happens?" Jasmine repeated, like she wasn't sure what it meant.

"Yeah, the way the schedule works, we should be okay." Indy left out the part about what Jack said about eventually choosing which to drop if she had to. Jasmine didn't need to know that part, at least not yet.

"So is that why you came all the way over here?"

"Yeah, and well, I wanted to, I guess apologize. All those things you said the day we fought, I'm sorry I made you feel that way. I didn't mean to."

Jasmine sat still for a second and then nodded. "I guess I knew that, at least now I do. I was just looking for someone to blame for, well for everything. This year isn't exactly going how I imagined, so I took it out on you."

"You sorry for smacking me?" Indy asked.

"No, you deserved that."

Despite herself, Indy smiled. "Maybe I did. Look, I think Dom's on to something here with this doubles thing."

Jasmine tilted her head. "I think so too."

"If we can just get our act together during your service games, I think we'll be fine," Indy said, hoping the joke didn't miss the mark.

Jasmine smirked. "Excuse me? The problem isn't my serve. The problem is your net game."

"Right, because I'm supposed to be able to cover the entire court when you serve up a meatball."

"I know it might be a foreign concept to you, but sometimes you have to hit more than one shot to win a point."

"Didn't have a problem doing that against you during the Classic, did I?" She saw the hurt flash in Jasmine's eyes and Indy cringed. That line she wasn't supposed to cross. It was behind her. "Shit, I'm sorry."

Jasmine shook her head, her eyes suddenly looking very tired. "Forget it. Are we still playing doubles or was this all a ploy to get me to drop out so you could play singles without Dom having a shit fit?"

"What? Of course I'm playing doubles. I just told you that."

"Good, then if you don't mind, I have some school work to finish up before we leave tomorrow."

Jasmine silently led her to the door. "I'll see you tomorrow," she said.

"Yeah, tomorrow," Indy said, but the door was already closed behind her.

CHAPTER 17

May 25th

Charles de Gaulle airport was a large, bustling international hub and yet their customs line was always painfully slow. The entire tennis world was descending upon Paris for two weeks and apparently someone forgot to warn the French Custom's Office. Penny could see fellow players, their coaches and families, along with dozens of tennis people—reporters, officials and their ilk—all trapped and waiting their turn.

Her eyes looked over the faces, wondering if Alex had arrived yet, but the familiar, tall frame, broad shoulders and sandy blond hair were nowhere to be seen. She exhaled through her nose and felt her stomach tighten. She hated having things so unresolved between them. The French Open deserved her total focus, but she wanted Alex in her life and that meant trying to strike a balance. It wouldn't be easy, but she was willing to try. It would be a lot easier if he would just talk to her, instead of the near complete cutoff the last few days.

At the front of the line a haggard-looking civil servant with a stern face asked, "Passeport?" rolling the R at the end of the word in that effortless way only a native French speaker could.

She slid her passport across the counter.

"*Où êtes-vous?*" the customs agent asked.

Penny couldn't speak French, but she'd done this enough to know what she was being asked. "North Carolina in the United States."

"*Pourquoi êtes-vous en France?*"

"Roland Garros," she said simply.

The agent's eyes flew up and lit with recognition. A tennis fan. The corner of the agent's mouth lifted in what could almost be called a smile.

"*Avez-vous quelque chose à déclarer?*"

"No."

"*Très bien. Bonne chance, Mademoiselle Harrison.*"

Her passport was passed back across the counter with a new stamp adorning its pages. "*Merci.*"

Jack's interview was just as fast and they soon found themselves dragging two weeks' worth of luggage and equipment toward the exit. They stepped out of the arrivals gate and into a rainy Paris morning. Raindrops dripping down from the overhang assaulted them.

Penny let out a sigh of relief when she saw a man holding a sign with her name on it. Having a waiting car was a large improvement over standing on yet another taxi line and hoping the driver wasn't in the mood to take a creative route to their hotel.

"You're welcome," Jack said.

"You rock."

"*Mademoiselle*," the driver said, drawing her eyes away from the rain as he held the door open for her. It was a Mercedes like so many of the taxis across Europe. That phenomenon had always fascinated her. A car that was such a status symbol in America was pretty much the standard cab across the Atlantic.

"*Merci*," she whispered and slid into the backseat.

The driver edged the car away from the curb and soon they were humming along down the highway through the outskirts of Paris—mostly open grass fields, modern office buildings and shopping centers—a view you'd find around almost every airport in every major city. Penny closed her eyes and rested her head against the seat. The vibrations of the car nearly lulled her to sleep.

"Don't conk out yet, Pen," Jack warned a few minutes later.

She opened her eyes. They were almost into the city itself and Penny didn't want to miss it. This was likely all the sightseeing she'd get. At first the road was lined with buildings built in the last half of the 20th century, brand names held aloft on their roofs by scaffolds. Then the car sped through an underpass, made a sharp right turn, and they were in the real Paris—at least the part of Paris that everyone imagined. The rain faded into a light mist, making the entire city glow.

The car pulled to a halt in front of their destination. During her last trip to the French Open, she'd stayed at this very same hotel, and since she'd won the junior tournament that year, Penny didn't see any reason to mess with good karma. La Metropolitan was a beautiful boutique hotel only a few minutes from Roland Garros, making the commute to and from the courts no longer than her drive to OBX, plus the upper floors of the hotel had some of the best views in Paris.

The driver opened her door, and as soon as she stepped out of the car, camera flashes barraged her. Shit, paparazzi, lots of them. They were yelling—mostly in French and she barely understood a word of it.

Then a voice rang out clear as day, "Penny, where's Alex?" The rest of the paparazzi took the cue, switching to English.

"Penny, do you know what Alex is doing in London?"

"How long have you two been together?"

"Did you cut the breaks on his motorcycle so he'd crash in Australia?"

Then a bellhop launched himself out of the front entrance, dodging through the throng of frenzied reporters. "*Allez,*" he said, waving them toward the door. "*Je vais porter vos bagages. Allez.*"

Jack came around to her and she pressed into him as the crowd of reporters pushed forward. Stepping easily into the role of bodyguard, Jack snaked an arm around her shoulders and used his bulk to shove the camera-laden men aside, breaking a path into the hotel.

Her heart pounding in her chest, Penny stared at Jack in shock. "What the hell was that?"

"Things are different now, Pen," Jack said, shaking his head in apparent disbelief.

"Yeah, I'm getting that."

"Next time we'll call ahead, come in through the back or something."

She nodded, still trying to catch her breath. That was so intense, a claustrophobic thrill—scary and beyond exciting all at the same time.

They checked in and followed the bellhop who'd rescued them into the elevator, up to the sixth floor and then down a long hallway to her suite.

"If you're with him, that crowd down there and the attention, it's only going to get worse. Are you sure this is what you want, Pen?" Jack asked as soon as they were alone.

Penny wandered toward the balcony and rolled her eyes.

"I can see your reflection in the window. Don't roll your eyes. Just be honest with me."

"Don't worry about it," she said, brushing off the question. Of course she wanted to be with Alex. She'd been fighting it for months now, but whether what she wanted was good for her, she had no idea.

"Fine. I'm going down to my room. You need anything?"

Glancing around the luxurious suite, she grinned at her brother. A large sitting room, the furnishings new and clearly expensive, an attached bedroom with a king sized bed, an en suite bathroom with a shower big enough for two and a soaking tub. It was nearly as big as the entire second floor of her parents' home. "I think I'll be fine."

The door clicked shut behind him and finally alone, Penny turned back to the balcony. Her suite was impressive, but the view—that was spectacular. The 16th arrondissement, one of the nicest neighborhoods in Paris, spread out before her with the Eiffel Tower looming in the distance as the sun began to peak through the fading rain clouds. She sat down on one of the chairs, a cushioned chaise lounge, and let her mind go blank, letting the scenery wash over her—not fully awake, but not quite asleep either.

Her cell phone buzzed in her pocket with a message from Indy, *We're here!* She wasn't sure how long she'd been sitting there and a quick glance at her watch told her nearly an hour had passed by in a blink. She was typing a response when a shrill ring from the phone sitting on the desk just inside the balcony door interrupted her. "I'm so popular," she mumbled, stepping back into her room to answer the phone, as she texted her room number to Indy.

"Hello?" she asked, balancing the receiver between her shoulder and her neck.

"Mademoiselle Harrison, there is a package for you at the desk," a woman with a French accent, not unlike Caroline's, responded. "Shall I have it sent up?"

A few minutes later, a knock sounded against her door. A bellman was on the other side, holding a small square black velvet box wrapped with a cream-colored ribbon, a card tucked into the bow. Then a flash of blond hair appeared just behind him. The bellman handed Penny the package and with a nod, was off down the hallway.

"Hey," Indy said, smiling. "What's that?"

Penny shrugged, as they went back inside her suite. "I have no idea."

The card slipped free of the ribbon easily enough and she opened it, smiling as she read the note.

For luck – Alex

Slowly, she pulled the bow free, but her hand paused before opening it. It was definitely jewelry, probably a necklace from the shape of the box. Why would he send her jewelry? Was he apologizing for his near-total silence for the last couple of days? Penny shook her head. She had to stop overanalyzing everything and just open the gift.

"Wow," Indy said, from just over her shoulder. "So I guess he doesn't hate you."

"It's perfect," Penny said, running a fingertip over the old British coin attached to the long chain. It was a 1936 penny, minted the same year Fred Perry won Wimbledon, the last British man to do so before Alex. It was exactly what she would have picked out for herself, except that she wouldn't have thought of it in a million years. The gift was beyond thoughtful. It wasn't just some expensive, shiny object, but represented both of them. Still, having him with her was what she really wanted.

"You're going to wear it to the gala tonight, right?" Indy asked. "If you don't, I will."

"It's a penny necklace, Indy. I don't think people will get it if you wear it."

"Ha! The paparazzi would probably make up some story about me ripping it off your neck and stealing Alex away from you. Caroline would love that. Think of the buzz that would stir up." Indy looked back at the necklace. "God, it's the most perfect gift I have ever seen. You two are just—you kind of make me want to vomit."

"Love you too," Penny said, checking her phone. No messages. Where was he? "How was your flight?"

Indy tossed herself back onto the bed and let out a long-suffering sigh. "Jasmine didn't speak to me the entire trip here. How do you think it was?"

"You can't take all that negative energy out onto the court. You guys will get destroyed."

"Don't sugarcoat it or anything." Indy stretched her neck and groaned. "I'm working on it, promise."

"Good, but for now I think I have something that'll cheer you up," Penny said, grabbing her phone and texting Jack. "The dresses will be here in fifteen minutes."

~

Penny couldn't quite reach the zipper of the dress she'd chosen for the player's gala. Strapless taupe silk embellished with beading at the waist and hem, it gave her an exotic look she usually avoided. She bent her arm back, gave the zipper one last tug and it slid into place.

"There," she said, turning and twisting in the mirror. Perfect.

A knock sounded against the door and she moved to open it. "Indy, hurry up," she called toward the bathroom, "We've only got like...." Her words were cut off by a hard body storming through the door and crashing against hers, strong arms enveloping her in warmth. Her body recognized Alex before her mind did, letting him press her against the wall of her hotel room. He engaged her lips in a searing kiss and his hands buried into her hair, totally ruining the tresses she'd meticulously arranged just minutes before. Penny didn't care as she curled her leg around his calf, pulling him even closer.

Ignoring the pointed throat clearing from just behind them, likely Indy emerging from the bathroom, Penny pulled away then kissed him lightly one more time, as Indy's gagging noises faded back into the bathroom.

"You got the necklace." His hand came up to where the coin rested against her skin, just above the neckline of her dress, rising and falling with every breath she took. "Do you like it?"

"I love it."

"I've had it with me during every Grand Slam I've ever played in and I wanted you to have it." She leaned forward again to kiss him, but he rested his forehead against hers, stopping her. "I'm sorry about how I left things between us," he murmured against her lips. "I couldn't figure out a way to say that over the phone, so I thought this might do it for me."

If he kept this up, all of her lingering doubts would be long gone in no time. This was how it needed to be, them talking things out, not stressing over stupid misunderstandings when their minds needed to be on the court. "You thought right. It's perfect. That doesn't mean I'm not going to worry about your knee, though, okay?"

He winced. "Yeah about that, I saw my surgeon in London while I was there. I told him about the pain and he took a look. Knee's fine, I promise, but worry away if it'll make you feel better."

"Oh," Penny said, the flurry of information making her mind whirl as much as his arrival. "You could've said something."

Alex shrugged. "Might have been a little embarrassed, about how I snapped."

"Next time, just talk to me, okay? Don't disappear."

"Promise," he said, pressing his lips against her forehead. She closed her eyes, reveling in the feel of the kiss, but her mind was still spinning, still unsure if she could let go enough to trust him completely

"I stand by what I said, you two make me want to vomit," Indy called from the opposite end of the room, balancing against the dresser to put on her black stiletto heels, pairing perfectly with an emerald green halter dress with a metallic sheen, hugging her long, lean figure tightly. Penny couldn't help the soft snort of amusement against Alex's neck. He hushed her lightly.

"You look lovely tonight, Indy," Alex said and Penny lifted her head in time to see her friend blush.

"Thanks. Now get out of here before I ruin this gorgeous dress," Indy said, grabbing her makeup bag and waving them out of the room. "I'll be right behind you."

They walked, hand in hand toward the elevator bay, but once they got there, Penny couldn't resist. She stood on her toes, leaning against his chest and kissed him lightly once, twice, and then slowly opening her mouth beneath his, letting her tongue nudge against his bottom lip. They broke apart and came together over and over again, neither willing to stop until they both pulled away, gasping for air, shaky breaths matching the trembling in her body.

"Jesus," he breathed. "How do you do that?"

"Do what?" she asked as his hands fell to her waist, squeezing gently.

Alex shook his head. "I don't even know. It doesn't matter. Just do it again."

Laughing a little, she pressed her lips to his again. "Your flight got in early?"

"Took an earlier one," he said, reaching around her to push the elevator call button. "I wanted to get here in time for the gala."

"So you could go with me?" she asked, only half-mocking him. "We can't even stay that long. I have my first-round match tomorrow."

"So I could see you in a dress like that and I don't care how long we stay. In fact, I'm all in favor of making an early night of it." He stepped back and let his eyes travel up from the floor over every inch of her body.

Penny laughed. "You're so smooth."

A deep chuckle echoed from his chest. "Apparently not that smooth."

"Smooth enough," she said, grasping the front of his crisp white dress shirt and pulling him in for another kiss.

A ding from the elevator behind them registered in her mind, but she didn't care.

"Damn it, could you two not do that in front of me, ever?"

Alex pulled away at the sound of her brother's voice. She fell back on her heels, turned and glared at Jack.

"Can we hold hands or is that too much for your delicate sensibilities?"

"Jack, nice to see you, mate," Alex said, extending his hand toward her brother.

Jack frowned, but shook the hand offered. The handshake lasted longer than it probably should have, the knuckles of both hands turning red and then briefly white before they both released their grip.

"Are you done?" she asked Jack sharply.

He ignored her question. "Is Indy ready too? Dom's downstairs holding a car for all of us."

As if on cue, Indy appeared around the corner looking like someone who belonged on a runway rather than a tennis court, long blond hair in wild waves hanging down her back, smoky eyes and gloss making her lips shine. Penny saw Jack suck in a breath and a sudden heaviness cut through the small space. She glanced between her brother and her friend, but as quickly as she felt the tension, it was gone again.

"Alright, let's go," Jack said, calling the elevator again. The door opened immediately. They all stepped inside. As the door closed and the car started moving downward, Alex's hand slipped around hers and squeezed.

~

"Penny! Alex!"

"When's the wedding?"

"Look this way!"

"Give her a kiss!"

Alex stepped out of the car and then offered her his hand as the camera flashes assaulted them. Penny steadied her heels against the cobblestone street and stood, feeling his arm slide around her waist. Indy, Jasmine, Jack and Dom followed behind, but the reporters were in a frenzy for tennis's new golden couple. No more unsubstantiated rumors. They were clearly together. And as if to emphasize the point, Alex's hand slid a little lower. Penny bit her lip and glanced up at him through her lashes.

He winked at her and then nodded at the red carpet. The flashes were blinding and it was almost impossible to understand anything in the cacophony coming from the camera pool.

"You okay?" Alex muttered into her ear about halfway down the line.

"This is insane," she said through her teeth, keeping her smile firmly in place, but moving closer to him, pressing her side into his.

She felt him exhale into her hair and then the brush of a kiss against her temple, his neatly trimmed five o'clock shadow scraping lightly against her skin. The paparazzi went wild.

If it hadn't sunk in that her life had changed forever when she arrived at the hotel earlier to a sea of cameras, the point was hammered home now. She wasn't just a tennis player anymore. Penny Harrison was a celebrity.

CHAPTER 18

May 25th

"Wow," Jasmine said as she watched Penny and Alex finish their red carpet walk and head into the party. Next to her, Jack, Indy and Dom were all gaping at the reporters going nuts for the couple ahead of them, but Jasmine just started making her way down the line. That jump-started the rest of the group.

The reporters weren't quite as enthusiastic as before, but she and her new doubles partner got plenty of attention from the cameras.

"Stand together for some," Dom muttered to them as he passed behind them about half way down the carpet. "Present a united front."

Their united front would last as long as their doubles run did because as soon as the junior girls' singles started it would be every girl for herself. Indy didn't look any more thrilled than she felt, but they smiled for the photographers' pool together. As if their personalities didn't clash enough, the tangerine sheath dress and funky purple belt Jasmine was wearing up against the green, metallic fabric of Indy's dress didn't really make a pretty picture.

They finally made it to the end of the row and immediately stepped away from each other and followed Dom into the party. The music was loud, but the buzz from the crowd was louder as people mingled in the dimly lit room. She looked around for a familiar face and couldn't find one. Things had changed a lot since her dad retired. Before, she would've known half the party before stepping through the door. Now she was in a crush of strangers, people who were supposed to be her peers, but none of them knew who she was and never would unless someone pointed her out as John and Lisa Randazzo's daughter.

"Screw this," she mumbled and turned back to the entrance. She'd have one of the staff call her a car, go back to the hotel and order some room service. She didn't need this party or these people. The only thing she needed was to get some rest and train well tomorrow. If she wanted to prove everyone wrong, she had to be at her best.

"Wait, where are you going?" Indy asked, grabbing her arm.

"Let go of me," she said, pulling free. "I'm going back to the hotel. This is such a waste of time."

"Don't be stupid. We're at the French Open. This is... You shouldn't miss this," Indy said, swiping a hand out at the party.

"Do you know how many of these I've been to?"

"Yeah, but how many of them because you were playing?"

Jasmine's shoulders dropped and she looked back out into the sea of partygoers. "But I don't know anyone."

Indy bit her lip. "We know each other."

"Yeah, me and you," Jasmine said, crossing her fingers and holding them up for Indy to see, "we're like that. Why don't you go find Penny, she's your new best friend, or is she just too busy for you tonight?"

"She is my friend," Indy said, "and she's obviously a little busy, but you're my doubles partner."

"Whatever," Jasmine said, trying to push past the taller girl, but Indy stood her ground.

"No, not whatever. Every time we take a step forward, we take like ten back. We have a couple of days of training to get past it before we have to go out in front of the whole world and compete together. We're both professionals. We should be able to put the personal stuff aside and just be..." She waved a hand through the air.

"Professional?" Jasmine finished for her.

"Exactly. Look I know you don't like me, but I mean look around, we're at the French friggin' Open. How many people can say they've been here? We should soak this in. Who knows if it'll happen again? We should just have fun and enjoy the whole thing."

She made a good point. Jasmine didn't know when she would be back at a tournament like this, especially if doubles didn't work out. She was only age eligible to play as a junior through the end of the year and then what? If Hodges was right, she was probably headed to the Challenger circuit, the minor leagues of tennis, or maybe even to a college team, thanks to her parents making her hang on to her NCAA eligibility. Maybe she could go to Duke with Teddy. They could rule the ACC together. That's what everyone expected of her now. They didn't think she should win just because her parents won all the time. Indy was right. There was no pressure...at all.

Her shoulders loosened, the tension she'd been carrying there, maybe for years, suddenly fell away. It didn't matter. None of it did. She just had to live in the moment. She could worry about the future and other people's expectations later...or maybe never again.

"Jasmine?"

She looked back at Indy, and for the first time, she didn't see the girl Teddy thought was hot or the girl who beat her at the OBX Classic. She saw her doubles partner. "Maybe we can just find a table or something."

"Great," Indy said, standing on the tiptoes of the five-inch heels that made her tower over most of the crowd even more than she already would have. "I see an empty one, come on."

Jasmine had to take two steps for each of Indy's long strides, but they got to the table and slid into the small booth. As soon as they were seated, Jasmine lifted her hand to call over one of the passing waiters. She was going to enjoy this party and that meant she wanted some champagne.

"Won't Dom mind?" Indy said as she took her own glass from the waiter's tray.

"He might for you. You're still seventeen, right?" Jasmine said and took a long sip.

"Yep," Indy said, pushing her glass away as her eyes focused on the crowd, darting from group to group. "Not eighteen until November." Then her gaze locked and Jasmine followed her line of sight straight to where Jack Harrison was standing, talking and laughing with a few party guests including several really gorgeous women. Despite that, his eyes seemed to be constantly searching the room, but couldn't find whatever he was looking for.

"So it's Jack, not Teddy, huh?"

"What?" Indy said, snapping her eyes away from the floor and staring at Jasmine wide eyed. "No."

"And yeah, that just confirmed it."

Indy pulled her glass back, taking a swig. "Fair is fair, I guess. I know about your secret crush and now you know about mine."

"So he doesn't know?" Jasmine asked, leaning forward in her seat.

"Oh he knows, but he's too...he's too Jack to do anything about it."

Jasmine giggled. "Too Jack?"

"Yeah, too *good*. I guess." Indy took another sip of her champagne, longer this time, nearly draining the glass.

"Plus, there are laws about things like that."

Indy snorted. "No, there aren't. I looked it up."

"I'm just saying, it's not as simple as I like you, you like me, let's make out."

"Right," Indy said, "but it still sucks."

"I know," Jasmine said, "believe me, I know."

They sat in silence, a much more comfortable one now and watched the party swirl around them, people dancing, flirting and lots of fake smiles followed by eye rolls behind someone's back. They drank their champagne slowly, but never let a waiter pass without grabbing another glass.

"So what do you think?" Indy said, nodding at a short, extremely buff man in his forties with an orange tan and way too much hair gel. His arm was wrapped around the waist of a girl nearly a foot taller than him, but probably half his age. "Still lives with mom, right?"

Jasmine nearly spit out a sip of champagne, but then smiled wickedly. "No way, he has a huge penthouse apartment to compensate for his other deficiencies."

A man stopped in front of their table and Jasmine looked up, her smile fading. "Hi, Dom," she said, cringing at their table of champagne glasses, some still full, but most of them drained.

"Ladies, I see we're having a good time," their coach said, a massive crease between his brows as he frowned down at them.

"We were," Indy muttered, "but I'm guessing that's over now."

"Damn right," he said, shaking his head. "Let's go."

They followed him through the party and to a side door where Dom had one of the tour officials call them a car.

"Straight back to the hotel," he told them before leaning in the window and telling the driver where to go.

Driving through the streets of Paris was an experience all its own. The streetlights reflected against the windows of their cab and each street looked like it was the set of an epic love story. Indy sighed from the seat next to her.

"It's beautiful isn't it?" Jasmine asked.

"Almost too beautiful to be real. Have you been here before?"

"Yeah, with my parents."

"Right, duh. Me too. My mom and I did the London and Paris thing when I was thirteen. I definitely didn't appreciate it at the time."

The car pulled up to the front of the hotel and the driver got out to open the door for them. As they stepped out onto the sidewalk, the Eiffel Tower—lit up for the night—twinkled in the distance, the rest of the city's lights a mere stage for the famed landmark to stand upon.

"Why didn't your parents didn't come?" Indy asked as they moved through the lobby toward the elevators.

Jasmine frowned. No one else had thought to ask that. Not even Dom, although it was possible he already knew why. "I asked them not to."

"Why?"

"I..." She hesitated as they got into the elevator car. "I wasn't sure how well we were going to do and I didn't want to, I don't know, disappoint them, I guess." Then feeling a lot more exposed than she had in a long time, she shot back, "Why isn't your dad here?"

"I doubt he even knows I'm playing."

Jasmine raised an eyebrow in disbelief and the elevator dinged signaling their arrival on the sixth floor.

Indy sighed and kept talking. "My dad loves his job. He loves his job more than he loved my mom and he loves his job more than he loves me. When my mom died, I started boarding at school, and in the summers, he just let me keep on living in the house I shared with my mom instead of bringing me to live with him. He hired a housekeeper, pays for the maintenance, and keeps my bank account full. I get a card from him on Christmas and a present on my birthday, but his secretary sends them."

"That sucks."

"Whatever. Life's not fair and all that. I have it a lot better than most people."

"I guess we both do."

"Yeah and look, I didn't mean what I said about your serve."

Jasmine snorted. "Yeah you did."

"Okay, maybe a little, but it's not terrible and you were right, my net game could really use a lot of work."

"If you miss, I'll be behind you to get it."

"Good to know."

Jasmine smiled. She should leave this newfound peace alone, but she couldn't help herself. They were getting everything out in the open, so why not this? "So if we get into the third round, which will it be?"

"What?" Indy asked, eyes wide.

"Women's Doubles or Girls' Singles?"

"How did you…?"

"Indy, I've been around professional tennis my entire life. I know how this works. Endurance isn't exactly your strength. I won't hate you forever or anything if you choose singles. I get it."

"No, it'll be doubles," Indy said finally.

"Seriously?"

"Yeah and not just because you're standing here asking me. I honestly wasn't sure until right now, but really, it's the opportunity of a lifetime to play in the main doubles draw at a Grand Slam tournament. I wouldn't be able to drop it, not even for a chance to win the girls' tournament."

A sudden surge of gratitude swept through Jasmine like she'd never felt before. Why should she be grateful to a girl she didn't even like all that much for taking advantage of an opportunity to play at a Grand Slam? It didn't really make sense and it was probably fueled more by the champagne than anything else, but before she could stop herself, she hugged Indy.

"Thanks," she said, pulling away before the other girl had a chance to react.

Indy narrowed her eyes. "You're welcome," she said, her voice lingering on that last syllable, making it more of a question. Jasmine ignored it.

"I'll see you tomorrow morning for training."

"Yeah, see you tomorrow." Indy turned and started down the hallway before she stopped and called back, "And I know I said we didn't have to be friends, but you know, I think I might like that."

Jasmine turned the idea over in her head as she stepped into her hotel room. She kicked off her heels and rummaged through her suitcase for some pajamas. It had been a long day and curling up in her bed sounded like a pretty good way to end it. After scrubbing off her makeup and washing her face, she stared at her reflection. Maybe Indy was right. Maybe they could be friends.

Switching off the bathroom light, she climbed into bed. On her nightstand her phone lit up, vibrating and playing Teddy's ringtone. Jasmine took a deep breath, exhaled and answered the call. "You'll never guess what happened."

~

"Good job, ladies!" Dom called from the sidelines as they finished up their workout with a set of Einstein sprints that made the other players on the practice courts stare in horror.

Jasmine slowed to a halt and held her hand up for Indy, who slapped it, hard. "Nice," she said and meant it. Indy looked fabulous during their practice session. Her conditioning level was finally catching up to Jasmine's, and they'd torn up the court for the two hours Dom had reserved it. Their sneakers and the lower halves of their legs were covered in red clay, but their faces were both lit up with smiles. Jasmine finally understood what Teddy meant about Dom being a genius. She felt it every time Indy served a bullet up the center of the court, or she got to a ball Indy couldn't quite reach. They had a real chance to open some eyes if what they brought at practice translated into their first-round match the next day.

"Ladies, I've got to get to Penny's match. Cool down, shower and then meet me there if you want."

They took his advice, and an hour later, both freshly showered and dressed in their OBX T-shirts, the closest thing they had to a uniform, they made it to the player's box just in time for the start of Penny's match. Jack's seat was on the aisle with Dom next to him and Alex the farthest down the row. She and Indy settled into the seats behind them.

It was as big a mismatch as Jasmine had ever seen: Penny Harrison, who defeated the number one player in the world in her last tournament, against some random French qualifier. The first couple of rounds at a Grand Slam tended to be like that. The highest-ranked athletes usually drew players who came through the qualifying rounds and spent most of the tennis season on the Challenger Circuit and not on the main tour.

Pulling her phone from her bag, Jasmine held it up to snap a picture of the court, where Penny and her opponent were warming up. Adding a quick caption—*Courtside at Roland Garros for Penny's match!*—she sent it out into cyberspace.

A minute later, her phone vibrated and a message popped up from Teddy: *Updates please!*

Don't you have twin ESP? You tell me how it's going to go.

Maybe I just want to talk to you.

Talked to you last night.

Too long ago. Call me tonight?

The chair umpire climbed up into his seat and said, "Play."

"Here we go," Indy said.

Penny got off to a blazing start, and after fifteen minutes of dominating play, she was just a point away from winning the first set. Her opponent looked exhausted and beaten, sitting in her chair, staring out into space.

Finally, during the break between sets, as everyone else stood to stretch their legs, Jasmine looked at the screen. Teddy had sent five messages, the last a picture of him sitting in the OBX library, crossing his eyes with one of the on-campus teachers glaring at him in the background. Laughing, Jasmine sent a message back: *Nice face. Penny's up a set.*

"What's funny?" Indy asked, sitting down beside her.

"Nothing."

Indy narrowed her eyes and focused on her phone. "Who are you texting?"

"Did anyone ever tell you that you ask too many questions?"

"Did anyone ever tell you that you have the worst poker face ever? You're texting Teddy, aren't you?" Indy plucked the phone from her hand.

"So what?" Jasmine said, stealing it back.

"So he's never going to appreciate you if you're always at his beck and call."

Jasmine shut the phone completely off and tossed it into her bag, then crossed her arms over her chest. "He's my friend. It's not like I'm never going to talk to him again."

"You shouldn't. Maybe if you cut him off it'll make him miss you."

"That's worked before."

"Wait, you've tried that?"

"Yeah and it worked. He missed me."

"But as what? His friend? You're never going to get over him if you guys stay friends. You should just end it now and stop torturing yourself."

Jasmine rolled her eyes and then flicked them up at Jack, standing in the aisle and talking to a rep from one of Penny's sponsors—Nike if the Swoosh logo on his shirt was anything to go by.

"Maybe you should take your own advice."

Indy's shoulders deflated a little. "Maybe I should."

CHAPTER 19

May 28th

The players' lounge was packed. Indy figured that made sense since it was only the second day of the tournament and almost no one had been eliminated yet. She took in the sight of players and their coaches discussing match strategy, some friends and family hovering in the background. Jasmine sat next to her, flipping through a magazine like she didn't have a care in the world, even though their first match was minutes away.

Sitting back, leg bouncing, her eyes darted around the room. She was a nervous wreck and the crowd wasn't helping. She hated this. Just like at the Classic, she felt fine until right before a match and then the jitters started. Except now there was no hope of stepping out onto the court against a weaker opponent. She was at the friggin' French Open and they were playing Zina Lutrova and Ekaterina Grishina. Though the two Russians hadn't played together before, they were training for Fed Cup doubles and were using this tournament as a practice run.

Jasmine glared at her and then glanced down at her knee. Indy muttered an apology and stilled the constant, nauseating motion. She squirmed in her seat, bringing her thumb to her mouth to chew on her fingernail.

"Ladies, good news," Dom said, throwing himself down in a chair across from them. "You two have a walkover."

"You're kidding." Jasmine said.

"Nope," he said, passing her an updated copy of the draw. "Lutrova withdrew from doubles. She wants to focus on singles. No match today."

"So, we won?" Indy asked.

"That's one way of looking at it, I guess. Next match is scheduled for the day after tomorrow. You've got a real opportunity here. Let's not let it go to waste. I reserved a few hours on a practice court so you can get some work in and stay fresh, but congrats, you're through to the second round." He stood and left, moving to the buffet.

"Wow, that was easy," Indy said, grinning, her nerves gone now that they didn't actually have to play.

"Not really. Did you see who our potential next round match would be?"

"No, I didn't look at the draw."

"Why wouldn't you look at the draw?"

"I thought you weren't supposed to. You know, like whenever anyone in an interview is asked if they know who they're playing next, they always say they have no idea. I figured it was bad luck or something."

"They're lying when they say that. Everyone looks at the draw."

"So...." Indy trailed off.

"So what?"

"Who are we playing?"

"Oh, right, sorry." Jasmine glanced down at the page Dom gave her and pointed out their likely opponents' next match. "The Kapur sisters, Pallavi and Ananya."

"Shit."

"Exactly."

The Kapur twins were one of the top doubles teams in the world and the number one seed for this tournament. They'd both given up playing on the singles circuit a few years ago and since then won dozens of tournaments, most notably, the Australian Open. Facing them in their first match together would be like deciding to run a marathon after a couple of hours of jogging on the treadmill.

"We are so screwed," Indy said.

"We could go watch them play. They're scheduled for right now."

"Why not?"

They made their way to one of the outer courts where the Kapur sisters were scheduled to play a wild-card team directly across from where their own match had been scheduled. The crowd was sparse and they found a spot along the chain link fence surrounding the court. There were stands on the other side, but the view was better against the fence.

"Indiana."

Indy turned her head, and her jaw dropped. Standing just a few feet away was a tall man dressed in khaki pants and a crisp, light blue Lacoste polo. His dark blond hair, beginning to gray at the temples, was cropped close. Caroline was beside him, hanging on his arm, her wide brimmed hat and sunglasses hiding her identity from passersby.

"Who's that with Caroline?" Jasmine asked.

"That's my dad."

"Your dad, but I thought..."

"So did I." Indy pushed off the fence and crossed the pathway between them. "Hi," she said, making sure to put a question in her tone as they both hugged her.

"I called your father," Caroline said, bussing each of her cheeks.

"Obviously."

Her dad had the gall to smile. "I hadn't realized things had progressed this quickly."

"So now that I'm playing in a Grand Slam I'm worthy of your attention?"

"Indiana!" Caroline scolded through a gasp.

"You should've asked me before you called him," Indy said, glaring at her agent.

"It is done," Caroline said with a dismissive shrug. "Now why are you not preparing for your match?"

"Jasmine and I got a walkover into the second round."

"Ah," her dad said, looking at Caroline. "Well, if there's no match, I should go back to the hotel and call into the office."

"Good," Indy said, trying to stifle the hurt. Of course he didn't want to spend any actual time with her, not that she wanted to either, but she would have liked the option of turning him down flat. "My next match is the day after tomorrow. Come if you want, whatever. I don't care."

She stomped away, catching Jasmine's eye as she walked by her. Pushing her way through the teams of spectators exploring the outer courts, she circled back toward the player's exit where she ran into Jack, her face almost colliding against the Nike swoosh logo on his black T-shirt.

"Indy?" he said, as she pushed past him. "Indiana, wait."

She whirled around and snapped, "What?"

His eyebrows shot up. "Are you okay?"

"I'm fine," she said, trying to step around him again. People around them in the busy hallway, athletes, coaches and staff alike, were staring at them. Most of them probably had no idea who she was, but they definitely knew Jack.

"You're not fine," he said, leading her away from the crowd and down a separate, empty hallway. "What's the matter? Maybe I can help."

Indy ran a hand through her hair. "My dad is here."

Jack studied her carefully, before opening his mouth to speak. She liked that about him. He always thought before he spoke. "And that's bad?"

"Of course it's bad. He's only here because...because..."

"He's your dad. He's here because he wants to support you."

She twisted her mouth into a pout and shook her head. Jack didn't get it. She hadn't met his parents, but she knew the Harrisons were a happy family.

"He's here because I'm interesting now. I'm doing something worthy of his attention, so he showed up."

"Indiana..." he said, sighing heavily, his eyes softening...pitying.

She felt something break inside of her. Pity was the last thing she wanted him to feel for her. "Don't. My dad is an asshole. He's always been like that, but I just I don't need you to feel sorry for me, okay?"

"I don't feel sorry for you."

"I…" She trailed off. "What?"

"I could never pity you, Indiana. I kind of want to go shake him for not realizing what an amazing daughter he has, but I don't feel sorry for you."

Her heart fluttered. "You think I'm amazing?"

Jack ran a shaky hand across the back of his neck. "You know I do."

He reached out and tucked a strand of hair behind her ear. His hand didn't fall away, but hovered over her cheek. He blinked down at her, hesitating for a moment before his hand descended, large and warm against her skin. Breathing in deeply, she leaned into the touch.

"Indiana, I…" He trailed off, finally bending his head to hers.

Since the day they met, she imagined kissing Jack more than she'd ever admit, but every daydream and fantasy she'd had didn't live up to the reality of having his lips pressed against hers. The electricity that accompanied their almost kiss a few weeks ago was like a tiny little sparkler compared to the fireworks exploding behind her eyes as his tongue gently pressed against her lips, deepening the kiss. His hands held firmly at her hips, his fingers flexing with every stroke of his tongue, pulling her closer. Then she felt him tense, and in the next second, he was gone, putting several feet between them, staring at her wide-eyed.

"I'm…"

"Don't apologize."

"I wasn't going to."

"Of course you were," she said, shaking her head, "because that's the kind of guy you are. Just like how you always show up whenever I need rescuing. I know you feel *something* for me, but you're just too damn good to do anything about it."

"I'm too good?"

Indy felt her anger building as she stepped closer to him. "If any other man were standing in front of me right now, he wouldn't be apologizing."

Jack's lips pressed into a thin line. "I'm six years older than you. Don't you think I'd rather just take what I want and damn the consequences? But I can't do that. That's not the kind of man I am."

"That's not what I meant and you know it."

"Then what the hell do you want from me?" he snapped, throwing up his hands in the air.

"I want you to stop being a coward."

The words were liberating. She'd been holding them in since the moment she first saw him and now he knew the truth, even if he'd never act on it—at least not again. The seconds ticked away and the longer he was silent, the clearer it was that he wasn't going to respond, but Indy wasn't finished. After that kiss, she was done pretending.

"If you don't feel the same way," she said, taking one step and then another toward him, until her body was nearly flush against his, "if you don't want me, that's okay. But if you want this as much as I do, well you know where to find me."

With her last words, she pushed up onto her tiptoes and pressed a soft kiss against his cheek, inflicting the same sweet torture he'd put her through back when they first met. Then she turned on her toe and walked away.

CHAPTER 20

May 29th

The sound of rain against her windows drew Penny from her sleep. Her eyes fluttered open; the room was still dark, a product of the overcast skies outside. She let her eyes drift closed and that's when she noticed it: a weight, heavy and warm against her stomach, an arm curving protectively around her body, two fingers tucked slightly into the waistband of her pajama shorts. She could hear his soft, even breathing on the pillow next to hers. She recognized the deep, slow rhythm. Alex was next to her and he was sound asleep.

She carefully rolled over. His arm remained around her, instinctively pulling her closer. He was practically radiating heat and she snuggled into it, pressing her lips to his shoulder. Penny closed her eyes again and let sleep slowly overtake her.

She woke later, sleepier than when she'd roused the first time, the rain still pelting her windowpanes. Alex was awake now, still holding her close, his eyes focused on her.

"Hey," he whispered, nudging his nose against hers.

"Hi," she breathed, their lips brushing together softly. "This is nice."

He nodded in agreement. "Mmm, more than nice. If I could wake up like this for the rest of my life, I'd die a happy man."

She tucked her head into the crook of his shoulder. "I think that can be arranged. I sleep better when you're here," she said, her fingers absently drawing patterns against the skin of his bicep.

They lay there for a few more moments. "I have to get up."

He groaned. "No you don't. You have to stay right here."

"I have to get up," she said again. "Dom booked a practice court for ten. I have to take a shower." A wicked grin spread across his face at the idea. "By myself. I need to get my head in the right space for my match tonight."

"It's raining. They're going to cancel your match," he argued against the skin of her neck, his hands already finding purchase against her hips, pressing her down into the mattress. Alex had dispatched his first round opponent in straight sets the night before, his knee not giving him any trouble at all, and his second round match wasn't until the next day. He'd earned a morning of rest, but Penny definitely had work to do that day.

"It's just drizzling and regardless, I have to prepare like I'm going to play," she said, despite wanting to agree with him in the worst way.

"Fine," he said, releasing her and burying his head beneath a pillow when she turned on a light.

"Drama queen," she muttered as she dug through her suitcase, pulling out the practice clothes Nike sent for this tournament.

Stepping under the hot spray of water, she let it soak her hair and her mind drifted to the tournament draw. Her opponent was Patricia Smyth, a veteran with a decent all-around game. They'd played once before, earlier in the season at Indian Wells. 6-3, 6-1, in an easy victory. There was nothing to be concerned about. What else did she know about Patricia? She was English, like Alex, which wasn't exactly information that would help her during the match.

She had to stop relating every single thing to him. She promised Indy she wouldn't become one of those stupid girls whose life revolved around a guy.

The water started to grow cool and she countered it by pushing the hot handle a little farther down. Every muscle in her body sang with relief as tension she hadn't realized was there slipped out through her pores. Letting her chin fall to her chest, she closed her eyes and exhaled heavily. Her mind drifted, imagining Alex's broad chest pressing up against her back, his hands exploring her skin, his lips trailing down her neck, over her shoulder…then she was jolted from her daydream by a buzzing against the vanity table just outside of the shower.

Wiping at the shower door to clear the fog away, she squinted through the glass. Alex's phone was plugged into wall, charging, its screen lit up with an incoming message. She turned off the water and stepped out of the shower, wrapping a towel around her body and tucking it closed between her breasts.

Leaning over, careful not to drip on the phone, she saw a message flashing over his locked screen, a picture message, from Caroline Morneau with a caption, *Just one more. I couldn't help myself.* The picture was tiny, just a thumbnail, but Penny could make out the gist. It was Alex, on the night of the gala. He had Penny pressed up against a wall, his mouth at her neck, his hand covered to the wrist by the skirt of her dress, disappearing between her thighs. Her head was thrown back, eyes closed, fingers digging into his shoulders. Penny swallowed back a wave of panic. They'd snuck away from the party briefly, not quite willing to wait until they got back to the hotel. Obviously someone had followed them and snapped a picture, then sent it to Caroline. Or had Caroline taken the picture herself?

The real question was, why the hell was Caroline messaging it to Alex?

Penny pulled the phone from its charger and swept out of the bathroom, tossing it onto the lump of covers she assumed Alex was buried under.

"Your phone was buzzing."

His head popped out from under the blankets and he picked up his phone, glancing at the screen before looking back up at her. "Did you see?"

"If you mean, 'did I see the screen and wonder why Caroline Morneau is sending you photos of us with your hand up my dress,' then yeah, I saw. What does she mean, she couldn't help herself?"

"Penny, love, listen," he said, sitting up, rubbing his hands over his face.

"I'm listening."

Alex let out a quick breath. "She's my agent."

"Your agent?"

"That night when we were on the court, when she interrupted us, I was meeting her to sign the papers."

Penny eye snapped up at the ceiling and shook her head. "I don't understand," she said, looking back at him. "What does her being your agent have anything to do with a picture like that?"

Alex looked away. "She probably wants to stir up some buzz off the court during the tournament."

A long breath escaped through her lips as it all clicked in her head. "Like she did before the tournament with the *Athlete Weekly* pictures."

"Penny…" He trailed off, but he didn't deny it or call her crazy or even have a moment of realization, like the idea had never occurred to him before.

"Did you know?" she asked, knowing the answer already.

"Penny, love…"

"Did. You. Know?"

"Yes."

The word was so simple that it took a moment for the implications to hit her. She sat down on the bed and felt the mattress shift as he crawled toward her, sitting beside her at the edge of the bed in just his boxer briefs, his thigh pressing against hers. He slid an arm around her waist, but she shook him off.

"Don't touch me." She felt him flinch and then move away, giving her some space.

"Penny, I swear, I don't know why she took this one and I'd never let her use it."

"Is that supposed to make it okay? And why did you let her use the others?"

He hesitated and then said in a soft voice, "I thought you hated me, that I didn't have a chance. She showed me the pictures and said they'd create a nice buzz around my comeback here, I thought, why not?"

"Why not? I don't know Alex, maybe because some of those moments were private? Maybe because I don't want my love life plastered all over the internet for everyone to see? Maybe because I trusted you. And that's really the point, isn't it? I'm an idiot for trusting you."

"No, you're not. I'm the idiot. I'm sorry. I'll fire her. I'll do it right now."

Penny shook her head. "I don't care that she leaked the pictures, Alex. I care that you told her she could. Were you ever going to tell me?" He looked away and that was all the answer she needed. "Of course not."

She stood up and went straight for her suitcase, pulling out her training clothes. She had a practice court reserved in a little less than a half hour and Dom would be there any minute. Chucking off the towel, she dressed quickly, not even sparing Alex a glance.

Then her own phone, charging on the dresser, started vibrating and message after message began popping up on the screen. Behind her, she heard Alex's phone doing the same, a steady stream of *blings* echoing in the large hotel suite.

"Fuck," Alex muttered, his eyes on his phone. Then he looked up at Penny, his eyes wide, but his shoulders slumped in defeat and she knew. Caroline leaked the photo.

She should have felt panic rising in her chest or her head aching from the onslaught of bombshells in the last few minutes, but instead a calm washed over her, a stillness that she'd only ever felt before on the tennis court.

"I have training soon. I should get going."

Moving back across the room, she grabbed a band and pulled her hair up into a quick ponytail. Through the reflection in the mirror she saw the eyes the man she'd trusted with her body and nearly with her heart, focused on her, total bewilderment on his face.

"Penny," Alex started as soon as she turned around, but she shook her head. Whatever he had to say, however he thought he could make this better, she didn't want to hear it.

"I knew something like this would happen. It was all just too damn good to be true." She couldn't look at him. If she looked him in the eye, it would weaken her resolve and she had to be strong.

"Penny, love, please," he tried again, but she ignored him.

She opened the hotel room door and then looked back at the man still sitting on her bed, head in his heads. "You shouldn't be here when I get back."

~

Neither Dom nor Jack asked her about what happened when she met them in the lobby, but by their tense silence, it was clear they knew about the picture. They walked in silence down through the lobby, out of the hotel and hopped into the car waiting to take them to Roland Garros. By the time they arrived, the rain had stopped and the sky was clearing to a bright blue.

Dom told her to warm up, so she did. Then they worked on a few footwork drills, followed by their usual pre-match routine, sticking to the basics, making sure her shots were strong going into her match that night. The workout got her heart rate up and a fine sheen of sweat coated her skin by the time they were finished, but it didn't do anything for her mental state. The odd calm that had settled over her at the hotel had disappeared as soon as they got on the court, replaced by a cloudy mess of confusion, and by the way Dom was looking at her, he definitely noticed. Penny didn't need him to tell her she'd practiced like crap.

Her hands shook, vibrating with frustration as she packed up her gear and left the practice court. She wasn't sure whom she was most angry at, but she quickly settled upon herself for letting herself give in. She was prepared for this tournament, thanks mostly to him. Playing with him every day had brought her game to a whole new level, her reaction time was shorter, her feet were quicker and no other player had ever tested her will, on and off the court, so thoroughly, but then it had all gone to hell so quickly. When had this become her life? Men and sex and drama instead of what she always wanted, to be the best tennis player in the world. Was it so wrong to want someone to share that with? A dull ache settled in around her heart, her chest tightening.

"Stop it. You have to snap out of it," she muttered to herself as she turned a corner nearing the street exit and nearly collided headlong with another young woman headed in the opposite direction. A long blond braid whipped against her cheek as the other girl tossed her head in annoyance.

Penny narrowed her eyes as she regained her footing and saw the owner of the blond braid. "Zina."

"Watch where you are going. Oh. It is you," her rival said with a small smile. She didn't sound all that surprised. "I did not expect to see you. I thought maybe you would withdraw."

"Why would I do that?" Penny cocked her head to the side, not letting the other girl's slightly larger frame intimidate her. There were a few people loitering around and she recognized most of them as reporters. This had set up written all over it.

"You have no chance to win."

"You have a short memory."

She wasn't going to give Zina or the reporters what they wanted; she wouldn't be goaded into a fight. Not even while every fiber of her being was screaming at her to haul off and smack the smug, superior smirk off the Russian girl's face.

"My memory is good. You play your best tennis. I play my worst. I have won two tournaments since that defeat and you have spent time since then not training, but, how you say, fucking Alex Russell."

Her stomach lurched at the mention of his name, but she kept her reaction off her face. "We'll see, won't we?"

Penny walked away, feeling every set of eyes fixed upon her. In a few minutes the internet would probably explode with pictures and reports of her little tête-à-tête with Lutrova, but at least for the first time since she arrived in France, they'd be talking about tennis.

CHAPTER 21

May 30th

Jasmine was ready to strangle her doubles partner. It wasn't the all-consuming envy from a few days ago, but she had no idea that being friends with Indiana Gaffney would be more torturous than being rivals. The other girl had made it her mission to find Jasmine a replacement for Teddy.

"What about him?" Indy asked and nodded to her left as a guy walked by them, studying the strings of his racket.

"Too short," Jasmine said, wrinkling her nose. She'd always preferred taller guys.

They were killing time in the players' lounge before Penny's match, rescheduled from the day before because of the rain. She'd asked them to be her cheering section and they were more than happy to oblige. The entire tournament was buzzing about the picture that leaked to every major media outlet she could find. Jasmine had barely glanced at it, but that was enough to tell it was a totally private moment that was put on display for the entire world.

"Okay," Indy said, scanning the men in the room. "Him, over there by the window, with the bright blue shirt."

"Gay," Jasmine said, dismissing him as a candidate.

Indy tilted her head. "Really?"

"Came out last year."

"Huh, okay. You're going to have to explain your type for me then, because I've pointed out like a dozen perfectly hot guys and you've shot down every one."

"It's not my fault the last one was gay. Otherwise, he would've been an option."

Indy narrowed her eyes, leaning forward. "I call bullshit. I think you don't want to be attracted to anyone else, so you're not."

Scoffing, Jasmine examined her nails, picking at a broken cuticle. "Attraction is biology, Indy. You can't just force yourself to ignore it."

Indy shrugged. "Love makes you blind."

"Maybe." Her eye caught on a flash of brown hair across the room. The hair belonged to a young man working his way down the buffet table.

"Paolo Macchia," Indy said when she saw where her eyes had focused, "I saw him play at Indian Wells last year."

Jasmine grinned. Olive skin and a floppy mess of dark hair, tall, but lean and like pretty much every guy on tour, in incredible shape. "He's cute."

"Very cute with an amazing Italian accent."

"Good to know."

Indy leapt to her feet and started in that direction.

"Where are you going?" Jasmine asked, following her.

"To say hi," Indy said over her shoulder, making a beeline for Paolo.

Jasmine grabbed her arm and tried to pull her to a stop. "You don't even know if he speaks English."

"He totally does," she said, stepping in front of Paolo as he started loading his plate with lettuce. "Hi."

He stopped and looked up, a wide smile spreading across his face as he looked back and forth between them. "Hello."

"I'm Indiana," she said, but leaned away, giving Jasmine a gentle shove forward. "And this is my friend Jasmine."

"It's very nice to meet you," Paolo said, his blue eyes crinkling as his smile deepened. His Italian accent was soft, his English very good.

Indy coughed. "And I've gotta go make a call. Be back in a second." She pulled her phone out of her pocket and walked away before Jasmine could say a word.

Paolo cleared his throat softly so she took a deep breath. "Sorry about that. She's a little crazy."

"Not so crazy. Your name is Jasmine?"

"Yes, Jasmine Randazzo," she said, waiting for the immediate flash of recognition in his eyes, but it didn't come. He just nodded.

"I am Paolo Macchia."

"I know." She cringed inwardly. What a stupid thing to say. He probably thought she was some silly girl with a crush who hadn't been brave enough to approach him on her own. The last part might be true, but the first definitely wasn't. She still had feelings for Teddy, and there wasn't room in her heart for anyone else.

Jasmine forgot her embarrassment when an unnatural quiet settled over the players' lounge. She looked around and saw Alex Russell had entered the room. Gray sweatshirt, hood pulled up over his head, hands tucked into the front pocket, he ignored the stares and the whispers that erupted as soon as they were sure it was him.

"People suck," Jasmine muttered.

"Yes, they do, very much," Paolo agreed. "*Scusi, signorina*, but he is my friend. I have to speak with him."

"Oh," she said, "of course."

Paolo left his tray of food and made his way across the room to Alex, who stopped and spoke to him for moment before they walked together out the door on the opposite end of the lounge.

Indy appeared at her side from nowhere. "So, how'd it go?"

Jasmine whirled on her. "Don't ever do that to me again."

"Please, both of you were all smiles before Alex dragged that black cloud in here. Look, Teddy Harrison isn't the only guy in the world. That's all I'm saying."

"Is this about Teddy and me or about the fact that it's been two days since you kissed Jack Ha—"

Indy shushed her, cutting off the last word, her face suddenly peaked and drawn. "That is *not* public knowledge."

Jasmine shrugged her shoulders in defeat. "I'm sorry. Anyway, you were right, his accent is amazing."

Indy brightened, latching on to the change of subject. "Told you so. Come on, let's go down and watch the match. Penny could probably use some moral support right about now."

"Yeah, sure."

As they made their way down toward the court, Jasmine's mind was whirling. Maybe she wasn't such a lost cause after all and maybe Indy wasn't either.

~

"Game. Set. Match. Harrison."

In the seats next to her, Dom, Jack and Indy all let out a collective sigh of relief as Penny looked up at the sky, thanking whatever higher power pushed her through the match. It was a close call, but she managed to squeak past her opponent, 7-5, 6-4.

"I'm going to talk to her," Dom said, standing and making a hasty exit from the player's box. "See you all back at the hotel."

They watched him go and Jasmine cringed. She could imagine the lecture Dom would give her if she ever played like that, and maybe for the first time ever, she didn't envy Penny at all. Then she realized she had her opening, the moment she had been trying to engineer in her head since they sat down to watch the match.

"Maybe you better go with him. She's probably going to need a friendly face after their *talk*," she whispered to Indy, who nodded and left, but not before glancing quickly at Jack, who was making a rather obvious show of not looking in Indy's direction. It made her decision to go through with her plan even easier. They just had to get out of their own way.

They sat in an awkward silence as the crowd around them started to disperse for the bathrooms and concession areas between matches. Jack stood, but Jasmine grabbed the cuff of his pullover jacket and tugged.

He squinted at her, obviously confused. She knew it was odd. In all the time they'd known each other, she couldn't recall ever having a full conversation with him—just the two of them—without Penny or Teddy around. Jasmine pushed past the awkwardness.

"I need to talk to you."

"What's up?" he asked, sitting back down, giving her his full attention. When their eyes met she was startled by how much he and Teddy resembled each other. They were different in so many ways that it was easy to forget sometimes that they were brothers.

"You've met my dad, right?" she asked, wanting to approach this the right way. She didn't want to scare him off before she could make her point.

"Yeah, of course I have."

"Would you say he's a good guy?"

Confusion clouded his eyes, but he nodded. "Yeah, your dad's a great guy. Are you okay, Jasmine?"

"Me? I'm fine. At least, I think I'm fine. I know I'm a little spoiled and I have a tendency to freak out sometimes, but I think my parents did a good job of raising me."

Jack's forehead wrinkled and he put a hand on top of hers. "Seriously, Jasmine, are you having some kind of issue with your parents? I don't think I'm the best person to talk to about something like that."

She rolled her eyes, pulling her hand free. "Jack, chill, I'm just trying to make a point."

He studied her carefully, but nodded. "Okay, I'll play, what's your point?"

"Do you know how old my mom was when she met my dad?"

"No, I don't."

"Sixteen. She was sixteen years old."

"Okay."

"Yep. She was sixteen years old and they've been together for almost twenty years now. Kind of nice right? That they've been together so long?"

"I guess so."

"You know how old my dad was at the time?"

Jack narrowed his eyes at her, obviously finally figuring out her point. "I'm guessing not sixteen?"

"Nope. More like twenty-one."

"Did Indiana send you to talk to me?"

Jasmine snorted. "What? God no. She'd kill me if she knew unless she died of embarrassment first. Then she'd probably haunt me for the rest of my life."

"Then I don't get it. I distinctly recall having to literally hold you back from beating her to a pulp. Why are you doing this?"

Jasmine shrugged.

"And this has nothing to do with my brother?"

"Teddy?" she asked, tilting her head. "What would he have to do with this?"

"If I were with Indy, then my very easily distracted little brother would be less distracted."

"Teddy's my friend. If I thought he'd be hurt by you and Indy getting together, I wouldn't be here talking to you."

Jack raised a skeptical eyebrow, but Jasmine pressed on.

"It's true and I think you're just making excuses. Indy's seventeen, not twelve. I'm not saying you guys have to get married or whatever, but seriously for two people like you, a few years just are not a big deal."

He didn't answer. She stood up and walked away, leaving him to his thoughts. As she left the stadium, her phone buzzed in her pocket. The screen lit up with Teddy's picture, but with a deep breath, she ignored the call and kept walking.

CHAPTER 22

May 31st

For Indy, the day between their walkover and second round match flew by faster than one of her serves. She had a good practice session with Jasmine, watched Penny win, even if it was just by the skin of her teeth, then it was straight to dinner and bed, avoiding all contact with both Caroline and her dad. Indy knew they were staying at the same hotel, but whenever she'd seen them in the distance, she'd done a quick about-face and even once hid behind a column in the lobby until they passed. She hadn't had to avoid Jack because it seemed he was avoiding her. She figured he was freaked out enough to stay away from her for good.

Now, she was back in the players' lounge, dressed in the match outfit she and Jasmine had picked out together, a traditional white pleated tennis skirt paired with a bright turquoise tank. The color looked good on both of them, a rare thing for two people whose features were so opposite.

If only the color of her outfit was her biggest worry. She wished Lutrova and Grishina hadn't dropped out. Then these nerves would already be gone and she wouldn't have to think about going out onto the court for the first time. Maybe the Kapur sisters would drop out too. Maybe they would wake up with a mysterious virus and withdraw from the tournament. Her throat tightened and her stomach lurched. Why was this happening again? When had she become this player who wanted to throw up before a match or hoped her opponents forfeited? That wasn't who she wanted to be. She had to get over this and get over it now. She felt like she did before the final of the OBX Classic, jittery and ready to burst out of her own skin. What had she done to calm down then?

Nothing. She hadn't done anything; she went out there a total wreck and fell behind in the match. She couldn't do that again. There was too much riding on it and their opponents were too good. If they fell behind, a comeback would be almost impossible.

"Hey," a voice said from just over her shoulder and she jumped in her seat. "Whoa, sorry. Didn't mean to scare you." Penny stepped into view. "Dom was looking for you. He needs you down in the prep room in five."

"Oh, okay, I'll just…I'll just go then." She stood, wiping her palms against the sides of her skirt.

"You okay?" Penny asked, tilting her head in concern.

"Hmm?" Indy stalled for a second. "Yeah, I'm fine. Just amped up, you know?"

"Look, I just…I'm not going to be there. I'm just all over the place right now. I don't want to bring any negative energy to your box, so I'm going to watch from here, okay?"

Indy tilted her head and shrugged. "Sure, whatever."

"Okay, I'll see you after then?"

"Definitely, see you after."

Indy took a deep breath, starting down the hallway that led to the locker rooms.

"Indy, hang on," Penny called out. "I almost forgot. Ana Kapur, her serve is tougher so that's who you'll be facing, she tends to start off really powerful and then back off later in the match, opting for more consistency than velocity. If you wait her out, you should be able to handle her no problem."

"Right. Thanks." Dom had reminded her of the same thing earlier, but she'd forgotten about it as her nerves took over.

"You're going to do fine. Just relax and let your training take over."

Indy nodded and made her way to the locker room. Jasmine was getting her ankle wrapped, but looked up with a smile as soon as Indy walked in.

"This is going to be so much fun," Jasmine said.

The last of Indy's nerves faded. She was about to play in the French Open, against two of the best players in the world. A month ago, she was just a regular girl sitting in physics, trying to hide her phone from her teacher. There were six thousand miles separating her from that classroom desk, but she may as well have been on Mars. Jasmine was right. The match, win or lose, would be the greatest moment of her life and she was going to enjoy it.

"We're ready for you," a tournament official said from the doorway, headset in place, instructions coming from outside on court.

Time was up.

They stepped out of the tunnel and on to the court. The sky was blue and the sun was bright. The Kapur twins were already stretching and getting warm. The stadium was at least twice the size of the OBX main court, with double the amount of speakers pumping in music. There was a sizable crowd and she caught sight of Dom sitting in the player's box. Just one row back, her dad and Caroline were both dressed to the nines and sitting with the bored disinterest that people who sat in expensive seats at any sporting event always seemed to exude. Indy looked away, focusing instead on the rest of the crowd, all of whom were there to watch her play. She wasn't going to let anything negative get in her head.

A tap against her arm drew her attention and she turned to Jasmine. "Let's go."

The chair umpire announced that warm-ups should begin and so they moved onto the court.

She just had to keep her feet moving. That was the key. Keep her feet moving and use her serve. Get as many aces as possible, so they could save all their energy for Jasmine's and their returns. And keep her friggin' feet moving.

"Time," the chair umpire called, ending the warm ups.

"You ready?" Jasmine whispered as they retreated back to their chairs.

"Damn right I am."

~

"Game, set and match, Kapur and Kapur."

Indy bowed her head and tried to catch her breath after watching her last shot sail wide. She wanted to win. Of course she wanted to win, but she couldn't be upset with the result. They'd gotten off to a bit of a slow start, but after that, they'd taken the second set and nearly pulled it out in the end, sending the third to a tiebreak. There was definitely a victory in this defeat.

"Final score, 6-2, 4-6, 7-6," the chair umpire said as they shook hands with their opponents, congratulating them with a kiss on each cheek.

"We will see you again, I think," one of the Kapur sisters said, grinning, before she released Indy's hand.

The crowd cheered their effort as she and Jasmine gathered their things and exited the court. Her eyes darted up to the player's box where Dom was standing and applauding for them. Caroline and her dad were nowhere in sight. She lifted her hand and waved a thank you to him and the fans.

About a half hour later, Indy and Jasmine were both showered and changed into their street clothes, packing up their gear.

"That wasn't bad for a first time out," Jasmine said and Indy turned to her.

"If we play like we did in the second set, we could really do some damage in our next tournament."

The door to their locker room slammed open and they turned to see Dom standing in the archway. "Ladies, that was amazing. Taking the best doubles team in the world to a third set tiebreak! Phenomenal."

"Thanks, Dom," Jasmine said. "And I really appreciate you giving me this chance, even after what happened."

"I take it you've worked out your differences." Looking between them, he grinned when they both nodded. "Good, because I have plans for the two of you."

Indy had plans too. This was just the beginning for her and Jasmine both on the court and off.

~

As soon as they arrived back at the hotel, Indy excused herself from the group, finding herself a chair in a quiet corner of the lobby. She just wanted to sit and think for a second. She and Jasmine had done really well and her nerves hadn't been a problem all. Now she could go into girls' singles and dominate, just like she had at the Classic.

"Indiana." Her dad's voice pulled her from her thoughts.

"What do you want?" she asked, her eyes snapping up to his. Why couldn't he just leave her alone?

"I wanted to say good-bye," he said, shifting awkwardly from one foot to the other and then running his hand through the blond strands of his slightly receding hairline.

She should've been thrilled that he was leaving, but her heart sank. "Okay," she said, trying not to betray herself. It was beyond annoying that she could want him gone and then be totally gutted when he decided to leave.

"Caroline thought it was best. She thinks it's too much pressure having me here and—"

Indy shrugged, cutting him off. "Well, whatever Caroline thinks is best and--Speak of the devil…"

Caroline emerged from amid the mass of people milling around the lobby and exclaimed, "Indy! *Très bien, chérie.* What a wonderful performance to build upon for the junior tournament."

"Thanks," she said, searching desperately for an escape route, but there was a wall behind her and she'd literally have to push them aside to get away.

"I was telling your father after the match that, despite the loss, with the way you played the sponsors will most certainly come knocking. I have already been in contact with Nike and they will submit an offer for outfitting by the end of the week."

Indy watched in horrified fascination as her father's hand landed upon Caroline's shoulder. "She's doing a great job, isn't she?" He squeezed gently and the older woman's blue eyes filled with warmth when she looked back at him.

Indy's jaw dropped. "Oh my god. Are you two…are you two friggin' sleeping together?"

"Indiana!" her dad scolded, but he pulled his hand away like Caroline's skin burned him. That was all the confirmation Indy needed.

"I cannot believe this. Is that why you hired her? And you!" She whirled on her agent. "First my coach and now my dad? Have you ever even heard the phrase conflict of interest?"

"Is everything okay over here?"

Jack stood behind her dad, his eyes trying to hold on to hers from over her dad's shoulder. He was coming to her rescue again and it made her stomach turn. If he cared, really cared, he would've been there to begin with instead of just showing up to help, only to disappear again a moment later.

"No, but it doesn't matter. I'm out of here."

Indy stormed forward, her dad and her agent pulling apart just in time to get out of her way. Most of the people in the lobby stared in their direction, fascinated by the sudden outburst, but she ignored them as she moved down a hallway through to the back of the hotel. There was a small courtyard lined with a large fence and trees, the cherry blossoms still flourishing even as the calendar moved toward summer.

"Are you alright?"

Jack. He must have followed her. She crossed her arms over her chest and hugged herself tightly, but kept silent, taking deep breaths, willing herself not to cry.

"Just tell me you're alright."

"I'm alright," she muttered. Seconds ticked away, but she didn't hear him leave, so she turned to face him. He was leaning against the outer wall of the hotel, arms crossed over his chest, studying her. "I swear to you, I'm fine, Jack. You can go."

"Maybe you are," he said, pushing off the wall and taking a step closer, "and maybe not, but that's not why I'm still here."

"No?"

"No." She saw the moment when his expression shifted, moving from concern to something else, something she'd only seen glimpses of over the last few weeks when he'd allow the wall he built up between them to slip.

"Why are you still here?" she asked, her voice no louder than a whisper, terrified the sound of her voice would break the moment.

He took slow, measured steps until he was just inches away from her. "A few days ago, a crazy, beautiful, incredible girl called me a coward and she was right."

"She was?"

"You were and I should have done this a long time ago."

It was just a soft brush of the lips at first and then that fire, that intensity and passion that swirled and built between them in the last few weeks, came bubbling to the surface as their mouths caressed each other, tongues dancing slowly. He brought her close, pulling her body gently into his, but she had other ideas. She pushed up against him, one hand twisting into the cotton of his shirt, the other caressing the back of his neck, keeping him close.

When they finally broke apart, he buried his face into her hair, inhaling deeply. They stood breathing each other in for a moment until he ended the silence. "Is this really what you want?"

"Yes," she said, wrapping her arms around his shoulders, pushing up on her toes to brush their lips together again.

Pulling back, their eyes locked and he lifted a hand to her cheek, stroking his thumb over the line of her jaw. "To hell with it," he said as he drew her mouth to his again and they lost themselves in each other.

CHAPTER 23

June 1st

There was too much time to kill. Penny glanced down at her watch, the gift Rolex sent in anticipation of her signing yet another endorsement contract. It was heavy on her wrist and nicer than anything she'd ever owned, but in that moment, all it did was reinforce the fact it was only six o'clock. Though she needed her rest before her match tomorrow against Lutrova, she couldn't reasonably go to bed before eight. Any earlier than that and she'd be wide-awake at some ungodly hour the next morning.

So instead of sitting around, staring at the walls of her room or watching random French television shows, she wandered down to the lobby, hoping the hustle and bustle would make the minutes tick by faster. At least, that's what she told herself.

She settled into a chair next to a large pillar. She would be well-hidden and still have a view of the lobby. Of course her motives for sitting there had nothing to do with the possibility of seeing Alex coming back to the hotel after his training. The television mounted on the lobby wall was airing his press conference from earlier in the day and she couldn't tear her eyes away.

"Last time, he gave me some opportunities and I took advantage of them," his image said on the screen. "We've played each other a lot over the years, so neither of us will be surprised by the other. It'll be a matter of executing and hopefully I'll be able to do that."

"Alex, much has been said about your relationship with American star, Penny Harrison," the reporter began.

"I'm going to say this and I'm going to say this once, so pay attention," he said, glaring daggers into the press pool. "Penny Harrison is the most genuinely good person I've ever met. She inspires me every single day to be a better man and she's definitely too good for the likes of me. Now, does anyone have any actual tennis questions? No? Fine, then we're done." He stood up quickly, knocking his chair over and marched off camera, the reporters shouting after him.

Her heart swelled against her ribcage. She knew he meant every word of it and she wanted desperately to forgive him, but it was just too much. She couldn't keep opening herself up only to be blasted by another disaster. She'd tried that and he ruined what could've been something great between them. She was not going to make that mistake again.

Glancing around the lobby again, she wondered if he'd returned, then she shook her head at how completely stupid she was being. This was ridiculous. She should go back to her room, put on a movie and try to zone out before going to bed. Sitting there waiting for him to come back, especially since she had zero intention of talking to him, was pathetic.

She was just torturing herself and she should be focused on Zina Lutrova, the matchup she'd been training for since Madrid. It was enough with the self-pity. A mellow, relaxing evening would be the perfect way to prepare for facing down her rival tomorrow. She started for the elevator bay when she caught a quick glimpse of sandy blond hair at the other end of the lobby, heading straight for the hotel bar.

Backtracking in that direction, she saw Alex taking a seat at the bar, the bartender pouring a drink into a shot glass. She watched, her heart rising into her throat as a woman took a seat on the stool beside him and ordered a drink. Tennis tournaments were notorious for attracting groupies. Alex looked up and glanced at the woman, took in her long legs, the deep cutting neckline of her dress and the clear invitation in her pouted lips and half-lidded eyes before turning away, studying his drink even more carefully than before. The woman took the hint and sauntered away toward a table of players at the other end of the bar.

Relief swept through Penny, but then she shook herself back to reality. It didn't matter if he hooked up with a random groupie. It wasn't any of her business, not anymore.

Alex still hadn't taken a sip of his drink; he just stared at it like he was looking for answers. He shouldn't be drinking. His next round match was early tomorrow morning, even before hers. Her instincts screamed at her to go to him, to figure out whatever it was that drove him there in the first place. Except, she knew that she was the reason he was sitting at that bar, and there was nothing she could do to help. Penny felt another piece of her heart crack.

Pulling her phone from her pocket, she shot off a quick message to Dom. He and Alex weren't just a coach and athlete. They were friends. Dom would know what to do.

Then she raced to the elevators and pressed the call button, but her patience wore out quickly. She pushed open the door to the stairwell and sprinted up the seven flights of stairs to her floor. Her breath came short and quick as she scanned her key and fell into her room, the sound of the door slamming behind her heavy and satisfying. Curling onto her bed, she let go, the sobs wrenching from her throat as she struggled to breathe. She hugged herself, shoulders shaking with the heavy emotions spilling out of her, but no tears came. She didn't know how long she lay there, rolled into a tight knot of anguish, but eventually her breathing slowed and her muscles relaxed. Enough. It was enough now. She would need all her focus tomorrow to beat Lutrova. Her pain could wait until later; after all, it wasn't going anywhere anytime soon.

~

She woke with her mind fixed on one thing, beating Zina Lutrova. There were no nagging injuries to fuss over, no sudden hitches in her game to tweak. She was ready and it was time to go out and win. Dressing quickly, she eyed the velvet box sitting on her dresser. Alex said the necklace was for luck and she'd need all the luck she could get.

"Morning," Dom said, when she answered a knock at her hotel room door. "Ready to go?"

"What are you doing here? Shouldn't you be at Alex's match? He didn't... Please tell me he didn't withdraw or something stupid."

"No, he sent me away, said I should be with you this morning, so here I am."

"Oh, okay," she said, pushing Alex's thoughtfulness out of her mind. "Let's go then."

By the end of the first week of a Grand Slam, the tournament was still in full swing, but the matches were spread into separate ticket sessions to ensure they made as much profit as possible. The player's lounge where she and Dom had breakfast was practically empty. Alex's match was on the television mounted against the wall, but she was determined not to watch. She would find out how he did later.

"Last night," Dom said, drawing her attention away from her oatmeal, "you did the right thing by texting me."

"It was nothing."

"It wasn't nothing. A lot of people would've just left him there to drown his sorrows and throw away his chances at this tournament. You're one of the best people I know, Penny. You don't deserve what's been happening to you the last couple of days, but don't let it get to you, okay?"

"I'm not. I promise. I'm ready for this."

"Good," he said, taking her at her word. "Okay, one last time. Game plan."

"Attack her back hand, make her move as much as possible and keep at her with the velocity. No letting up or getting cute with shots, just keep at her."

"Good." He took a bite of his grapefruit. "She's expecting an aggressive game, but honestly, I don't think she can handle it."

Penny took a sip of her orange juice, not quite as sure as he seemed to be. "Well, we'll see, won't we?"

"I'm sure of it. As sure as I've ever been of anything in my entire career. You're better than her, Penny. I know it, you know it, and maybe most importantly, she knows it."

"Thanks, Dom."

"I mean it," he said, though she didn't need that reassurance. He never said anything he didn't mean. "And don't thank me. Prove me right."

~

It was overcast and gloomy as they entered the court. Court Philipe Chartier was the premiere court at Roland Garros. The stands could hold more than 14,000 fans and every seat was filled. The media was billing this match as the real championship, declaring over and over again that whoever won would be the clear favorite to take home the title at the end of the fortnight in Paris.

Lutrova won the toss and chose to serve first. Excellent, Penny thought, she would have the first chance to break. She bounced up and down, getting used to the clay surface, testing with little shuffle steps how it would play during the match.

The chair umpire climbed to his chair overlooking the court, and after a brief warm up, silence reigned in the sold-out stadium, but the hum of anticipation was nearly palpable on the court.

Lutrova bounced the ball at her feet, before bringing her arms together, tossing it into the air. Just as it reached the pinnacle of its rise, she slammed her racket head through it, sending a low-lying rocket of a serve across the court. Reacting instinctively, Penny stepped into the shot, returning the ball so fast Lutrova barely had time to recover her feet. The ball bounced in and then slammed in the wall behind the service line.

For a moment, the stadium remained silent, stunned by the speed and perfection of the point.

"Love – 15," the chair umpire said and the crowd finally applauded, cheering the statement she just made with that shot; she was here to win.

Penny stared across the court. Zina met her eyes and Penny let the corner of her mouth lift up in the smallest of smirks. That return, that's what Dom had wanted when he brought in Alex to train with her. He wanted her to take Zina's best weapon, her serve, and shove it back down her throat. The hurt of the last few days hadn't faded, but lifting her hand to the neckline of her shirt, she pressed against the coin through the material. Alex had helped her get here and she wasn't going to let that go to waste.

Three more serves and three more short points later and Penny had the lead.

"Game, Harrison."

She turned to the box just behind her. Dom, Jack, Indy and Jasmine were all sitting in the front row.

"You go, girl," Indy said, loud enough for her to hear even over the buzz of the crowd.

Penny held out her racket to the ball boy who placed three balls on it as options for her serve. She tucked one into the hidden pocket beneath her skirt and let another fall back to the ground in his direction before she approached the baseline.

Lutrova was standing on the other side of the net, bent at the waist, racket spinning in her hands, poised on the balls of her feet. Her forehead was creased, blonde eyebrows knit together, face pinched in concentration.

Penny would go right at her, just like she and Dom discussed. It was time to see if the best player in the world could handle her game. She coiled her body, every muscle in her body tensing, then releasing. The serve was perfectly placed, right where the lines crossed in the center of the court. It whistled past Lutrova before pounding once again into the wall lining the backcourt.

"15 – Love."

~

The match was a whirlwind as they went back and forth. The Lutrova she'd beaten in Madrid was nowhere to be found. The Russian superstar had won two tournaments since then and was at the top of her game. Her shots were crisp and accurate. They exchanged blows, making each other race around the court.

Penny served, a screaming line drive down the center of the court. Lutrova fired a return back, and it began again, a rally from the baselines. Penny sent a slice backhand, short and spinning, into the clay and Lutrova came storming up to the net. A forehand rocketed into the far corner and Penny raced after it, letting her last step fail, sliding across the clay, legs fully extended as she swung into a winner down the line. Her momentum failed and she stopped in a full split, before popping up into the air and back onto her feet. The crowd erupted.

"Game. Harrison *remporte le premier* set, 6-4."

Sitting in her chair, she placed her racket down on the ground beside her and downed half a bottle of Gatorade, before burying her face in her towel, wiping off the layer of sweat. She allowed herself a huge grin while the terrycloth shielded her from the cameras.

Lutrova called for the trainer between sets and was having her legs rubbed down. Maybe it was an excuse for dropping the first set, getting the trainer out there, making everyone believe she was hurt, a rope-a-dope, or a ploy even, to make Penny think she was injured so she would let her guard down in the second set. Whatever game she was playing wasn't going to work. Dom was right; she was better than Lutrova, she was better than the best player in the world. And that meant—shaking her head, she cleared out those thoughts. She could think about that after the tournament was over. Right now, it was time to finish off this match.

"Time," the chair umpire called and Penny leapt to her feet, striding quickly out to the baseline, getting her muscles loose for the second set. This was in stark contrast to the other girl, who stood up slowly and walked across her side of the court, examining her racket as if it might tell her how to win the match.

~

Whatever Lutrova's racket told her didn't work. Penny waited in the corner of the court for a serve that would never arrive as Lutrova buried her shot into the bottom of the net and yet another double fault brought her within one game of victory.

"Game. Harrison *conduit le second ensemble*, 5-4."

For a moment she let her focus slip away and she listened to the crowd cheering. Turning to her box, they were all yelling wildly.

"Let's go, Pen," Jack yelled. "Finish it."

She stepped up to the baseline.

"*S'il vous plaît, soyez tranquille*," the chair umpire said as she prepared to serve and the crowd quieted, but only a fraction.

With a small groan, she sliced her serve, putting an arching spin on it. Lutrova sat back on the shot, handcuffed for a split second by the angle and the change of speeds. She shuffle stepped and swung, but mishit, sending a soft lob over the net.

Penny sprinted forward, feet light as she sped up to the net, getting her racket under the ball just in time. A quick flick of her wrist sent it back over the net. The ball bounced once and then again before Zina could reach it.

As Penny tried to stop, her toe slid into a divot, her ankle twisted and then rolled under. She caught herself with her other foot, but a sharp, blistering pain shot up her leg and then back down again before settling on the inside of her ankle. She tried to put her weight on it. Bad idea.

Thankful the last shot brought her near the sidelines, she hopped quickly over to her chair and she looked up to the umpire to call for a trainer, but he'd anticipated her, waving a member of the tour's medical staff in from the edge of the court, the same man who'd worked on Lutrova's legs before the start of the set.

Before she could react, her sneaker and sock were lying on the ground and gentle, well-trained hands were examining her ankle, checking the range of motion—almost none—and the amount of discomfort—a lot—and then he asked, "Do you want to continue playing?"

Withdrawing hadn't even crossed her mind. How could it? It had all happened so quickly, but she was not going to give up. A forfeit wouldn't just mean a loss. It would practically hand this tournament championship to Lutrova. She wasn't going to let that happen. Even if she couldn't play her next match, she wasn't going to give her rival a free pass to the next round. She glanced around quickly and saw the Russian girl standing just off to the side, watching intently, a brief flash of victory in her gaze. Oh, hell no.

"Wrap it and give me my racket."

"It's a pretty bad sprain, could be worse than that. It might be your Achilles. I can't tell for sure unless you get an MRI." Penny raised an eyebrow and the trainer shook his head. "Fine, but it's against my recommendation."

"Fine," she agreed and winced as he reached for his bag and jostled her ankle in the process. Her hand came up to her throat and she pulled at the chain secured around her neck. The penny slipped out and she held it in her palm for a second. It was warm from resting against her skin, and she began to breathe slowly, closing her eyes and letting her mind go blank. Like lying on the court with Alex, her hand wrapped in his.

The trainer wrapped her ankle tightly. He had to, it was the only way to stabilize the joint, and as she slid her sneaker back on, she bit her lip to keep from crying out.

Tucking the necklace back inside her shirt, she checked the scoreboard quickly. She was three points away from the win and she had to get those points as fast as possible. She had to get the next three serves past Lutrova because there was no way her ankle would stand a rally. She had to keep the ball away from Zina, nothing into the body and definitely nothing off speed. It would have to be three serves. Three aces. That was the only way.

This was going to hurt. A lot.

Trying to minimize her limp as she moved to the baseline, she took a ball from the ball boy and breathed deeply, focusing instead on the feeling of the penny against her skin.

With a small prayer that the joint wouldn't give out, she pushed down into the ground and then up and out, lining the ball dead center as hard as she could.

"30 – Love."

The crowd murmured, clearly unsure about her decision to play. She could practically feel their concern. "*Allez*, Penny!" someone shouted from the stands and the rest started to applaud.

Pressing her lips together, she shuffled her feet, keeping the weight on one foot. The ball boy ran to her and placed one on her racket. Lutrova inched up in front of the baseline, clearly anticipating a softer serve.

"That's a mistake," Penny whispered to herself before tossing the ball up into the air, using every ounce of power she had to send the ball hard, straight and flat down the center of the court.

"40 – Love," the chair umpire said, but his voice was nearly drowned out by the crowd's roar of approval, shouts and whistles and the pounding of thousands of hands together.

Match point. She had match point and her ankle hurt so much it was actually pulsing inside her sneaker. The pain made it impossible to hold her focus and the sounds from the crowd started to invade her ears—a blur of voices and noise that was actually helping distract her from the throbbing in her foot. One more, just one more.

Lutrova wasn't having a great match, but she wasn't an idiot. She set up for the next serve a step behind the baseline, near the center of the court, cutting off the easiest route for an ace. What Lutrova didn't know was that over the last month or so, Penny had learned something important. The easiest path wasn't always the right one.

She launched her serve, a high kicker, skidding off the edge of the service line, spinning up and away.

"Game. Set. Match. Harrison. 6-4, 6-4."

The stadium practically exploded around her, but Penny couldn't move. She was frozen at the baseline, weight leaning entirely on her good ankle, using her racket to try to balance. She didn't want to take a step, but she had to. The match was over; she needed to shake her opponent's hand. She stared down at the court for a moment to catch her breath, willing the pain to go away, when another set of sneakers invaded her vision.

"Good match," Lutrova said, extending her hand. She'd come all the way over from her side of the court. If Penny didn't know better and the pain wasn't totally clouding her judgment, she'd have thought it was a sign of respect.

Nodding, Penny took her hand and shook it firmly. "Good match."

A moment later, the trainer walked out to her, clucking his tongue in disapproval as he helped her off the court, skipping the on-the-court interview because of the injury. He muttered something about stubborn, crazy girls who don't know what's good for them, but Penny ignored him in favor of listening to the crowd cheer before they made it into the tunnel.

"Penny," a voice echoed against the concrete of the hallway, followed by the pounding of feet against the ground. "I've got it from here, mate."

The trainer glanced at her, confirming it was all right to leave her with him. She nodded and stood on one leg as he switched places with Alex. He wrapped his arm around her waist and she hooked hers over his shoulders, but before he could lead her down the hallway, she pressed herself into him, letting her other arm circle around his shoulders and rested her head against his chest. He held her tightly, pressing a kiss into her hair and then she pulled back, nodding to a changing room just a few feet away. Once inside, he led her to a table and helped her on to it. She lifted her leg up onto the padded table top to keep her ankle elevated.

The trainer *tsked* at her, but she rolled her eyes. "Could you give us a minute?"

He left the room, but Alex stayed just a few steps away. He was still in his match clothes, the black and black look he'd started wearing during the *Athlete Weekly* photo shoot. Tennis's very own rebel. He ran a hand through his hair.

"Did you win?" Penny asked.

"Yeah, I did," he said, but then shook his head. "What were you thinking? That was insane, love." She snorted, uninterested in his disapproval. "Insane and bloody incredible. I was in a press conference when I heard what happened. I ran over here as fast as I could, knocked over a few reporters come to think of it." He took her hands in his and squeezed gently. "Are you okay?"

She was in too much pain to lie. "My ankle hurts," she admitted.

Alex's hands cupped her cheeks, his thumbs stroking against her skin softly over the line of her jaw, down to her throat. His index finger hooked into the gold chain at her neck and he tugged. "You wore it." His voice held disbelief and awe in it.

"For luck," Penny said, swallowing roughly, trying to find the voice to say the words she wanted to say. "But really, I needed *you.* I didn't realize how much until I was out there all alone and it felt like my ankle was going to fall off and I just needed you."

"Yeah?" He leaned forward, resting his forehead against hers.

"Yeah."

His hand slid from hers and brushed back a strand of hair that fell loose from her braid. "I fired Caroline. I know you said it didn't matter, but she published that last picture without my permission and I swear to you, love, I never want to hurt you again." He bent his head to hers, pressing a soft kiss against her lips. "I am just so bloody sorry."

"I know," she said, pulling away just enough to get the words out. "I just...I can't go through that again, Alex. I need you to promise me, we're in this together, you and me, or not at all. Please."

"I swear it, love. I promise. I—"

His words were cut off as Dom, Jack, Indy and Jasmine all poured in through the doorway, words of censure and congratulations spilling over each other. She smiled at them, but felt Alex try to slip his hand from hers and her attention snapped back to him.

"Don't leave," she said, tightening her grip.

He raised her hand to his lips. "I won't."

They still had so much unsaid between them, so many things to talk about and work through, but for now, she just needed him. Maybe forever.

SNEAK PEEK

LOSING AT LOVE
an Outer Banks Tennis Academy Novel

PROLOGUE

June 9th

La Metropolian Hotel
Paris, France

Indiana Gaffney gasped, her eyes flying open and locking on the glistening object across the hotel room. It reflected the muted television behind her, the French Open final, the red of the court blurry in the polished silver. A large, round plate, innocuous to the untrained eye, with the sizeable laser carved logo of Roland Garros at the center was braced against the mirror hanging on the hotel room wall. The mirror reflected the match clearly, the broad steps and fierce rallies of two men battling it out for the French Open Men's title. But those men were mere afterthoughts as her eyes caught on a set of shoulders stretching the material of his t-shirt thin, not a mere image from the television, but broad and warm and real. Strong hands slid down her back, fingers twining into the ends of her long blonde hair, tugging on it gently, drawing her gaze away from the mirror and back to the green eyes of the man in her bed.

He kissed her soundly, sending shivers down her spine and making her hips rock against his and her legs tighten around his waist. "It's not gonna disappear if you take your eyes off it," Jack Harrison muttered into the skin of her neck, nipping at it lightly with his teeth.

"Feels like it will," she whispered back, tilting her head to give him better access. Most of her mind was focused on what he was doing with his hands and mouth, but that plate, the one that declared in no uncertain terms that she was the new French Open junior champion, would not be ignored. Not even for the guy who made her heart pound like no one else ever had before, the guy who, up until a few days ago could barely look at her without his shoulders slumping with guilt. Their age gap hadn't shrunk in the days full of soft kisses and nights far more intense – though perhaps not as intense as she'd like – but he wasn't fighting their attraction anymore. She hadn't chased him, not really, but he'd known she wanted him, almost from the moment they first met. Then he'd found out how old she was and he started treating her like a flashing red SEVENTEEN was stamped across her forehead, every year between them creating an accompanying foot of distance. In the end, the attraction had been too much even for someone as painfully good as Jack Harrison.

"Hey, Champ, you in there?" Jack's voice brought her back, his lips spelling out the words against her shoulder.

"Champ?" Indy hummed and smiled. "I like the sound of that." In fact she liked the sound of it so much she planned on winning again the next chance she got, on the grass courts at Wimbledon.

"I bet you do. Get used to it, baby," Jack said, his whole face lighting up as he shifted his weight forward, tilting her back onto the bed. A shriek bubbled up through her throat and the giggles followed as he leaned over her, bracing himself on his elbows and then smothered her laughter with the press of his mouth. As his tongue slid against hers, she turned herself over to it, letting herself revel in the dreams of future victories and the celebrations that would follow.

~

Randazzo Residence
Outer Banks, North Carolina

Jasmine Randazzo shifted her weight back and forth from one foot to the other, trying to appear interested in what the man in front of her was saying. He'd been talking about something to do with eligibility and options for the future, but Jasmine's eye was drawn by the large screen over his shoulder. As was tradition, her parents were throwing a party during a Grand Slam final. The next best thing to being courtside was to rub elbows with the US's tennis elite and make everyone feel like they weren't missing anything, when in fact they weren't watching the match at all. If they were sitting at Chatrier they would all be silent during the points, heads whipping back and forth with the force of each groundstroke, nothing but the grunts and groans of the two men on the court echoing in the stadium.

"Do you understand what I'm trying to say, Jasmine?" the man asked, shifting into her view over his shoulder and trying to grab her eyes with his.

"Of course I do," she said, meeting his gaze for a second. "If you'll excuse me, I'd like to watch this last game."

Alex Russell was leading Henrique Romero of Brazil in the third set and was just a few points away from victory. Any other year and Jasmine wouldn't care at all that the best men's player in the world was about to win yet another Grand Slam, but this year was different. He'd spent the last few months training at OBX with them after coming back from a horrific knee injury. If he won, which all signs pointed to, that trophy would be displayed in the front entry of the training facility, letting everyone know exactly the kind of athletes that trained at OBX. It would bring an influx of talent, but it would also set a new standard of expectations. OBX wouldn't just be a training facility anymore. It would be the place you came to if you wanted to be the best tennis player in the world.

Finding an unimpeded view of the screen, Jasmine focused in on the court, a court she'd played on less than a week ago with her doubles partner, Indiana Gaffney. They'd faced the best doubles team in the world and after an embarrassing first set, they'd fought hard, made the final score respectable, and impressed a lot of people in the stands. Including, hopefully, the committee who'd issue wild card entries to the next Grand Slam, just a few weeks away now, in Wimbledon. That's what she had to focus on, not the other stuff, like losing in the second round of the French Open Girls Singles while Indy had won the entire damn tournament. And not the confusing mess that was her relationship with her best friend, Teddy Harrison. And definitely not that the man she'd tried so hard to ignore for the last few minutes was a college recruiter her parents had invited to the party specifically to talk to her about waiting until after college to turn pro and spend the next few years playing NCAA tennis.

The television was on mute so as not to disturb the conversations going on around her, but the closed captioning was on and a shot zoomed in on Alex Russell, tall, blond, and British, barely looking like he'd broken a sweat under the Paris sun. The black boxes and white lettering scrolled across the bottom of the screen: *Alex Russell, the man who everyone counted out just a few months ago, will serve for the championship and prove all of us wrong.*

"Come on, Alex," Jasmine muttered under her breath. People were counting her out too and one day when she is standing on a court like that, just a game away from a championship, those people are going to eat their words.

~

Philipe Chatrier Court
Roland Garros - Paris, France

Penny Harrison reached down, her fingers skimming the top of the walking boot encasing her foot. The strength of the sun, combined with the body heat of nearly fifteen thousand people was pressing down upon the court and a rivulet of sweat slipped down from the back of her knee, making her skin itch where the plastic rubbed against it.

Though she stayed seated, her ankle protesting against carrying any weight at all, the crowd around her was on its feet, applauding and shouting, letting their appreciation be known not just for the championship match, but for two weeks of tennis at its highest level played in the red clay baking under the new summer sun.

"S'il vous plaît, Mesdames et Messieurs. Merci." The chair umpire's voice boomed through the speakers, his words implicitly demanding and receiving silence or as close to silence as possible before such an important point. Everyone settled back into their seats, the cheers morphing into a buzz, electrifying the moment, the last one in Paris until next year.

Alex stood at the far end of the court, as far away the player's box as he could be, trying to use the shadow cast by the court's walls for some relief. He was just a point away from another championship and proving to the world that he was back at the top of his game. Penny scratched at her irritated skin again, twisting her mouth into a frown. Maybe in a month that would be her, standing on the grass courts at Wimbledon, back from an injury and celebrating a championship at a Grand Slam. It would be the first in her career, compared to what had become routine for Alex.

"Come on, Alex," she whispered, knowing that even if he couldn't hear her, he'd feel her support across the court. Her fingers caught on the chain of her necklace, a large old-fashioned penny dangling from the end, Alex's good luck charm and his gift to her before the tournament. Now clutching it in her fist, she took a deep breath as he went out to serve the final point.

Alex bounced the ball beneath his racket into the clay, a complete mess after three sets of hard fought tennis, especially down at the baseline. Romero was opposite him; bent over at the waist, shifting back and forth, ready to receive the serve. One last fan let his voice be heard, a deep British accent from somewhere in the crowd bellowing, "C'mon Russell!" A few anxious people shhh'd him, but Alex didn't even glance up. He coiled his body down, building power through his legs before tossing the ball high and with a lightning fast stroke, attacking the bit of green fluff. He sent a low-lying laser beam across the court, skidding off the white T on the other side of the net and then past the outstretched racket of his opponent. The crowd erupted and Penny lost sight of him as everyone leapt to their feet, screaming, totally drowning out the umpire's call of, "Game. Set. Match." He came into view again as he was shaking Romero's hand at the net, then he looked up into the stands, his eyes finding her immediately. She blew him a kiss, but he smiled and shook his head. Jogging over to the stands and climbing in, passing rows and rows of people who patted him on the back before he reached her, covered in sweat and mud, he leaned over the wall surrounding the player's box and slid his hand into her hair, the other catching her hand and pulled her up against him, getting red clay all over her white eyelet dress as they embraced.

"I love you," she whispered against the whisker-roughened skin of his cheek.

It was the first time she'd said those words to him and they just slipped out. Panic shot through her for a moment before he pulled her closer, held her even tighter and said, "I love you too."

CHAPTER 1

June 14th

Outer Banks Tennis Academy
Ocean Hill, North Carolina

The rough terrycloth of her wristband soaked up the sweat at her brow as Indiana Gaffney swiped it across her forehead. Grass stains on her elbows, a gigantic bruise blooming on her knee, cheeks red from exertion, she turned to her doubles partner Jasmine Randazzo with a wild smile. The breeze off the ocean whipped over her, cooling her overheated skin as she raised her hand into the air and Jasmine clapped hers against it. Her chest rose and fell heavily as her lungs tried to pull in as much of the salty air as they could, the effort from that last rally catching up with her, but not nearly as bad as it used to, her conditioning finally at an acceptable level after her year away from the game. Of course acceptable for most people was vastly different than acceptable for a professional tennis player, especially one coached by Dom Kingston.

"Nice one," Dom called from the sidelines, actually standing up and applauding with a broad smile slipping over his tanned features. But he then turned his attention to their training partners, two young men from OBX's Elite Boys squad standing flat-footed and winded, grumbling to each other in low tones. "And what the holy hell do you two think you're doing? Last I checked this was the Outer Banks Tennis Academy. We train the best in the world. Did you think because they're girls they'd be easy pickings? Take two tours and then report back to the Junior Courts, I'm sick of the sight of you."

The young men trudged off the court still muttering and Dom's eyes narrowed. "Changed my mind. Three tours. Want to make it four?"

The taller boy nudged the smaller one with his elbow as they both shook their heads and said, "No, Coach."

"Good. Get lost."

They took off down the path at a measured jog, conserving their energy for the three laps of the entire facility, a circuitous route that would take them through the maze of forty-five practice courts, finishing up with a sprint across the sandy beach that lined OBX property.

Jasmine raised her eyebrows towards Indy who smiled back. In her short time at OBX she'd endured Dom's wrath enough to simply enjoy when someone else was his target.

"Ladies, that's enough for this morning. Cool down. Indy get some ice on that knee before it blows up like a balloon," Dom said.

"It's fine," she said, glancing down at it. "I bruise easy."

"Fine, video analysis after lunch," he said before leaving them for his next training session.

Indy grabbed her water bottle and swished a mouthful before spitting it out. Too much water would weigh her down for the rest of the day, but she had to stay hydrated under the hot North Carolina sun as the weather shifted from a warm spring towards what promised to be a humid summer. Though if she had her way, most of that summer would be spent a long way away from OBX, on courts around the world, starting with the grass lawns of Wimbledon. She swung her arms around in slow circle, letting those muscles slowly recover from the intense workout she'd just put in, before moving further down her body, twisting and bending at her core, then lunging and reaching for her legs.

"Better every day," Jasmine said, as they left the court headed in the direction of the locker room for a shower and a fresh set of clothes.

Indy nodded, pulling her long blonde hair free from its ponytail and running her hands through the sweaty locks. "I just wish they would make a decision."

"They" were the Lawn Tennis Association or LTA, the English equivalent to the USTA and the people in charge of her fate for the next month or so. It was within their power to grant wildcard entries into the Championships at Wimbledon. After she and Jasmine pushed the number one doubles team in the world to a third set tiebreaker, it made sense that they'd be granted a wildcard into the main doubles draw, but sometimes sense had very little to do with what went on in professional tennis. They would both be headed there regardless, having earned entry to the Girl's Singles tournament, and they'd play doubles anyway, but after more than holding their own against the best in the world, playing doubles against juniors again felt like a total waste of time. Now it was just a waiting game and patience had never been one of Indy's virtues.

"It should happen soon, maybe tomorrow," Jasmine said as they entered the locker room, the buzz of dozens of girls echoing off the tile floors and metal lockers soon faded. Since their return from France, the atmosphere at OBX had been strange to say the least. Indy was used to it. She'd been an outsider from the moment she arrived at the Outer Banks Tennis Academy, but her stomach twisted for Jasmine who'd spent her entire tennis career training inside the high fences of the best tennis school in the world. The other girl didn't know how to handle the silent glares and fervent whispers that followed them everywhere. Their partnership and burgeoning friendship was one of the hottest stories in the tennis world, but at OBX, where everyone wanted to make it to the top and most had the goods, it simply made them the targets of soul crushing envy.

They walked side by side down the long hallway at the center of the room and made a quick left to their lockers. Indy tapped the second one in as she walked by. Penny's locker, empty while it's tenant was off in England recovering from her ankle injury and watching Alex Russell, the newly crowned French Open Champion, destroy the competition at Queens, the main prep tournament for Wimbledon.

"Have you talked to her?" Jasmine asked, nodding towards the locker while grabbing her shower kit from her own.

"Yeah," Indy said, wrinkling her nose. "She's pissed off that she can't train."

"Sucks," Jasmine said, before walking off to the shower room.

"Totally," Indy agreed. She'd never been hurt before, but just talking to Penny on the phone told her all she needed to know. She could hear the longing in her voice to get back on the court, to *do* something. Sitting on your ass while the people around you were working hard, getting better, as far as tennis was concerned, Indy couldn't imagine anything worse than that. Life of course, that would bite you in the ass over and over again and Indy wasn't a stranger to that, not with her mom gone for nearly a year from cancer and her father – who'd barely noticed her existence most of the time – spending his nights with her agent, the high powered Caroline Morneau.

~

The hot water was heaven after the morning workout. She took her time, letting her muscles recover as much as they could because she'd need them again during that afternoon's single's training. The locker room was blissfully empty as she emerged from the showers. Jasmine had headed to lunch with her parents, the facility's founders. She left her hair alone, knowing the warm air outside would give it a natural curl, and pulled on a pair of white, terrycloth shorts, then a bronze t-shirt with the Nike swoosh blazoned across the chest in black. The shirt was a gift from Penny who had more Nike merchandise than she knew what to do with after signing a lucrative sponsorship deal to become the face of their tennis line. Indy smiled to herself, knowing that one day soon she'd have her own sponsorship deal. Caroline had said as much over and over again since they returned from France, had made contact with all the big tennis outfitters and it was just a matter of waiting for the best deal and negotiating terms that brought in the most amount of money for the most exposure.

Indy grabbed her bag from the locker, stuffed with textbooks and her laptop. There were just a few weeks between her and her high school diploma. Just a few more tests and she'd graduate in absentia from her former high school back in California, so instead of a nice, relaxing mindless lunch she'd be tackling her off the court nemesis, AP Calculus. It wasn't something she had to do as she'd easily qualify for a GED at this point. Her course load was completely made up of classes above and beyond the requirements for a high school diploma, but Indy was done quitting things. She'd given up tennis for a year and nearly lost her dream because of it. So she'd slog through calculus and all the rest and get that diploma even if the equations made her brain melt inside her skull.

Stepping into the sunshine, she shouldered her bag and turned towards the OBX library, running through the assignments she still had to complete when a shadow crossed over her path, a large body falling into step with her, close, but not touching, their strides matching.

"Jack," she said, glancing up at him sideways, a small smile threatening at the corner of her mouth.

"Indiana," he said, echoing back her name, sending a shiver down her spine. He was the only one allowed to call her that, the only person who made the name she'd hated since forever sound friggin' good.

They walked together without another word, turning the corner that separated the courts from the residential area of the complex, but her stride was suddenly cut off when Jack shuffled his feet, sliding his arm around her waist and pulled her into a shady walkway between buildings. Her bag slid off her shoulder, but he caught it before it crashed to the ground and smashed her laptop to smithereens. He let it settle on the ground gently before leaning over her, forcing her to step back into the wall.

Walls were their thing. Their first kiss had been against a wall in a random hallway at Roland Garros, their second pressed against the wall of their hotel in Paris and now that they were back in North Carolina, they found any excuse to push each other against a wall and kiss until they were gasping for air and their bodies begged for relief. Jack's lips trailed from her temple, using the wall behind her as an anchor before bending his head to hers. Pushing up onto her toes, Indy met him halfway. She'd never been so grateful for every millimeter of her five feet ten inches as she was when she was kissing Jack. His hands slid through her hair, twisting it around his fingers, then cradling the back of her head, drawing her mouth more firmly against his. Indy brought her hands to his torso, gripping his t-shirt, letting her palms press against the cut of muscle that disappeared into his cargo shorts. The skin on skin contact made his breath hitch, his mouth opening just enough to allow her tongue to slide in, deepening the kiss, before letting her teeth nip at his bottom lip. A groan rumbled in his throat as he stumbled forward, pressing his body full length against hers. He wrenched his lips from hers, trailing his mouth over the line of her jaw to the spot just behind her ear. It was her turn to gasp and her head fell back as she arched into him. No one had ever kissed her there before. Jack smiled against her skin as her fingertips dug into his sides and she let a moan slip free as he focused his attention on that spot, scraping his teeth against it then soothing that small pain with a flick of his tongue. Her hands scrambled to get purchase against his shoulders, desperate for some leverage, anything to help her slide her body against his. Then he was gone, his hand gone from her hair, his mouth gone from her neck and his body inches then feet away. Indy blinked at him, trying to figure out where he'd gone when the voices echoing down the pathway towards them finally reached her ears.

Bending down, he lifted her bag as she ran her fingers through her hair, knowing he'd made an unholy mess of it. "You're fine," he muttered, handing her the bag, then keeping the distance between them as a group of junior boys stomped past them, none giving them a second glance.

"You have good ears," Indy said, biting her lip at the close call. If those boys had seen them, the news would have spread like wildfire through the OBX campus and everyone would have known by the end of the day. She was only seventeen for another few months, but that wasn't really the problem, seventeen or eighteen wouldn't matter to other people. She was a young tennis pro, he was an up and coming agent. The last thing either of their careers needed was the heightened publicity of a controversial relationship, even if Jack Harrison was far more of a gentleman than any guy she'd ever met. Sometimes a little *too* much of a gentleman, truth be told.

Jack shrugged, glancing back over his shoulder again before facing her fully. "I'm sorry about this."

She reached out and took his hand, "We both agreed," she said, entwining their fingers together, "it's just between us for now. It makes sense for the both of us." Pressing his lips together in a thin line, he nodded, but she knew he wasn't entirely convinced. "Jack, we talked about this. You said you were okay with it."

"I just wish it were different," he said, tugging her closer, pressing a soft kiss to her forehead. His hands released hers and dropped to her hips, the edges of his thumbs brushing against her hipbones in slow circles sending shivers over her skin.

"Me too." She wanted to scream it from the rooftops that this amazing guy was hers. That he had deep green eyes and a smile that brightened them whenever he looked at her. That he was brilliant in ways that she couldn't even fathom with his degree from Harvard. That he'd fought their attraction for so long because of that ingrained sense of honor, like one of those heroes in a fairy tale, except Jack was real, flesh and blood.

"Have you thought...maybe we should tell Penny?" Indy asked, her fingertips landing on his forearms, gently stroking up to his elbows and back down to his wrists.

Jack let out a heavy breath. "Penny has a lot on her plate right now."

"I know, I just feel funny keeping it from her. Jasmine knows."

"We'll do whatever you want to do. This is your show, baby."

"I don't need a supportive…" she hesitated, almost using the word boyfriend, but that didn't really fit, did it? Not if they were keeping it a secret, "I need honest Jack."

He leaned back, looking her in the eye. "Honest? Honestly, my sister doesn't do well with change. It freaks her out and right now, I'm not sure that the idea of you and me will go over that well. On the other hand, if we don't tell her and she finds out?"

"She'll be pissed."

"Yep."

"Maybe we wait a little longer. We could tell her in London?"

Jack nodded, "Face to face instead of over the phone."

"There's always Skype," she said, not really sure if she wanted to know what Penny, the only girl who'd made an effort to befriend her when she first arrived at OBX, would think if she found out she and Jack were together.

"There's that."

Indy shook her head. They should do it in person. They should have done it before they left

Paris, but Penny had been so devastated by withdrawing from the tournament that it hadn't felt like the right time then either. "In London. We'll be there in less than a week. We'll tell her then."

"Okay, in London." They stood there for a moment, just breathing each other in until Jack leaned away. "I've gotta go. I have a meeting with a potential new client this afternoon and I've got to prep."

Indy snorted a laugh. "Right, like you don't already have a complete profile worked up along with potential sponsors to contact if they sign."

"You know me so well," he said, leaning around the building, checking the pathway for any more unwanted spectators. "I'll go this way."

Indy nodded back in the opposite direction. "And I'll go that way."

With a bow, he was gone, around the corner and out of sight, so she turned and adjusted her bag over her shoulder, heading out from between the buildings and towards the library. She'd have about half the time to get her Calc done than she originally planned. Fingertips pressing against that spot on her neck lightly recalling the feel of his mouth and the way her entire body was lit on fire by his touch, it was totally worth it.

"Are you sure that is a good idea?" a voice rang out from just a few steps behind her, the French accent giving its owner away, if the superiority and condescension weren't enough of a clue. Indy spun around and came face to face with her agent, tall, blonde, perfectly put together in a silk blouse and linen skirt, somehow looking completely cool and calm despite the blaze of the sun. She was in town before they all left for England, mostly to go over her plans for Indy's future off the court.

A denial formed on Indy's tongue, but she knew it was useless. Caroline had seen them and it probably just confirmed what she'd suspected for a while. Her agent was damn good at her job and it wasn't like she and Jack had been super careful about keeping private moments behind closed doors. "Good idea or not, it's none of your business."

Raising her eyes to the sky and shaking her head Caroline said, "You are my business, Indiana."

"How many times do I have to say it? Don't call me that, and my *tennis* is your business," Indy corrected. "Keep your nose out of everything else."

"It is not that simple," Caroline insisted, her voice inching up in pitch.

"It really is." She turned on her toe and walked away, wanting to look back, hoping that Caroline's brow was furrowed and her hands were on her hips, lips pursed in aggravation. But looking back would ruin the moment because despite getting in the last word, Caroline now had the upper hand and it was only a matter of time before she used it to her advantage.

COMING FEBRUARY 2015

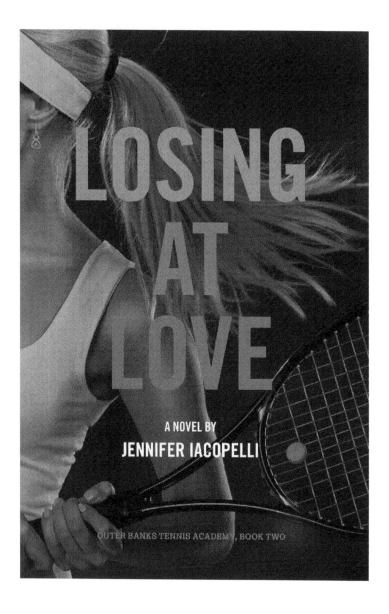

LOSING AT LOVE

A NOVEL BY

JENNIFER IACOPELLI

OUTER BANKS TENNIS ACADEMY, BOOK TWO

ACKNOWLEDGEMENTS

What they don't tell you before you write a book is that eventually, you're going to have to thank everyone who helped you do it. Thankfully, I kept a list, but even if I hadn't, these names wouldn't be hard to remember.

Michelle Wolfson, my incredible agent. You were the first to believe in this book (and me) and for that I'll be forever grateful. Thank you for your support, your enthusiasm and your guidance through this whirlwind!

Melanie Downing, editor extraordinaire. I can't even begin to describe how thankful I am for your insights and for pushing me to make this story and these characters the best they could possibly be.

Lisa, Waynn, Jennifer and the entire team at Coliloquy, thank you for "getting" this project and for taking this journey with me. I am so grateful to all of you for this opportunity!

To Erin Fitzsimmons for the original cover design and Anna Kovatcheva for the gorgeous re-design. You made GSM shine!

My fantastic team of critique partners and beta readers, none of this would have happened without you: Kaelyn Christian, Trish Smyth, Jess Swann, Jessica McCormack, Rachel Russell, Megan Weaver and Alycia Tornetta.

My parents, Tom and Joan Iacopelli, who only looked at me like I was half crazy when I told them I wanted to be an author; my sister, Annie Iacopelli, who gets to read everything first; my brilliant, beautiful grandma, Jennie Hennessy; my fantastic aunt and uncles: Carolyn Hennessy, Eileen Hennessy, Jimmy and Lore Hennessy, Al Stedina, Stella Mary and Tony Surowitz; my crazy cousins, Jill, Madison and Jimmy. I love you all so much.

ABOUT THE AUTHOR

Jennifer Iacopelli was born in New York and has no plans to leave...ever. Growing up, she read everything she could get her hands on, but her favorite authors were Laura Ingalls Wilder, L.M. Montgomery and Frances Hodgson Burnett all of whom wrote about kick-ass girls before it was cool for girls to be kick-ass. She earned a Bachelor's degree in Adolescence Education and English Literature quickly followed up by a Master's in Library Science, which lets her frolic all day with her books and computers, leaving plenty of time in the evenings to write and yell at the Yankees, Giants and her favorite tennis players through the TV.

Follow her on twitter @jennifercarolyn or on her website www.jenniferiacopelli.com

10231150R00197

Printed in Great Britain
by Amazon.co.uk, Ltd.,
Marston Gate.